The Jubjub Bird

Books by William Hardy

THE JUBJUB BIRD

A TIME OF KILLING 1962

WOLFPACK 1960

YEAR OF THE ROSE 1960

The Jubjub Bird

by William M. Hardy

Coward-McCann, Inc. NEW YORK

Beware the Jabberwock, my son!
The jaws that bite, the claws that catch!
Beware the Jubjub bird, and shun
The frumious Bandersnatch!
—"The Jabberwocky" by Lewis Carroll

The Jubjub Bird

one

"You know what your trouble is, don't you?"

"Don't want to know."

"Man, that's the trouble with you."

A blatant plagiarizing of classic dialogue from that classic comic strip *Peanuts*.

Do you know what's wrong with you? No, and I don't want to know. That's what's wrong with you, Charlie Brown, you don't want to know what's wrong with you.

Venable says, "Go to hell, Lucy."

Andy says, "Man, what is with this Lucy bit?"

"That's your trouble, Andy Brown, you don't even know whose material you're stealing. You don't read the important parts of the newspaper. Me, when I lift dialogue from my betters, I do it deliberately and therefore cleverly which shows the advantage of my superior education."

"Superior shit!"

Now that was getting better. That had a kind of sound to it. It marched. It was alliterative.

And it was also a time for decision. The completion of the third beer is always a time for decision. To pee or not to pee.

9

There exist several schools of thought on the general subject area of beer drinking and urination. One holds to the theory that periodic emptying of the bladder gives stamina over the long stretch, while another contends that the self-discipline of containment contributes to overall character development. This latter school of thought also gives birth to story— enormously funny to beer drinkers, only moderately so to nonbeer drinkers—dealing with man who drinks beer in a tavern from midmorning until closing time without ever getting up from his chair. When followed by uneasy bartender to front door of establishment, subject unzips fly and proceeds to aim instrument. Dialogue:

Bartender: Say, buddy, you ain't gonna pee here!

Subject: Naw, I'm gonna pee way way way WAY over there.

When queried, Andy says he has not heard story, so I relate it with highly gratifying reception, following which the decision is made to pee, more a tribute to power of suggestion than to any philosophical conclusion. First Andy, then Venable, then back to face round four, endowed with stamina at the possible expense of overall character development.

"You," says Andy, "may be the most screwed-up ofay professor I know."

After two beers this remark would constitute an insult. After five, a compliment. We wallow somewhere in the middle ground, so I reserve judgment until I send up my own trial balloon.

"And you are the most screwed-up coon student I know."

The beginning of number four puts us closer to five than two. White teeth grinning against all that black shining face and the familiar Amos and Andy routine.

"Mistuh, ah don' know what you talkin' bout, mistuh. Me'n Amos jes tryin' to do de bes we kin, mistuh."

10

"Tell me something, did your parents know what they were doing when they hung that Andy Brown on you?"

"Sure they did. Man, my folks thought those two cats were the greatest. It was either Lincoln Brown or Andy Brown, and Andy won."

Beer number four goes very rapidly. Number five arrives and is welcomed as old friend.

"Like I was saying, you don't know what your trouble is, and you don't want to know, but I'm going to tell you, man, so listen."

"I could go pee again."

"Listen now, pee later. Your trouble, man, is two things."

"Give me a slide lecture. That's what Lucy does."

"Man, you been making out with some chick named Lucy, that's your problem. Your trouble is, first off, you don't believe what old Tom Wolfe had to say."

"But I'm not afraid of his sister, Virginia."

"Old Tom Wolfe said you can't go home again, man, and you're trying, but you can't make it."

Touch me not on sore spots, Andy Brown. Even on the fifth beer this can be trouble.

"I came home."

"Naw, man. You just tried to come home. You've been ten years up North, freezing your butt off and thinking how liberal you are, and you decide to go back where the magnolias bloom and the birds make music all the day and the old folks are at home and where they now let the nee-grows go to school with the anglo-saxons. You've been away up North writing some books so you are now a real live author, so you get a chance to come down home again and be a writer-in-residence, and you say, man this is the greatest. I can go home again. Just like old Tom Wolfe never said a damned word."

And I hit back a little because the sore spot is definitely sore.

"You know something, Andy Brown, you are the blackest nee-grow I ever saw. Up North we have a lot of shades of brown, but you are *black*."

No sore spot there for Andy Brown.

"Maybe that's why you got so liberal, man. All those cats up there you figured maybe one of your great-granddaddies got into one of their great-grandmothers. Now I am pure stock, man, undiluted nee-grow. All my great-grandmothers knew they couldn't get half as much from old massah as they could from Uncle Tom. You are afflicted with what the sex-oriented shrinkers call penis envy of the Caucasians for the Negroids and Asians."

"Merde!"

"Shit is shit in any language, man. Now, mistuh, ah'm gonna tell you dis one mo thing dat's yo trouble. You don' pay no tention to whut you says in yo class dere."

Ease up on sore spot number one and begin to apply pressure on number two—which is infinitely sorer.

"You've been moaning and groaning because you can't write that book, man. You've even got so desperate you're reduced to sitting here and drinking beer with a nee-grow student and telling him your problems because that book won't fly, man."

The spot is more than sore. It is agonizing.

"Don't tell me it isn't topical, Andy. For Christ's sake, everything I hear from my agent is make it topical. If the right-wing menace isn't topical, what the hell is?"

"Sure it's topical, man, but what the hell do you know about it? You read the papers and you look at the tube and that's all you know."

"I've spent a year researching the right-wing movement."

"And you sit there in that air-conditioned classroom, wear-

12

ing that suede vest and smoking that white pipe and you tell all us creative writing students that the first rule of writing is to stick to personal experience."

"I am substituting research for personal experience." A difficult statement to make on number six and manage to camouflage the pompous quality. I did not succeed.

"Substitute shit!"

Another score for alliteration.

"Man, you wrote one book that scored and that was all about the big shoot 'em up in the sky. And that was great, man, because you were up there looping the loop and flying by the seat of your pants and shooting down Zeros by the dozen. I read that book, man, and I was right up there with you in the wild blue yonder. Then you tried it again, and it was just a wee bit forced because you decided you wanted to be an important writer so you tried to mix in a little of that philosophy bit, and I don't think you were a goddamned philosopher when you were playing zoom zoom. You were having one hell of a time—scared shitless and exhilarated and *living,* man!"

This is my cue for yet another pompous statement. "That was twenty years ago. I've lived all the time in between."

Picture of Andy Brown, black as the ace of spades and halfway through number six beer, laughing with those incredibly white teeth at me.

"I don't rightly think so, Professor. I think maybe that was the onliest time you ever really lived, and you wrote your book about it, and suddenly the well's run dry. And that's what your trouble is."

"Show it to me on a black slide, Lucy."

"You keep up that Lucy jazz, man, and folks're going to think you're queer."

"You ought to read *Peanuts.*"

"Man, I eat peanuts."

On six beers I can get pleasantly drunk. The seventh sobers me, and I decided to go for sober.

It was depressing. Because Andy Brown was hitting the nail on its highly sensitive head.

"So that's what my trouble is?"

"Sure, man, and you know how I know?"

"Because you're a wise ass?"

"Not entirely, but it helps. I know because that's my trouble too. That story I gave you last week. You haven't had the guts to talk to me about it yet, and you know why."

"It's phoney. All the way down the line."

Number seven turned the magic corner, and the spell was shattered. Slat's Tavern changed back into a pumpkin. A flyspecked, dirty-tabled, jukeboxed pumpkin. Number seven tasting flat and green. Andy Brown looking cadaverous and sooty black and hostile. My weakness and his weakness exposed, mine by him and his by me in acts of mutually destructive friendship based on nothing in common. White on one side and black on the other and a few million light-years in between.

Seven is the charm.

"Man, I'd better cut out, I got work to do."

"Yes, it's later than I thought. My wife'll be wondering where I am."

Take a closeness born of a mixture of shared frustrations with half a dozen cans of beer. Add that one additional can. Add a carefully selected assortment of honest and hurtful words. Stir well.

Result. End of closeness. Hackneyed excuses and pushing back of chairs and clumsy, unfriendly mutterings about who pays for what and walking through doors into the night. White man and black man, each into his own night.

"Give you a lift, Andy?"

"No thanks, Professor. Need the exercise."

14

"You want to come in on Monday and kick that story around?"

"Throw it away, Professor. You said the word. Phoney."

Hopefully, Venable detects no anger in his voice and attempts minor salvage operation.

"Andy, thanks. You got me where it hurts. Right in the truth."

Operation reasonably successful. "What the hell, man. You wrote one good one. That's more than most of us'll ever do."

"But it's not enough."

"You and me, man." Andy Brown, long and lean and hollow and black, leaning on my car now. "We're sitting here in this town and making a goddamned point of missing the boat. You made the big shoot 'em up and I made the little one in Korea. And you got a book and I got a couple of stories, and we both got gun-shy, man. We like our wars over there in gook land. Now we got our own home-grown war right here in West Brandon, but we don't want to even look. We got the black boys and the white boys, and we go along walking right in the big ham fat middle of it, and we don't want to look one way or the other because we're scared of what we might see."

"You want to demonstrate?"

"Hell no, man. I want to make it all by myself. You're the liberal, Professor. Why don't you demonstrate?"

It is a question I cannot answer.

So I say good night to Andy Brown and I drive away, through the village and the campus and into the pleasant suburb where professors live.

But the question rides with me. I take it in to say my hello are you still up to Cathy. I take it up to bed with me while she tucks her cold feet in under my warm ass and talks about the fact that Jimmy may need glasses and isn't that a shame at the age of only eight and the fact that Elaine is worrying because the other girls in her class have boy friends and isn't that ridiculous for a kid of twelve.

And before I can comment on these shameful and ridiculous things, the question goes to sleep with me.

two

WRITERS-IN-RESIDENCE get to sleep on Saturday mornings because the CREATIVE people who take CREATIVE WRITING courses cannot be CREATIVE on Saturday mornings. They can be chemical, historical, geometrical, biological, French, Spanish, German, Latin, Greek, or even Russian. But thank God, they cannot be CREATIVE. CREATIVITY comes on Mondays, Wednesdays and Fridays at ten and eleven o'clock which are pleasantly CREATIVE hours.

And so on this Saturday morning, Venable finds himself frightfully and hopelessly awake at seven o'clock. He resists being awake, but the Venable brain is crammed to overflowing with IDEAS for the book. He knows, lying in the warm nest of his Saturday morning with Cathy's ass, now also warm, burrowed into his belly. He knows all of the things that are wrong with his book, and he must crawl out of bed, sneak his quick breakfast and lock himself in his study because this very morning will be the breakthrough.

Cathy is frightfully and hopelessly asleep so my parting squirm of my private parts against her does not disturb her, only gives me a comfortable sense of having some haven for my private parts.

Breakfast is not to be sneaked. In the warmth of a Saturday morning bed one forgets that downstairs two products of other warm beds in other years wait to exact the Saturday morning ritual of hot cakes. Cathy makes hot cakes, but Cathy is frightfully and hopelessly asleep and the process of getting her up and with the world of hot cake making could only delay the WRITING.

Jimmy pounces. Elaine pounces. Being the CREATIVE children of a CREATIVE father, they have CREATED a song. And they sing it.

> *"Cheer, cheer, cheer, it's Saturday at last!*
> *Cheer, cheer, cheer, another week is past!*
> *So get out the syrup and get the butter too,*
> *There'll be a hot cake in the old plate today!"*

Talent, I decide, is definitely hereditary, and I announce with a flourish that on this particular, special, and never-to-be-forgotten Saturday morning the hot cakes will be made by Robert M. Venable who is appearing as a last-minute substitute for the announced star, Catherine Venable who, if you will bear with us, ladies and gentlemen, has been unavoidably delayed by a chronic case of oversleeping. The cheers from the crowd are stimulating, but mixed with the general applause, I detect murmurings of doubt and distrust.

"He never made hot cakes before."

"He makes scrambled eggs pretty good, but . . ."

"Maybe we ought to settle for french toast."

The Venable ego is stirred. The male Venable tradition as culinary giants rises to the occasion. The box of hot cake mix is studied carefully. There is a formula which of course must not be taken too literally. One level cup of mix is wisely increased to one slightly heaping cup of mix. Three-quarters of a cup of milk goes in and is supplemented by a Venable inspiration in the form of an added dollop of milk. The single egg is used as directed, my tribute to the integrity of the manufacturer, but the two tablespoons of oil are daringly cut in half. Now my full inventive genius comes into play. Without the slightest hint from the printed instructions, I add a pinch of salt. Further inspiration is to melt butter in small cup, placed on 450-degree skillet. Served up to Elaine and Jimmy to the accompaniment of squeals and exclamations of admiration which settle once and for all time the question of superiority over the sleeping Cathy. I apply the masculine *coup de grâce* by mounting the stairs bearing a heaping plate smothered in melted butter and ersatz maple syrup arranged tastefully upon a tray along with orange juice and coffee. Mission accomplished. Triumph overwhelming. From this moment on, Cathy, warm and sensual with late sleeping and served-in-bed hot cakes, grants the crowning accolade.

"Bob, from now on, you must always make the hot cakes. Mine simply cannot compare."

The male Venable is irrevocably ascendant.

On Saturday mornings I will make the hot cakes.

I have been had.

Two cups of coffee as a mark of sharing with Cathy as she sits propped up in bed stuffing her lovely face with my lovely hot cakes, my syrupy and melted buttery petard upon which I find myself hoisted. Then a shower, a shave and a donning of corduroy slacks and Orlon sports shirt which go well with CREATIVE WRITING. I am ready to lock myself in my study and put to paper the IDEAS with which I awoke in the dim distant, pre hot cakes, pre coffee, pre shower and shave.

The fourth draft of the first fifty pages of the Venable masterpiece on the radical right wing is extracted from its manila folder and placed upon the rack. The reliable Underwood is unveiled and a clean sheet of yellow paper is inserted. rolled, leveled, checked for margin. The white pipe is filled with English tobacco and lighted, and the Venable fingers hover above the keys.

And there are no IDEAS. Goddamn you, Andy Brown! Goddamn the war which was long enough to have furnished me with a dozen books, but I put it all into one, and now it is finished.

What to do when the well runs dry? Easy solution is furnished by Elaine and Jimmy who pound on the locked study door.

"Daddy, it's in the paper! You promised you'd take us! This afternoon, will you take us to the new Jerry Lewis picture? It's going to be real funny! It's all about a big department store!"

Hot cakes and Jerry Lewis in one day. Venable can be a GOOD FATHER and a real DAD and who gives a damn about being a creative writer?

Jimmy and Elaine piled into the back of my red sports car which is unmistakably the proper car for a forty-year-old AUTHOR and Cathy happily left alone on a Saturday afternoon as DAD goes to the movies with his kids.

"Do we have to get popcorn or can we have a candy bar this time?" Jimmy, shrewd far beyond his eight years, going for the bundle.

And getting it thanks to DAD's defiance of a mother-dentist edict.

We park on the campus because it is easier to find a place there and walk a couple of blocks to the village. The last stretch down a small alleylike side street, onto Main Street and into chaos.

Down the middle of Main Street a long line of marchers, black, white and shades of brown, mostly young, some middle-aged, a few old, all carrying signs on sticks and poles. No words. No music. No sound. Only marching, black, white and various shades of brown faces set straight ahead, letting the signs scream for them.

FREEDOM IS FOR ALL
SEPARATE IS NOT EQUAL
BLACK AND WHITE TOGETHER

Elaine squeals with delight. "It's a demonstration, Daddy! It's a real demonstration! Can we watch it? All the kids in school have seen them. I'm the only one who hasn't."

Jimmy perplexed. "What're they doing out in the middle of the street?"

"It's a demonstration," Elaine explains. "The colored people are demonstrating."

"So what? Let's go to the movie."

"It's exciting, Jimmy. It's just like on TV on Huntley-Brinkley."

I cannot watch those faces. I can watch my television set and see the faces in Birmingham and Atlanta and Jackson and Detroit and New York and I can feel the righteous indignation of a LIBERAL swelling within the Venable breast and I can sit with my father over two glasses of his home brew and argue the case of the nee-grow with eloquence and passion because my father is a southerner of the old school and cannot understand the changes which are blowing in the wind and the fact that nee-grows are after all human beings too and all they are asking is that they be allowed the dignity of human beings and does he have any idea how he would feel if he were a nee-grow and had to explain to his children why they could not stop at a motel or go into a restaurant to eat a meal when they are out traveling on the highways and get hungry.

"Come on, children. You don't want to miss the first of the picture."

"Daddy, I want to watch the demonstration. Maybe they'll

start fighting. Will the police come and drag them away? I saw them on Huntley-Brinkley and they were stretched out on the sidewalks, and the police had to pick them up and put them in trucks and take them to jail!"

Oh, Christ, don't let them do that while I am standing here with my children!

I take Elaine firmly by one hand and Jimmy by the other and I walk toward the theatre where Jerry Lewis will save us all.

"Can I see a demonstration sometime, Daddy? I've never really seen a real demonstration, and all the other kids have seen them."

Promise them anything but give them Jerry Lewis.

"I'll bring you down to see one someday. I promise. Now come on or we'll miss the first of the picture."

Due to the extreme complexity of this motion picture, the management advises its patrons to see it from the beginning.

I purchase one adult and two children's tickets. This is the last year for Elaine at thirty-five cents. Next year it goes up to eighty-five. This is too great a jump. Fifty cents in one lousy birthday and when I was a kid it cost me ten cents and for that one thin dime I could go to the Byrd Theatre in Richmond to the Mickey Mouse Club on Saturday mornings and without having to wear any silly goddamned ears on my head, see four cartoons, an Andy Clyde comedy, listen to Art Brown play the mighty Wurlitzer while we sang along, thrill to the latest chapter of the Flash Gordon serial and stay on to see the regular feature. Oh, sweet Jesus, for only a dime!

Taking the tickets from the vacuous-pretty bleached-blond high school girl at the box office window, I have to turn back toward the street to drag Elaine away from watching that silent line of marchers. As I do, my eyes happen to meet the gaze of one of the marchers, a huge, shapeless black woman who ought to be grinning from ear to ear as she fixes hot vittles for the white folks in my Old Kentucky Home Far Away down upon the Sewanee River. But there is no grin. She looks at me, through me, into me, and the Saturday afternoon sun glints sadly on the tears that run down her fat, mammy cheeks.

Retreat and run. Jerry Lewis will save us all! Let the children buy candy bars, fifteen-cent candy bars that are no bigger than the ones I used to ruin my teeth with for a nickel. Herd them down the aisle to the cacophony of the opening titles. Coats off, candy unwrapped and at work in support of the dentists of America, eyes wide opened to Jerry Lewis and mind fighting to be shut against the face of that black fat woman who had the audacity to let me see her tears.

Betty Mills!

Betty worked for my grandparents when I was a kid. Huge, black, shapeless Betty, married after a fashion to John Mills, half her size and the obvious inspiration for Stepin Fetchit. Jolly, ageless Betty who washed and cooked and ironed and worked in the fields and tied tobacco at the barns and laughed most of the time to the accompaniment of the shaking and quivering of mountainous breasts, belly, buttocks and intermediate vast areas of black flesh.

Betty Mills, regularly each summer saved by Grace at revival and newly baptized in the muddy waters of the Halifax River. My one memory of the salvation of Betty Mills when I was ten and the visiting revival minister was a little runt of a brown man who weighed in at about one hundred and twelve pounds. In the devil's corner, introducing Betty Mills at three hundred, six and one-half pounds. Down to the riverbank and the Lord God gets hold of old Satan and Betty's mountain of flesh is the battle ground. Ten year old Robert M. Venable, future AUTHOR and LIBERAL, rolling in high glee up on the opposite bank as the struggle rages. Betty being dragged and pushed by the preacher and half the congregation into the river to be saved. Betty shouting in the unknown tongue. Betty going under the yellow water for redemption and pulling that little preacher with her not once but five times until they are both hauled out of the river. Betty soaked, saved, and subdued. The preacher gasping and flopping like a freshly caught catfish on the bank.

Oh, Jesus Christ, Betty, why have you come out of your grave to look at me with tears running down your face!

Jerry Lewis is doing his best. He is in the sporting goods department of this store, see, and he's looking at this goddamned elephant gun, and he's aiming the gun and Jesus Christ, it goes off and the recoil knocks him ass backwards through the whole bloody store, onto this little boat and through the glassware department and the lingerie department and the whole goddamned store is in chaos and you can laugh your ass off at Jerry Lewis and forget Betty Mills.

Betty Mills steaming black in the kitchen and showing her yellow and gold teeth in silent laughter while my grandfather in the dining room tells the story of Betty's and John's wedding night. Betty as bride weighed slightly under two hundred and fifty pounds while her groom was approximately one hundred pounds lighter. The setting, a one-room cabin donated by my grandfather to the happy couple. The time, midwinter. The weather, cold as a witch's tit.

My grandfather, toothless and white of hair, rheumy and blue of eye as he spooned up his bread and milk and sugar, telling the story I had heard a hundred times before and which was always new and uproariously funny.

My grandfather speaking in a tongue which was virtually indistinguishable from the colored people who worked on his farm, speaking of these people he loved in his way which is no longer comprehensible, of these people who owed their bread and clothing and hovels to him and who loved him in their way which is also no longer comprehensible.

24

"Betty, she got herself all ready for bed that night, gigglin' and bouncin' round like she was somethin' crazy and John, he knew danged well he was gonna have a job on his hands takin' care of all that gal. But he finally crawled in the bed, and I reckon he done the best he could cause their first young'un, Ephraim, was born exactly nine months later. Anyways, after awhile, old Betty she fell asleep, and she woke up way somewhere in the night and John, he wasn't in the bed. Betty, she was feelin' like friskin' some more, I reckon, so she hollered out, 'John! John! Where is you, John?' And John, he answered from the darkness, soundin' kinda weak and feeble, 'I'se sittin' over here by the winder.' And Betty says, 'John Mills, what you doin' over there by the winder and it freezin' cold. Now you get yourself back in this here bed.' But John, he just sit there, so after awhile, Betty hollers at him, 'John! John, what you doin'? I say.' And John says, 'I'se just sittin' here fannin' myself.' 'You doin' what?' 'I'se fannin' myself.' 'What you doin' a fool thing like that for?' And John, he says, 'Cause I'se hot!' "

And my grandfather chokes on the mouthful of bread and milk and sugar as the tears run down his face, and in the kitchen, Betty Mills throws her head back and whoops, "Laws, Mistuh Bobby, don' you pay no tention to yo granddaddy. Ain't he de one now? Ain't he jes de one!" And the tears ran down her face.

But those were tears of laughter, Betty Mills. Why don't you laugh at me now? You are not supposed to shed tears of sorrow when you look into my face.

Jimmy whinnies with laughter and grabs my arm in a hand smeared with chocolate. "Look, Daddy! Look!"

Jerry Lewis is running amuck in the department store with a monstrous vacuum cleaner which is sucking up everything in sight. An entire set of china is swooshed into its omnivorous mouth. A shapely salesgirl enters and is derobed down to her black bra and panty girdle as an offering to the horny daddies who take their children to see the picture. A fat lady is upset, and—plop! swish!—there goes her girdle over her ankles and across the floor into the insatiable maw of the machine. Around me children are howling with laughter and somewhere in the distance I can hear the wailing of sirens. The cops are coming to get Jerry Lewis and his wonderful vacuum cleaner, but no cops appear on the screen and I know the sirens are behind us, beyond the rows of screaming children, beyond the pimply-faced usher who guards the aisle, his mouth working frantically on a wad of gum, beyond the wondrous candy counter where for a quarter you can get a few pennies' worth of hot buttered popcorn, beyond the dried and pitiful old man who has been taking tickets there for thirty years, beyond the two-sheets proclaiming such coming attractions as *Who's Been Sleeping in My Bed* and *Blood Feast* and, for adults only, *Passion Holiday!*—beyond the ticket window and in the bright glare of Main Street the sirens are coming for the fat black woman whose tears now run down my face.

Oh, Jesus Christ, let it be over before we leave!

And after Jerry Lewis is done, there is a Bugs Bunny cartoon, a sports short about water skiing in the Everglades and the previews of *Who's Been Sleeping in My Bed?* and *Blood Feast* and Jimmy covers his eyes and Elaine leans across him and wants to know why she can't come to see *Blood Feast* because all the kids at school would probably go to see it because it looked cool and weird.

And we got up and went out into the sunlight. And there was no sign of the marchers. Traffic moved as usual and shoppers strolled along Main Street on this Saturday afternoon.

And we went home.

26

three

There is this nice thing about Sundays which is called a hangover, a direct derivative from the fact that Cathy and I have these good friends who are still in West Brandon after all these years and since they are so glad to have us back and we are so glad to be back, WE DRINK TOGETHER ON SATURDAY NIGHTS.

Mostly we drink martinis which are cleverly mixed in an old Lime Crush fountain dispenser which is mounted on the bar in their recreation room and which holds one hell of a lot of martinis so that whenever your glass gets empty from drinking it is a simple matter to fill it up again and drink some more. The evening does not end with martinis. It ends with brandy or scotch or bourbon or sometimes a little of each and at some ill-defined point in between, food is consumed, but it is mostly for drinking on Saturday nights with these good friends.

And that is how I get my hangover. And the nice hangover is my excuse for not working on my book, and it lasts me all through Sunday and sometimes a little into Monday morning. On one memorable occasion when I think we forgot to consume that food, my hangover excused me from working on my book until half past seven on Tuesday evening. I treasure those hangovers because the only other excuse I can ever come up with for not working on my book is that I do not have a frigging thing to say in my book, and that hurts.

But Jerry Lewis and Betty Mills and Andy Brown combined to screw me out of my hangover on this particular Sunday morning because I could not get myself into the proper drinking rhythm the night before and I ended up hideously sober and clearheaded, a condition which, to my horror, persisted into Sunday morning. And do you think my little family would come to my rescue? Cathy slept in until noon because she had her hangover and she was too goddamned selfish to share it with me. Elaine and Jimmy slept in because they had been permitted to stay up and watch the late show the night before so I could not save myself by doing a return engagement with the hot cakes. At eight o'clock on a bright Sunday morning, all I had to protect me was the morning paper and orange juice and coffee.

There was a time when Venable was called a brave man. What he really was was an idiot and slightly confused because he thought his wing man was where he was supposed to be when Venable went after those five Zeros, and by the time Venable realized his wing man had hauled ass because he was almost out of juice, it was too late for him to avoid being a goddamned hero.

If you will read my first novel—the good one—you'll see how brave I was thought to be. What I really have is a kind of desperate animal courage which manifests itself only when I am cornered. As for example, on this Sunday morning.

Venable, there is just you and this thing, and there is no way around, over or under it. Cathy is not going to save you. Elaine and Jimmy, ungrateful little brats that they are, are not going to save you. You are cornered.

All right, I said, looking it straight in the eye. It's you and

28

me. You think you've got me, don't you? Well, you didn't count on the Venable guts. Brace yourself, friend, I'm coming after you!

So Venable charged Venable, and we went to it, out the front door, complete in hand-knit sweater, suede cap and —no white pipe—a cigar. White pipes are for writing. Cigars are for looking at the monster who is yourself when he has you cornered.

Once upon a time there was a graduate student named Venable and he studied his graduate studies at this great university in the southland where there was green ivy crawling over old brick walls and the names of the sons of the university who had served the CONFEDERACY inscribed on stone plaques and a football team and a sprawling campus with huge oak trees and dogs of all shapes and sizes which chased squirrels of a fairly uniform size and an honor system and a daily student newspaper which was usually in hot water with someone and a pleasant little town called West Brandon which was attached to this university and had a wide pleasant Main Street with shops and a post office and several drugstores and some eating places and two movie houses, one on each side of Main Street.

And this great university had a LIBERAL TRADITION.

The graduate student named Venable fell in love with the L.T. Before the big shoot 'em up he had attended another great university which did not have a L.T. While he was shooting 'em up and trying to drink all the booze and diddle all the girls at home and abroad, he became a LIBERAL.

So it was only natural after he had stopped shooting 'em up and tried his hand at half a dozen jobs and liked none of them that he would decide to be a graduate student and prepare himself for something lofty and that he would do this at this great university which did have an L.T.

At what precise point did Venable decide to become a LIBERAL?

Venable lights his cigar, considers the pleasant suburban neighborhood and selects a direction for his Sunday morning walkie-thinkie.

In 1944, Venable met his first nee-grow. In fact, it was only in 1941 that he had known any colored folks. Before that time, he had been acquainted with a large number of niggers.

In 1944, Venable found himself in San Francisco by the bay awaiting transportation to Pearl Harbor where he was going to start being a hero. Venable knew only one person in San Francisco, a girl he had gone to high school with who was remarkably plain and remarkably good-natured and possessed a swell personality which meant she would go to bed with almost anybody. So Venable called her and she said sure she'd love to see him and there was going to be a great old party up on a place called Montgomery Street where there would be a bunch of people she knew Venable would like and why didn't they look in on that party first and then take it from there?

So they did and it wasn't half bad because this girl had learned enough about fixing herself up since high school to make her face socially acceptable and she still seemed to have this swell personality, so Venable figured he had himself a pretty good one-shot going in San Francisco by the bay, but at this party there was a colored fellow who turned out to be a nee-grow in disguise.

It was a great old party and Venable ended up the next morning going to bed with a redheaded woman who was a total stranger and whose face was just naturally a lot more socially acceptable than the old high school chum's and who had every bit as swell a personality, but all that was really so much inconsequential hauling of the Venable ashes, a process which, even then, was not unique.

30

The unique and IMPORTANT thing about that evening on Montgomery Street was the colored fellow who became a nee-grow and whose name was Al.

Venable and Al talked most of that night. They talked over drinks of hard-to-get bad wartime whiskey. They talked in corners, over the blasting of music, on the edge of at least two fights between a couple of fairies and during a long walk along a deserted Montgomery Street at four in the morning.

Al was not only a nee-grow, he was a labor organizer and very left-wing and very bright and very articulate. He came very close to being the brightest and most articulate man Venable had ever known. And during that night and into the morning right up to the time that Venable decided to check in on this woman with the good face and the swell personality, Al and Venable became very good friends and Venable became a LIBERAL.

He never saw or heard from Al again, but it struck him that there might be a lot of Als in the world and that up to that night he had been denied them for one reason only.

Initial Venable definition of a LIBERAL.

A man who chooses his friends solely on basis of compatibility, EVEN IF THEY ARE NEE-GROW.

Typical manifestation of Venable's new LIBERAL TRADITION. If you are driving your car and another driver cuts in front of you after having run a stop sign and almost makes you have a wreck and you see he is a nee-grow, you do not yell, "You stupid sonofabitch!" at him.

So Venable comes to this great university just before the Supreme Court makes its big decision and he agonizes along with many other students because nee-grows are not admitted as students despite the fact that they are welcomed as janitors. Venable is active in his agony. He signs several petitions with his own name and he writes a letter to the editor of the local newspaper and, most important of all, he writes a play which

31

is about a college professor who is a young LIBERAL and who has a father-in-law who is a FACIST and a Dean and the struggle between these two mighty opposites over the admission of a nee-grow to a university which is very much like the university Venable is attending. Not only that, but the student drama group staged this play, and Venable became a minor and momentary figure as a LIBERAL voice on the campus to the point that he received several anonymous letters from people who referred to him in glowing terms as a "dirty mother-diddling COMMUNIST" and a "shit-eating nigger lover," and Venable felt very warm and good about all of this.

Because he was a graduate student.

After the great university gave Venable a MASTER OF ARTS, he got married to a beautiful girl named Cathy and got a job teaching freshman English at a university in the frozen North and wrote a novel which was well received and a book club selection and made Venable more money than he had ever seen before so that he became an AUTHOR. As an AUTHOR he performed a number of public services like joining the Author's Guild and having a Literary Agent and giving talks to Women's Clubs and autographing copies of his novel in department stores and buying a sports car and subscribing to a clipping service. He also produced two beautiful children with the assistance of his beautiful wife.

Then his Literary Agent suggested that he should write another novel which would be well received and a book club selection and make more money. So Venable wrote another novel which was not very well received and which did not become even a paperback reprint selection and which never made back the publisher's advance.

And all the while, Venable was still teaching in the frozen North. He was teaching CREATIVE WRITING courses now because he was an AUTHOR. And, of course, he was still a LIB-

ERAL. He was still very proud of the great university in the sunny South and he constantly bragged to his frozen northern friends about the L.T. of this university. Because it had already admitted nee-grows as students and the little town of West Brandon which belonged to this great university was far ahead of any town in the entire sunny South in INTEGRATION.

So when an invitation came from this great university for Venable to come back for a year as a WRITER-IN-RESIDENCE, he had broken the icicles from his nose and kicked his heels in the air and rented his big house in the frozen North and gathered Cathy and Elaine and Jimmy and his typewriter together to RETURN.

The great university looked exactly the same as it had ten years ago. Venable walked down Main Street and spoke to familiar faces which spoke back to him. His old friends had him and Cathy out for drinks and for dinner. And he met his classes in CREATIVE WRITING and he was inspiring to them.

But something was wrong.

My cigar is dead and too short to be brought back to life again. I have seen as much of the pleasant suburban neighborhood as I can stand. I am too tired and too depressed to know what is wrong with the great university and the town of West Brandon and with myself. I go back to the house and go to bed and sleep all of Sunday afternoon. And that night I say hello to Cathy and the children and eat dinner with them and watch the Ed Sullivan Show and Bonanza with them and go to bed.

I have survived a Sunday without a hangover, but something is wrong.

And I know as I drop off to sleep with Cathy's cold feet tucked under my warm ass that I am going to do something about what is wrong. But I do not know what.

four

I said, "Andy, do you know what's wrong with that story you handed in Monday?"

"You going to give me that Lucy routine, man?"

Andy Brown relaxes in my office on the second floor of the English Building. It is a pleasant office with a large desk and a swivel chair and a file cabinet and a bookcase and a wastebasket. There is also a chair for students who come in to talk with me about their CREATIVE WRITING. Andy Brown sprawls in that chair and I lean back in my swivel chair with my feet on the desk and we both smoke fine maduro cigars which Andy has furnished. To complete the picture there is also a large window in my office which affords a spectacular view of the main quadrangle of this great university and my chair is aimed so that I can enjoy that view by merely turning my head a little to the right. It is class-break time and the quadrangle is inhabited by students and the sight of them gives me hope.

"You've written that same story three times already just since I've known you. You keep changing the names and the details, but it is the same story. It was pretty good the first time, but it gets weaker each time like soup when you keep adding water."

Remember that one, Venable. It makes the point.

"Yeah, I guess you're right." Andy Brown, also relaxed and too comfortable to rise to a fight. We sit and enjoy the cigars which are dark and rich and strong.

"Professor, I'll make you a proposition."

"Does it require me to remove my feet from this desk?"

"Not right this minute."

"Cost money?"

"Freebies."

"So proposition me."

Andy Brown being serious in the light of day makes me vaguely uncomfortable, but I listen from behind my dark maduro smoke screen.

"You and me, Professor. Like I was saying at Slat's the other night, we got the same disease. We're walking down the middle of the street, only there's no traffic there. Man, they're whooping it up over on the sidewalks, but the middle of the street is calm and peaceful and the grass is growing up through the pavement. Like we're sitting in our easy chairs right in the eye of the hurricane, man, with our feet up and our peckers down. And all around us that old hurricane is tearing up the world."

"Leave my feet where they are and leave my pecker out of it."

"You can't grin and make a joke and think it'll go away, Professor. Neither can I. Now you still want to hear my proposition?"

I don't want to hear it, but I am going to.

"Let's at least find out what the water's like, Professor. It won't hurt us to get just a little closer to where that wind is

35

blowing. Man, we can sample it, that's all. Just a little taste. There's a meeting tonight."

The Venable heels dig into the desk top for security. "What kind of meeting?"

"Students for Freedom, boss man. Better known as the S.F.F." Soft, sibilant Andy Brown voice, mellowed by the rich dark leaf. Strong northerly winds coming up and small craft warnings posted.

"I should work tonight."

"Boss man, you ain't gonna work tonight. You maybe gonna roll some nice clean paper in the machine and stuff some of that nice mild tobacco in that white pipe and play like you was workin', but you ain't really gonna work."

You are on my back, Andy Brown. I saw a preview of a movie with Dean Martin where this Japanese girl gets on his back and does wonderful things to tensed muscles with her toes. If you have to get on my back, Andy Brown, why the hell don't you do something for my tensed back muscles?

"Meetings scare me."

"Meetings scare me too, Professor, but there's something else scares me more. You know what scares me more?"

"Do I get to guess?"

"Not too many guesses."

"Impotency?"

"No such thing as an impotent black man. That's just for white folks."

"The bomb?"

"Love the bomb. Old bomb's gonna blow up every place but Africa."

"I give up. Don't tell me."

"Being in a vacuum scares me, Professor."

"You see that Jerry Lewis movie, Andy. He had this crazy vacuum cleaner . . ."

"There's action going on, Professor. Now I don't intend to

36

be a part of that action, but I do want to see what it is. Man needs to see what the action is. I think you need it too. Let's you and me go to that meeting, man. Let's take one little bitty peek at the world and see if we can get out of the vacuum just long enough to grab us a little piece of that action and then run back in the cave and gnaw on it some."

Venable makes a short speech.

"Andy, this town is already integrated at least eighty percent. What are there? Maybe a couple of lousy eating places and half a dozen little stores still back in the Stone Age. It's better here than any place in the South and most places up North. What do you people want?"

Lazy laughing Andy Brown. "What people, Professor? I don't have any people. I just want to watch a little of the action."

This road is under construction. Proceed at your own risk.

"What time is the meeting?"

"Eight o'clock, boss man."

"Where?"

"Calvary Baptist Church down on the south side of town."

"Sit near the back in case we want to leave?"

"Sure, boss man."

"Strictly spectator sport?"

"We'll take a bag of popcorn."

"Perhaps we ought to get there a few minutes late and sort of sneak in."

"Man, we'll take off our shoes."

Excitement stirring in the valiant Venable breast. A sense of daring. The natives are restless, Bwana. White man no safe in jungle tonight. Damn the natives! I just want to get the feel of the situation. No use trying to talk me out of it. No, I won't wear a gun. Let them see me out there unarmed. Give them a taste of backbone, what?

"I'll pick you up at eight."

"Crazy, Professor."

Crazy professor. Crazy Andy Brown. Crazy crazy crazy crazy whole goddamned world!

At fifteen minutes after eight.

Last previous Venable appearance inside a church three years ago at wedding of three-months pregnant daughter of colleague in the frozen North. Very fraught ceremony. Venable born a Baptist, raised a Baptist. Very big in Sunday school. Very active in Baptist Young People's Union better known as B.Y.P.U., better known as Button Your Pants Up.

Baptized at the age of eleven and none of this sprinkling crap either. All the way under. Strip down to your drawers and put on the long white robe and wait in the little antechamber while the organist plays "Shall We Gather by the River" and you hear the water running in the font because the janitor goofed and forgot to fill it before the service and you wonder if old Dr. Parker still has the strength not to drop you when you go under. Most of all the sound of the running water makes you want to pee and you pray to God whose army you are about to join that you won't pee in the baptismal font. Then someone calling your name and you walk through the door to where Dr. Parker greets you with a rotten-toothed smile and takes you by the hand. Napkin in your hand held by his hand. His other hand raised above your head and the painted picture of the River Jordan on the wall behind you and between you and that wall the baptismal font filled with water that looks cold. Dr. Parker whispering, "Just relax, Bobby." Dr. Parker raising his nasal voice for the congregation out there in the darkness to hear. "I baptize you, Robert Venable, in the name of the Father and of the Son . . ."

38

Oh dear God receive my soul to Your service and do not let this old fool drop me in the water!

And of the Holy Ghost! Amen!

Hand now behind my back and I am being carried down into the saving water and it is cold and the napkin slips just enough to fill my nose with water and I kick and want to yell but I am gagging and then I am up and shoved back through the door dripping and cold and scared and SAVED.

Venable at the age of eighteen screwed a woman and found God and left the church.

"Come on, Professor. Couple of seats here in the back row just like I said."

It is not a very big church and there are perhaps two hundred people already there which leaves only a few empty seats. A few heads turn to watch Venable and Andy Brown as they ease into a pair of folding wooden chairs. Perhaps two dozen white people in the church, most young, probably students from the university. Very nice church with white-washed walls rising above dark oak paneling. Stained-glass windows. A pipe organ and a baptismal font behind the platform stage where the pulpit stands. At the pulpit is a tall, hollow-cheeked coffee-creamed man wearing a black suit and a white shirt and a black tie. I recognize him as local minister named Clifford James. He is speaking. Behind him are four chairs. From left to right, a graduate student I recognize as Mac Kirkpatrick, campus president of Students for Freedom. A stocky, intense young man with a crew-cut blond head and heavy black-rimmed glasses and a good set of teeth. Next, a bulky black man, bald and bullet-headed, low-slung jaw and ANGRY of expression. Identity unknown to Venable. Next, young, cleric type with reversed white collar above black bib and gray suit. Very sharp. Very white and pink. Very golden of wavy hair. This one Venable knows to be the Reverend Alexander Nichols. Local, Episcopal and LIBERAL.

Stop at the next chair. God has wrought another miracle!

God has taken a vat of golden honey and poured it into a mold in the shape of a WOMAN and he has breathed life into it so that high pointed breasts rise and fall under soft clinging white wool. He has made it long of gleaming leg. He has made it with shining black hair pulled skin tight back over the ears and parted down the center of the head in a bold slashing line. He has given it huge yellow green eyes and a tilting nose that flares ever so little at the nostrils and a bold hungry red mouth.

Oh Sweet God this time you have really loused up your servant Venable!

Andy Brown's elbow nudges the Venable ribs. "Hey, man, you dig that chick?"

Venable asking in a whisper that croaks like a frog, "Who is she?"

"Don't know, man, but if she's with the Cause, I'm liable to join up."

Venable in heat, straining to listen to the words of the coffee and cream man.

"They tell us to be PATIENT! I want to know if you recognize that word. You recognize that word?"

They recognize that word and they cry out against it.

"They say the day is gonna come! They say give them time! I say the day has already come and passed!"

They agree.

"I say the time is NOW!"

They agree that the time is now. They shout their agreement. They clap it with their hands and they stamp it with their feet. SHE agrees too, but she does not clap. She does not stamp. She opens her red slash of mouth and a tip of tongue flicks out and touches the top lip, then vanishes again.

"They say this town is better'n most! We say this town is not good enough! They say be grateful for what has hap-

40

pened here! We say what has happened here is only the beginning!"

Venable worries about the clapping and the foot stamping. He knows he is impressionable and he whispers to Andy Brown.

"He needs new material, Andy. That's the same routine they used in Alabama. I saw it on the television."

When Venable makes a feeble attempt at humor, it is FEEBLE. Andy Brown does not even look in my direction. He is concentrating on the speaker and this is a worrisome thing that leads you to sing the blues in the night.

"Now before we hear from our other speakers I want you all to join in a little singing. You know what I want to hear, don't you?"

And the voices thundered back that they knew what he wanted to hear.

How odd, Venable thinks, that after reading about the song so much he still has never heard it sung.

> *We are not afraid. We are not afraid.*
> *We are not afraid today.*
> *Deep in my heart, I do believe*
> *We shall overcome someday.*

And the woman on the platform was singing with the rest, but she was not like the rest. She sang the song to Venable.

How in the hell did she know I was here? This is not the song you want to sing to me. Oh Sweet Jesus make that woman into a real nigger for me! I cannot fight her as a nee-grow or even as a colored woman. Make her into Miranda and I can be excited by her without wanting her.

Miranda! Tall, lean of leg, broad of hip and full of bosom. High-yellow Miranda. Miranda with thick lips and mean eyes and kinky hair. Miranda working for my grandmother. Mi-randa living in that little cabin just down from my grand-

41

parent's home with her two little boys and never a husband for them to call Daddy. Miranda sullen and sensuous, making her way in her own narrow world.

We shall overcome! We shall overcome!
We shall overcome someday!
Deep in my heart, I do believe
We shall overcome someday!

Thirteen-year-old Bobby Venable going with his father to the nigger Baptist church down by the river. Better than a circus his father tells him. "Never saw anything like that, son. They tell me Miranda's going to shout tonight." The one-room frame church is already rocking when they arrive. Betty Mills, ready to be saved again, meets them at the door.

"Howdedo, Mistuh Venable. Howdedo, Mistuh Bobby. Praise de Lawd, we havin' a great revival tonight. That preacher from Bear Swamp is got de debbil by de tail, fo sho, Mistuh Venable. You give Betty bout fifty cents and she really gonna shout!"

My father laughs and reaches into his wallet for a dollar bill.

"Lawd Jesus! Dis nigger gonna really be saved this night! Thankee, Mistuh Venable, suh. Thankee kindly!"

"Betty, is Miranda going to shout tonight? I told Bobby she might."

"Lawd, Mistuh Bobby, yo daddy done tol you da truth. Dat sinful nigger gonna holler this night cause dat preacher done swore he was gonna git de ol' debbil by de tail and pull him right outta Miranda fore dis revival is over and dis de las night! You gonna see somethin' sho!"

God is on our side! God is on our side!
God is on our side today!
Deep in my heart, I do believe
We shall overcome someday!

Don't sit there and tap the pointed toe of that high-heeled shoe at me! You should be barefoot with broad flat feet and dust between your toes like Miranda.

Miranda! Miranda in the very first row sitting still as stone, wearing a cotton calico dress and barefoot. Staring up at the lean blacksnake preacher who is just rising to begin to speak. He stands coiled and ominous, his slitted yellow eyes drifting over the hushed congregation. They drift until they come to rest on Miranda and the thick lips pull back in a snarling grin. Like a whip one long arm snaps out and a finger is pointing straight at Miranda.

"Woman! You'se a sinner!"

Miranda does not move a muscle as a great sigh goes up from the congregation.

"Lawd God look down on you and He knows you fo a sinner!"

And that long black finger twists and turns boring into Miranda and the blacksnake's right foot begins to tap very slowly to build the rhythm.

"Debbil's got you holdin' tight! You a sinner! Jesus love will sit you right! Pray sinner! Debbil's fire will burn yo soul! Jesus love kin make you whole!"

And the church rocked to the roaring PRAY SINNER!

Now the blacksnake throws his arms straight up and turns his snake head to the ceiling and starts to pray.

"Sweet Jesus look down on dis woman! She sittin' here, Jesus, full of de debbil! She a sinner, Jesus! Ol' debbil's got her in his claws, draggin' her straight down to Hell, Jesus! Ol' debbil got de fire roarin' to burn her fo a thousand years, Jesus! Heapin' on the red hot coals to roast her sinful flesh!"

AMEN! SWEET JESUS!

Miss Melted Honey of 1964 does not belong in this place. Transport her to a dimly lighted cocktail lounge in Manhattan. Perch her upon a high barstool and place a very dry martini before her and add the soft murmur of a piano in the background.

> *Let there be you.*
> *Let there be me . . .*

Blacksnake, whipping and lashing now under a full head of evangelical steam.

"Ol' debbil he say drink likker and you grab fo de jug! Ol' debbil he say gamble and you grab de dice! O' debbil he say FORNICATE and you grab holt of de first pair britches you see! Next thing ol' debbil gonna say to you, woman, is BURN IN HELL!"

Miranda moving now. Swaying from side to side with the blacksnake.

"Sweet Jesus help dis sinnin' woman! Sweet Jesus make her know her sin! Gonna go down and rassle with dat ol' debbil, Jesus, and give me yo strength. Look out debbil, me'n Jesus comin' to git you now!"

Seated at the next barstool is a suave, hair-gently-touched-with-distinguished-gray WRITER. She leans toward him with just that smile.

> *Let there be cuckoos*
> *A lark and a dove . . .*

Blacksnake coiling over Miranda now, snake head darting forward ready to strike.

"Now I got hold of de debbil, Jesus. He twistin' and turnin' but I ain't gonna let him loose!"

PRAISE JESUS! PREACHER GOT HOLT DE DEBBIL!

"You listen to me, sinner! Me'n Jesus fightin' de debbil in yo soul! You feel Him don' you sinner?"

Thirteen-year-old Bobby Venable frightened by the hair that rises on the back of his neck and the unknown excitement in his secret thing. Listen to the clap clap clap of hands.

44

Listen to the stomp stomp stomp of feet. Listen to the YES LAWD! Listen to the SWEET JESUS! Listen to the grunt grunt grunt. Smell the sweat! Feel the charge! See the black black black BLACK!

"Oh SWEET JESUS!"

Miranda on her feet now and wild. Miranda river-mud yellow under flimsy cotton twisting and squirming hip to hip and belly to belly with the blacksnake.

"SWEET JESUS I A SINNER!"

Miranda with high round buttocks jerking out of control. Miranda with head thrown back and her face gone wild. Eyes open and rolled to whites. Saliva bubbling from thick lips.

Black and white together! Black and white together!
Black and white together someday!
Deep in my heart, I do believe
We shall overcome someday!

And in the dimly lighted cocktail lounge the WRITER leans forward to whisper something in the honey ear of the honey woman and the red slash of mouth opens and a tip of tongue flicks out to touch the top lip, then vanishes in a smile and a nod of acquiescence.

But most of all please,
Let there be love.

Bobby Venable sick and retching being taken from the church by his father. Bobby Venable sick and frightened and lying in the big bed in the big room at his grandfather's house and hearing his father laughing and talking to his uncle in the next room.

"Those fool niggers really got religion tonight. You should've seen Miranda. That black preacher from Bear Swamp was turning her every way but loose. One of the boys told me they saw him taking Miranda home after the meeting. I'll bet there's some tall humping going on right now. They tell me that preacher's got one that hangs down around his knees and Miranda's probably got that black pecker stuffed clear up to her gullet. She's going to be saved if it kills that preacher."

And five hundred miles and twenty-seven years away Miss Honeypot unlocks the door to her exotic apartment in mid-Manhattan and the WRITER walks in and there is barely time to close the door behind them and rip away his suave WRITER's clothing and rip away her white clinging wool and the honey melts and runs all over him in sweet sticky burning urgencies and he pants into her honey ear.

"Your name! You didn't tell me your name!"

And strong teeth gnaw at his shoulder and he smells the rich sweaty smell and her head is thrown back so that thick lips laugh at him.

"Lawd, Mistuh Bobby, yo knows Miranda! Cmon, Mistuh Bobby, give Miranda dat big ol' thing you got!"

No!

Now approaching the pulpit is Mac Kirkpatrick the IN-TENSE young man. He stands waiting for the applause to die away and he looks upon his colored brothers with love and sorrow and dedication.

"What do you want?"

"FREEDOM!"

"When do you want it?"

"Now!"

Andy Brown looking at Venable with concern. "What's the matter with you, man? You look sick. You all right?"

I nod. I am sick, but I know the cure. Look at Mac Kirkpatrick. Look at the ceiling. Look at my hands. Look anywhere except at her.

"I am very pleased to see such a fine turnout tonight." The Kirkpatrick approach is SINCERE. "I will not take up much of your time because there is someone else here we all want to hear."

Oh God, he is talking about HER!

"I do want to report that there was a meeting of our university chapter of Students for Freedom this afternoon, and the membership voted unanimously to support every demonstration, every sit-in, and every boycott in West Brandon."

Loud cheers and applause and a few AMENS.

"S.F.F. wants to be at your side when the police come! This will be our fight as well as yours!"

More of the same.

"And now we come to the moment we've all been waiting for. The national headquarters of S.F.F. has recognized the extreme importance of the crusade for a one hundred percent integrated community in West Brandon, and they have sent one of the most successful fieldworkers in the entire nation to help us plan an all-out campaign to sweep away every racial barrier which rears its ugly head in our town. All of you know her by her deeds in this great cause, and it gives me great pleasure to introduce her to you now—your sister in the fight for freedom—Miss Alise Hungerford!"

Bedlam! Even Andy Brown is clapping his hands and stamping his feet as everyone in the church stands and begins to sing.

> *Oh freedom, oh freedom,*
> *Oh freedom over me!*
> *And before I'll be a slave*
> *I'll be buried in my grave*
> *And go home to my Lord and be free!*

Everyone but Venable who has reached the end of his short rope. He stumbles past Andy Brown and gropes blindly for the door.

"Man, where you going?"

No time to answer. Only time to run. Run for the street. Run for the car.

JESUS WHERE ARE MY KEYS!

Gun the engine! Lay the rubber! How will Andy Brown get home? That is Andy Brown's problem. Venable on the lam and running and making it to suburbia and into the garage and up the stairs and answering the questions about did you have an interesting evening and saying I'll tell you all about it tomorrow only dear God let me crawl into bed right now and shut out everything in the blackness and maybe with any luck I can sleep three days and wake up and it will all be gone.

BLACKOUT!

five

NOT FOR THE WEAK OF HEART!
FILMED IN LIVING
BLOOD!
BLOOD FEAST

Lucy had sent Charlie Brown a bill for $143 to cover her services as a psychiatrist. He was reluctant to pay so she had written a letter to the A.M.A. to seek their assistance. It was not very funny, and, Jesus, when *Peanuts* was not very funny, what the hell kind of day could you expect!

The University's basketball team had lost the services of its star player because he had failed three courses in the first semester. He had been taking four courses. Why is it that one somehow expects basketball players to be better students than football players? Perhaps it is because they look so goddamned clean-cut running around in their underwear. The fact of the matter is that I am not very fond of basketball. But on this morning I read everything about it in the sports section. I also read about something to do with golf, of which I am even less fond than I am of basketball.

Moving on studiously to the society section, I discovered a

49

number of fascinating items. The Ladies' Auxiliary of the Elks Club was holding a rummage sale. A female with buck teeth was betrothed to a gentleman named Harold Pfeiffer. Some vows had been said in a simple ceremony at the First Presbyterian Church. Nuptials had been set for early June between a Miss Agnes Higglesworth and a Mr. Strumberger, while a double ring ceremony had united one Abner Coxworthy and a triumphant-looking wench named Patience Jones.

One might have got the notion that I was stalling for time.

But time ran out. I turned to the front page.

We were still up the creek with no visible sign of a paddle in South Vietnam. Four high school kids had been killed instantly when their late-model car had tried to take the right of way from an interstate bus. The bus driver had suffered only minor bruises. A big score for the bus company. Castro had accused the C.I.A. of torturing Cuban fishermen picked up inside U.S. territorial waters. The State Department had accused the Russians of murdering U.S. fliers shot down over East Germany.

Oh, Jesus!

NEW DEMONSTRATIONS PROMISED BY
ALISE HUNGERFORD

There was a picture of her taken at the meeting of the previous night. I was thankful for the lousy reproduction of photographs in the local paper. There was no sharpness. I could close my eyes just a bit and she became a blur.

New and "unique" demonstrations were promised for the local Civil Rights Movement by a field representative of the national Students for Freedom organization. Addressing a gathering of nearly two hundred persons at the Calvary Baptist Church last

50

night, Alise Hungerford of Philadelphia pledged an all-out campaign aimed at ending "every vestige of racial discrimination in West Brandon" by Easter.

Miss Hungerford is a graduate of Vassar and holds a Master of Arts degree from Columbia. During the past two years she has been active in the work of the S.F.F. organization in Philadelphia, New York and Chicago. She expressed herself as being "greatly thrilled and honored" to have been invited to take part in "one of the most significant areas of the Civil Rights movement in the entire nation."

She told the audience that this was her first visit to the South and that her reaction was one of "deep humility and determination."

Introducing Miss Hungerford was the student president of the University's S.F.F. chapter, Mac Kirkpatrick. Following the meeting, neither Kirkpatrick nor Miss Hungerford would reveal any details of the new demonstrations which are being planned other than to say that they would be of a completely new and "dramatically different" variety.

There was a comfort in the cold factual news story. Nothing of Alise Hungerford shone through. She was a name, and the events were removed from reality. I began to feel better, as I turned to the editorial page for hints on how I should think about controversial matters.

BEWARE THE JABBERWOCKY!

One of the advantages enjoyed by a newspaper published in a university town is the literary editorial writer. West Brandon had one.

One of the most charming bits of double talk and nonsense in all literature is Lewis Carroll's "The Jabberwocky," one stanza of which reads as follows:

> "Beware the Jabberwock, my son!
> The jaws that bite, the claws that catch!

Beware the Jubjub bird, and shun
The frumious Bandersnatch!"

This kind of poetic fluff, while it makes little sense, is a lot of fun. Unfortunately, when double talk and nonsense reasoning are applied in matters relating to the human condition, the results are far from fun for anyone. Our community is currently the prime target for some of the most dangerous nonsense and double-talk in the history of the Civil Rights movement. This newpaper and a majority of the citizens of West Brandon have consistently presented a forward-thinking attitude to the fully justified quest of our Negro fellow citizens for a just and equitable solution to their proper grievances. It is with a deep sense of pride that we have watched this community assume a place of leadership in the South in racial equality. In recent weeks, however, we have seen West Brandon made the target for senseless vituperation by militant integrationist leaders who demand that a record which is already far superior to that of any other southern community is not enough. They insist that we must achieve what few communities or individuals ever achieve—perfection. To reach this Utopian goal, they are making a serious error. Outsiders, people who have no understanding of local conditions or attitudes, are being imported to direct this "all-out" campaign.

The good citizens of West Brandon may find themselves forced into a correspondingly ridiculous and nonsensical position as regards Civil Rights. When it is no longer possible to maintain a reasonable position on moderate ground, the only alternatives are to leap to either one nonsensical extreme or the other.

How tragic it would be were we to find ourselves divided into Jubjub Birds and Bandersnatches on the one side and childish zealots brandishing our vorpal swords on the other!

I was saved! Once again the power of the printed word had worked its miracle. When something is printed in a paper, it is true, I thought, and how foolish all my doubts and worries seemed. Gratefully, I pictured my contribution by way of a Letter to the Editor.

To the Editor:
Congratulations on your timely and comforting editorial entitled "Beware the Jabberwocky!" It is with a deep sense of relief that I found myself reassured that I was not, as I had feared, a complete horse's ass.

ROBERT VENABLE, AUTHOR

six

I was armed with that most blessed of convictions that actually I had been right all along, so what the hell was I worrying about with all that conscience crap, so I was carefree and gay and giving my Creative Writing classes the full treatment, white pipe and all, ignoring the fact that Andy Brown was absent—in fact, relieved as hell that Andy Brown was absent— and generally being an all-around Writer-in-Residence.

Item. I even accepted an invitation from two of my colleagues in the English Department to go to the Faculty Club for lunch.

Introductions are in order.

The Director of Creative Writing in the English Department was afflicted with the name of Dr. John Allen, unpublished. Blessed by nature with a face and figure and personality which could easily have supported some such name as Ichabod Clutterbuck or Ferdinac Frigglesworth or, Golly Moses, a whole collection of magnificently appropriate names, he had been restricted by the gross inadequacies of unimaginative parents who chose to christen him Dr. John Allen.

And the other half of the regular staff's Creative Writing

team was a native of West Brandon who, twenty-five years earlier, had written and had published a novel dealing with the Civil War. One of the more startling and striking things about this novel was that it was not made into a motion picture starring Clark Gable and Vivien Leigh and Leslie Howard, a fact which had embittered and disillusioned its author, Miss Samantha Simms, to the point that she had never written another word. Incidentally, *her* parents had chosen names well. She *looked* like Miss Samantha Simms.

And she conducted classes. And she planned new novels.

There is nothing so comforting as to gather for repast in the company of one's peers in a Faculty Club. It matters little that what one is actually gathering in is a discarded cafeteria formerly used for the feeding of the football team. In the proper course of events the football team had been moved on to a more lavishly appointed establishment, and the faculty had been fortunate enough to secure this facility. In the Faculty Club, by standing in line for a remarkably short period of time owing to the fact that only a desperate handful of the faculty could stomach the fare, one could make a choice from such items as BREADED PORK CHOPS or COUNTRY STYLE STEAK or BEEF POT PIE or, on Fridays, FRIED SCALLOPS.

The three of us agonized over our choices and made our way past the other two tables of unhappy lunchers to our chosen spot at the far end of the room.

Dr. John Allen was a man who would pursue a point of knowledge relentlessly until every effort to dislodge truth had been exhausted. Accordingly he began our conversation by asking me the same question he had asked on some fourteen previous encounters since I had arrived at the University to take up my duties as Writer-in-Residence.

"Well, Robert, how's it going with you? Found any future Hemingways yet?"

I searched my mind to discover some new and exotic response but decided at last on the tried and proven one.

"Well, I think it's going fine. There're some very interesting kids in those classes."

"Great bunch of kids! Been a long time since this University turned out a really top-notch writer, though. Now, I don't think that's any reflection on the writing program or us, Samatha, but it's good to stir things up every once in awhile. I had a lot of trouble convincing the Dean that this Writer-in-Residence thing was sound, but by golly, we finally built the right kind of fire under him."

The noonday meal being no place to challenge one's colleagues, I did not comment on reports I had heard from various students to the effect that a Dr. John Allen had fought the student-sponsored move to secure the services of a Writer-in-Residence until the students finally went over his head to the wife of the Dean who threatened to suspend the Dean's already dwindling bedroom privileges unless he approved the program. After all, it could have been some other Dr. John Allen.

"I am finding my own classes quite discouraging this year," said Miss Samantha Simms. "And I attribute this directly to all the terrible things the colored people are stirring up in West Brandon. I finally had to lay the law down to my students. Any story dealing with this subject will simply not be accepted. After all, there is still a place in literature for beauty and things of the spirit."

While I was a graduate student at the University, I had read Samantha Simms' novel about the Civil War, entitled *The Gallant Gray.* It was a moving tribute to the OLD SOUTH. Plantation owners who loved all their nigger slaves. Nigger slaves who loved all their owners. Wasp-waisted, full-bosomed virgins who waited bravely for the return of the dashing

56

heroes in gray. Dirty, swinish Yankee sons-of-bitches who burned and pillaged and raped.

There is a quotable quote made by Andy Brown who had taken a writing course under her instruction.

"That Miss Simms, she likes colored folks. Tell the truth, she loves colored folks. She loves us so much she'd like to own about a dozen."

What ensued was a three-way conversation among two BIGOTS and a LIBERAL.

Dr. John Allen said, "I could not agree with you more, Samantha. It is totally incomprehensible to me that these things could be taking place in West Brandon." Then Dr. John Allen sighed. "I have lived here and taught in this University for more than twenty years, and I have watched with a real sense of pride the way both the University and the community have responded to the agonizing pressures brought about by these so-called Civil Rights people." Dr. John Allen chuckled tolerantly. "Mind you, Robert, I do believe in the principles they stand for. They are human beings with the same feelings and sensitivities that we have. Shakespeare put it best, I suppose, in those marvelous lines he wrote for Shylock. All one has to do is substitute the word *Negro* for *Jew*, and there you have it."

He was followed by Samantha Simms who gushed, "Precisely. Now, as you know I have always lived in the South, and I simply cannot change a basic attitude with which I have lived all my life. I do think, however, that I have made a good adjustment to the changing times. When the University was opened to these people, I did not resist it. I won't say I like it, but I accepted it. I have even had one or two of them in my classes, and I pride myself on having bent over backwards to be fair to them. As a matter of fact I think this entire community has bent over backwards to be fair to the colored people, and this is the thanks we get."

I said, "Would anyone like some more coffee?"

Dr. John Allen added, "As for myself, I have always prided myself on having what I feel is a liberal attitude, despite the fact that I am a native southerner. On at least two occasions I have written rather strongly worded letters to the editor in support of the basic principles of limited school integration. But over and above all that, I am a member of the faculty of this University and an adopted, but nevertheless loyal, citizen of this community. Now my University and my community are being attacked and maligned—without cause, and I must confess I find myself in opposition to this."

And Samantha Simms agreed. "It's those outsiders who make the trouble, Dr. Allen. The local colored people have always been so easy and contented with their way of life. There is the dearest old soul who has worked for my family for nearly forty years. That's Aunt Annie, Dr. Allen. I'm sure you've seen her. She worked for my dear mother, and now she works for me, and there is nothing in this world I would not do for Aunt Annie, and I know she feels exactly the same way about me. Now, only yesterday Aunt Annie was ironing in my kitchen. I've fixed it so she can sit down while she irons, because, after all, she is in her sixties now, and I feel an obligation to take care of her. Anyway, I asked her right out what she thought about all these demonstrations, and Aunt Annie looked right at me, and she said just as honest as you please, and she is honest—just as honest as the day is long—she said, 'Miss Samantha, that's them crazy niggers doing all that. Most of us colored folks won't have nothing to do with them.' Now those were Aunt Annie's exact words."

At which point I mumbled, "Well, I will say this much. It's a distressing thing. It is—distressing." And to drive my point home even more conclusively, I muttered, "Well, I have a student coming for a session in five minutes, so I'd better dash."

58

This was the end of the conversation among two BIGOTS and a LIBERAL.

I ran! I ran to find myself a real bigot. For Christ's sake, I thought, I will put myself in juxtaposition to someone against whom I will be forced to take a stand. After all, what was the point of arguing with those two idiots? They counted for nothing. They were so obviously phoney that it would have been a waste of the Venable brand of fiery liberalism to joust with them. I wanted to go where the fighting was the heaviest.

There was this little store on the west side of town, just inside the West Brandon city limits. Here one could purchase a loaf of bread or a carton of milk or a six-pack of beer or other minor needs. It had no charm. Other than the fact that it remained open late at night and on Sunday, it offered no unique advantages. It was simply a place. And it was a target. Painted in bold yellow letters across the front door there was this message.

NO NIGGERS OR DOGS ALLOWED

Here the bigotry was blatant, and here I would confront it. However, being an AUTHOR, I was much too clever to just charge into this citadel of evil and blunt my liberal lance against the windmill of intolerance. I had a role to play—the role of an ordinary, casual customer who would strike up a conversation with the proprietor, lulling that villain into loose talk and then—at the proper moment—I would run him through.

I parked my red sports car and entered casually, pushing through the door with its sickening warning inscription and managing to avert my eyes so that I was not forced to read the admonition. There was no avoidance of any issue involved there. I merely recognized the potent anger which lay dor-

59

mant within me, and I was properly wary of releasing it too soon.

The villain was behind the counter accepting payment for a quart of milk and a package of hamburger buns from a dirty man in dirty overalls. Biding my time, I browsed casually at the soft drink stand, apparently debating the relative merits of Pepsi-Cola and Seven-Up and waiting until the other customer had departed.

"Help you with something, mister?"

Controlling the hard, tight smile which might have betrayed me too soon, I turned casually to confront the enemy. The enemy was a huge man of some fifty years. He wore a soiled pair of brown trousers, a short-sleeved gray shirt which exposed a massive chest and huge arms, both of which were heavily matted with thick, curling black hairs. Hands resembling two small hams rested on the counter top. His head was completely and indecently bald. His face was red and blotched and unshaven. The enemy had been typecast.

"Just a loaf of bread and some drinks." I placed a carton of Pepsis on the counter and turned to select the bread from the rack behind me.

"Anything else?"

"Not today." I managed to keep my tone quite casual. "How're things going?"

"Can't complain."

"Business pretty good?"

"Fair. Could be better."

I began to sense that the bait was being nibbled. "You're kind of on the spot, I guess, with . . ." I made a vague waving motion with my arms. "All this."

The villain swallowed my bait in one ugly gulp. "Only goddamned spot I'm on, mister, is this one where my place of business is standing. And I'm stayin' right on this spot just like I want to."

60

I had to struggle to keep my eyes innocent. My hand held the line lightly, but I was ready. The hook was almost in. "You expecting any new trouble from . . ." Again I made that meaningful gesture. "All this?"

Now the eyes of the enemy narrowed to evil slits, and I could see the muscles in the enemy's upper arms appear to swell perceptibly as the hams closed into red fists.

"Any trouble those black sonsabitches start around here, I can finish." He leaned forward, resting his weight heavily on those fists so that the muscles in his lower arms bulged noticeably. And his mouth split in an ugly grin. "I been running this here little old store for near twenty-five years, and there ain't never been a nigger in here less'n it was to deliver somethin' off a truck and then git his black ass out. And what's more, mister, there ain't never gonna be no nigger comes into this store long as I got the breath of life left in me."

The ugly grin exploded into a hoarse and raucous laugh.

"Them black sonsabitches talkin' about how they're gonna try some new tricks. Well, you just listen to me, buddyrow, I got me some old tricks I can use. I killed me a nigger once in my life, and I ain't a bit against doin' it again if I have to."

At last I was ready to strike. I placed the loaf of whole-wheat bread casually on the counter beside the carton of Pepsis, let my gaze drift contemptuously over the enemy—his evil, slitted eyes, the knotted, bulging muscles of the lower and upper arm—and I opened my courageous mouth to deliver the killing remark.

But the mechanism failed! The wrong record had been set on the spindle!

"Uh—how much do I owe you?"

Frantically I tried to find out where the trouble was before it was too late!

"You didn't bring no bottles with you, did you?"

Oh Jesus, I prayed, let me find the error! Where did it all go wrong!

"No. No bottles."

I was all thumbs trying to put the damned thing right!

"Well, sir, that'll be twenty cents for the bread and fifty-three cents for the drinks countin' the deposit on the bottles. Comes to seventy-three cents plus tax makes it seventy-six cents."

It was no damned use. I had the wrong record but the correct change, and I grabbed the loaf of bread and the drinks and went out through the door, past the yellow letters on the door and into my little red AUTHOR's car.

And I drove home. And for the first time I was beginning to know who the real enemy was.

seven

There are times when the life of a hermit seems infinitely desirable to me. A hermit is spared such complicating extensions of the human condition as wives and children and telephones. A hermit, hung upon the agonizing hook of his own moral cowardice, can jolly well crawl into his hermit's cave, pull the leaves up over his miserable carcass and suck his goddamned thumb in peace and quiet. A hermit, even within the context of suburbia, can take his loaf of whole-wheat bread and his carton of Pepsi-Colas into his split-level cave and crawl into a tub of hot water or into a dry martini or into something which can give him solace.

Not having the good fortune to be a hermit, I was not spared either wife or children or, for that matter, the telephone.

Elaine and Jimmy met me at the door, gleefully at large on a school day at the hour of half past one.

"There's a big teachers' meeting," Jimmy explained. "We got half a day off!"

"All the schools in town let out at one o'clock," Elaine added. "Isn't that keeno, Daddy?"

I clutched my bread and Pepsis to me and muttered my agreement at how keeno it was.

"Mom says maybe you could take us to the library." This was Jimmy, the patron of the literary arts.

"Mom says you might be able to take us to a movie if there's anything good playing." This was Elaine, the patron of the cinematic arts.

"Hi, honey. Someone's been trying to reach you on the phone." This was Cathy, the patron of the art of getting kids out of her own hair and into mine.

"Who was it?"

"I don't know."

"Didn't he say?"

"*She* wouldn't say, but *she* left a number for you to call."

Her emphasis on the feminine pronoun was actually more subtle than indicated here, but it is important to make it clear that the emphasis was there.

"Probably one of my students."

"She didn't sound like a student."

It was a conversation which was leading us nowhere, so I let it end there, taking the slip of paper on which Cathy had written the telephone number and retreating to the hall to study it before returning the call.

965-3002.

I have a way of retaining telephone numbers. It is a part of an overall talent for the near-perfect retention of nonessential information. I can recite the 1939 batting average of Billy Horstschmidt who played second base for my high school baseball team, name the entire cast of *It Happened One Night,* render "The Raven" in its entirety, and tell the telephone number of Alicia Boyd, a plumpish girl with whom I enjoyed considerable exploratory sex play in the tenth grade.

965-3002 meant nothing to me.

But I dialed the number, uncomfortably aware of Cathy who had taken up station a few feet astern of me and was watching me with an unsettling curiosity.

The ringing stopped, and the voice murmured, "Hello." I knew who it was, though I had never heard the voice before, and I could feel the magical transformation of good solid bones and marrow into jelly.

"This is Robert Venable. Someone left word for me to call . . ."

"Yes, Mr. Venable. I'm so glad you called." There was that little extra breathiness which insisted that she *was* so glad I had called. "This is Alise Hungerford."

Immediate problem—how to keep my voice steady and unaffected with Cathy's mildly, suspiciously curious gaze threatening me from the rear and that voice launching a frontal attack. One thing was certain—any hope I might have entertained that Miss Alise Hungerford's voice would sound like anything other than exactly the way *her* voice ought to sound, had gone down the drain. I had escaped from the Calvary Baptist Church before she had started to speak, and I had been able to hopefully imagine that she would really sound like Butterfly McQueen, but now that saving illusion was shattered. Miss Melted Honey sounded like Miss Melted Honey, and I was getting all sticky sweet inside . . .

I made a cautious response. "Oh, yes . . ."

"Although we haven't met yet, Mr. Venable, I have been hearing a great deal about you from one of your students, Mr. Brown . . ."

A Mr. Brown, I snarled to myself, who has just been shot down in flames over his Creative Writing class for being a big mouth.

"Yes," I said. "Oh, yes . . ."

"Mr. Brown was telling me that you attended the meeting with him last evening, but that you had to leave before it was over. He also told me how very much you are interested in our problem here in West Brandon."

Oh, Andy Brown, I thought, you have really done it to your friend and mentor, Venable. You had better never show your black face in my class again, Andy Brown!

"Well," I said. "Well, yes . . ."

"We need the help of men like you, Mr. Venable—artists of all sorts, but especially writers, men who understand the power of words and ideas. Because these are the weapons we must fight with, don't you agree?"

"Well, yes," I said, "I suppose so . . ."

"I'm so glad you agree. Mr. Brown assured me that you would. Now, Mr. Venable, let me come straight to the point. We want to have a meeting, a rather exclusive meeting with a few key people in West Brandon's Civil Rights movement. And we would like to have you there, as a man who is in sympathy with our program who, for various reasons, has not yet actively associated himself with our work. The purpose of this meeting will be to explain to you just what we are striving for and how we plan to achieve our goals. There is no obligation on your part, but we do want you to get a firsthand picture of our situation. Then it is up to you to decide how you can help."

"Oh," I said. "I see. Well . . ."

"I know this is terribly short notice, Mr. Venable, but then, time is of the essence, don't you agree? Could you possibly make that meeting tonight? We will be at the Calvary Baptist Church again, down in the basement in one of the Sunday school rooms. At eight o'clock, Mr. Venable, and I can't begin to tell you how much I am counting on your being there."

The unfunny joke had gone far enough. Having just been put to rout by the Hairy Ape at the neighborhood grocery store, I was in no mood to suffer the same fate from the Sex

Goddess of the Freedom Marcher Set. Screw you, beautiful, sexy lady, I said bravely to myself. Screw you and all the lovely little traps you are setting for me, using poor gullible Andy Brown as bait.

She beat me to the draw.

"Mr. Venable, are you still there?"

"Well, yes. I was just . . ."

"Good. I thought perhaps we'd been disconnected. Now, we can expect you at eight, can't we?"

"At eight? Well, I suppose . . ."

"Wonderful. I'm looking forward to meeting you in person. Good-bye."

I considered the telephone in my hand for several seconds before putting it down, debating seriously the possibility of ripping the entire installation from the wall and smashing it with a hammer for the wrong it had done me.

"Well, you certainly were a charming conversationalist." Cathy had *that* sound. "Was it a student?"

I took care not to turn my head so she could see me. There is this thing about Cathy. She knows me too well, and she has developed a nasty little knack of knowing when I lie to her just by watching my mouth. Her own way of describing it is that my mouth "doesn't work right." I'm not sure what the hell she means by this, but she has me conditioned to the point that when I am even considering lying to her about something, the muscles around my mouth seem to tighten up, and I have trouble moving my lips when I speak. Since my instantaneous decision was not to tell her the truth about this particular phone call, I preferred to keep my face averted from her wise-ass gaze.

"Yes," I said, forcing my lips to move so as to articulate carefully. "I don't think you know her. Brenda Adams. She's having a bad time with one of her stories, and she's anxious to talk with me about it."

"Oh," said Cathy, in a tone which led me to suspect that she could see right through my head to my lying mouth.

And, of course, having committed myself to the lie, I immediately wondered why the hell I had bothered. After all, there was nothing to hide from Cathy. But I had hidden something, and I was stuck with it.

"Yes," I said, getting up and edging into the bathroom to get a glass of water. "She's got some real promise as a writer, but she has a way of getting bogged down on little things, and sometimes it's best just to sit down with her and talk her clear of whatever's bothering her. I'll run in and see her at the office tonight."

"All right."

I had a second glass of water, made a quick check of my mouth in the mirror, was pleased to see that it seemed to be working normally, and, thus encouraged, went out to face Cathy. It was my experience that the mouth routine operated most strikingly in the very earliest stages of the lie. Once I was underway, it was rather easy to carry it along.

So I made a test run on Cathy with a smile. "Damned nuisance, honey, and I'm sorry. I'd looked forward to staying home tonight and getting some work done on the novel."

"Well, that's the price you have to pay for being a teacher."

And she was returning my smile with her own smile which was just enigmatic enough to worry me and make me want to kick my ass for having lied to her in the first place.

There is another thing about Cathy. She is a bug on communication. This has always been a problem with us, because I am not basically a good or willing communicator. I prefer not to expose myself by means of the spoken word, and in times of personal stress, I have a nasty tendency to withdraw into my own private little shell to ride out the storm alone. And while there are undoubtedly many things about

68

the Venable personality which Cathy finds mildly irritating, I know damned well that this is something which really drives her up the wall. Over the years of our marriage, we have had some dandy brawls over this point, and I usually wind up promising to try to do better. But there is no point in such promises. I know this, and Cathy knows this, so we try to live with it, but it is not always easy.

Now I was not communicating, and she knew it, so she smiled that smile, and I had wistful thoughts of her warm ass which would be cold that night.

That night!

I arrived at the Calvary Baptist Church a few minutes after eight. An ancient black man in a faded blue suit met me at the front entrance and directed me to a stairway with instructions which he mumbled in reassuringly southern darkie accents as to how I could find the meeting room "jes down de stairs, Cap'n."

In the basement there was a long hall with doors opening off from it, undoubtedly to rooms where Sunday school classes were held. I remembered those rooms in the church I had attended as a child—little cubicles with a table and some chairs where every Sunday morning we would gather at ten o'clock to "study" the lesson for that week. What actually took place was a desperate effort on the part of whatever poor Christian adult who had volunteered to teach us to maintain some degree of order for the better part of an hour—a task to which various teachers applied themselves in various ways, ranging from telling us ghost stories to threatening to beat our brains out if we didn't hold our voices down to a mild roar.

In this hallway of the Calvary Baptist Church, I found myself trying to remember if I had ever thought of little black children in a Sunday school class just like the one I was in. It was not likely that I had.

Only one of the doors was open, and there was a light in that room, so I cleverly deduced that the meeting would be there.

Not actually.

She was in that room, and, from the moment I passed through the door, I was in that room, but there was not anyone else in that room.

At this point, I should probably go into a somewhat detailed description of Miss Alise Hungerford as seen at close quarters in an eight-by-nine Sunday school classroom. I will be succinct in the manner I was told that Billy Wilder was succinct in his script for the Jack Lemmon film, *The Apartment*. According to a Hollywood type I once met, Wilder, when writing his opening sequence, had described a rather important building as follows:

It is a gasser.

With apologies to Billy Wilder whom I have never had the pleasure of meeting, Miss Alise Hungerford was, as seen at close range, a gasser.

And she was alone.

"You're Mr. Venable?"

I was, and I was man enough to admit it.

"I'm so glad you did come. At the last minute, we decided to change our meeting place, so I stayed here to let you know. The others should be there now, so perhaps we ought to get started right away."

She moved toward the door and me, and I backed away from her as she reached the door, switched off the light and closed the door behind us.

"I hope you won't mind, Mr. Venable, if I catch a ride with you. I have the address, and I think I can give you instructions how to get there. It's the home of the minister of this church, Reverend James."

Up to that point, if I had said anything intelligible, I

cannot remember it. We went back up the stairs and past the old Negro at the door who bobbed his kinky white head and muttered something obsequious. My sports car was parked at the curb, and she made approving noises.

"Oh, it's a love!" She slid into the bucket seat and flashed a smile up at me as I closed the door for her. As I did this, I was trying to recall if I had ever before opened the door for a Negro. A small thing, but bothersome at the time. When I had eased myself into the other bucket seat, she continued, "This reminds me of the TR-Three a boy I used to date in college drove. He was so much in love with that car that I don't think he would have given it up for anyone."

I cleared my throat and groped cautiously for the stick shift, aware as I did that it brought my hand within a fraction of an inch from the silken sheen of her knee. If I had needed to put the car in reverse, I might actually have brushed that knee, and I breathed a silent prayer of thanks that the required gear was low.

"This," I said, after two more distinct throat clearings and a starting of the engine, "is a TR-Four."

"Yes, I know. Do you like it?"

We pulled away from the curb and were on our way. "Yes, it's a great little car." I have this knack of being able to express myself in a remarkably fresh and unclichéd way at times.

"I don't think I like it as well as the Three, though," she said. "I hope that doesn't hurt your feelings."

"No. Of course not."

The hell it didn't hurt my feelings!

"I mean, the Three is more along the lines of the classic sports car. There's something so elemental about riding in it, and I loved the long hood and the cut-down sides. Why, you could actually trail your fingers along the road."

"That could be pretty painful."

71

She laughed, and it was a good laugh—the kind that girls you like and take out to movies and dances and dinner laugh.

"Well, you know what I mean, don't you?"

I knew what she meant, because I had felt the same way when I bought the Four. What I had done, of course, had been to sacrifice my own instinctive preference for the older model to gain the luxury of roll-up windows. It had been as simple as that, and now I was damned ashamed of myself. Who, for Christ's sake, needed roll-up windows?

"Oh," she said suddenly. "I forgot to tell you where we have to go."

I didn't care where we had to go, but I wasn't about to let her know that. So I applied the disc brakes and looked attentive while she gave me instructions on how to reach the residence of the good Reverend James.

He lived about half a mile from the church in a section which represented the highest level of the Negro society in West Brandon. The house was a two-story frame building set fairly well back from the unpaved street. Several cars were already parked in front of the house, among them Andy Brown's aging Plymouth.

I commented on this to my companion.

"Yes, Mr. Brown is here. He—" She stopped abruptly and turned to look at me just as I was reaching for the door handle. "Mr. Venable—just a minute. Before we go in, there's something I'd like to discuss with you."

I had been vaguely aware of the fragrance of jasmine, but up to this point I had managed to ignore it. Now it did its best to envelop me. I kept one hand on the door handle. I have this sort of instinct for escape from close quarters. For example, I always try to sit next to the emergency exit in planes.

"It's about Mr. Brown," she was saying. I permitted myself

one quick look. In dimly lighted profile, she was still a gasser.

"I gather he is one of your students."

I had been gassed by the gasser. "Who?"

"Mr. Brown."

"Oh—Andy—yes."

The profile tilted slightly to a quarter view. "His name is Andy?"

"Yes."

"Andy Brown?"

The quarter-view gasser frowned. "How unfortunate."

"You mean because of Amos and . . ."

Sharply. "Yes!"

"He told me his folks were great fans of Amos and Andy."

"That's terrible. Don't you agree, Mr. Venable?"

"Did you ever listen to them?"

Decisively. "No!"

"They were very popular."

"That kind of humor at the expense of an oppressed people is, I'm glad to say, no longer acceptable."

End of conversation about Amos and Andy.

"You were talking about Andy—our Andy Brown . . ."

Her quick smile efficiently put all unpleasantness to rout. "Yes, of course. Well, I met him after our meeting last night. He came up and introduced himself, and we had quite an interesting talk."

I was surprised and said so. "My feeling was that Andy didn't want to get involved in—all this."

She gave a strange little laugh. "He didn't. He came up to ask me to go out with him."

Foxy you, Andy Brown.

"Andy's quite a guy."

She nodded. "Yes, he struck me as being rather brilliant, but he seems to lack direction and purpose."

"So you didn't give him a date?"

"Oh yes, we went out that very night and talked for a long time. That's when he told me about you."

That damned jasmine was getting to me. I had grown up with the popular southern myth that colored people smelled differently from white people. I can still hear my sainted mother saying, "It's the way they *smell*, honey. I just couldn't stand sitting next to one of them the way they *smell*."

Alise Hungerford smelled great!

"Mr. Venable?"

"Yes?"

"Don't you agree that he lacks direction and purpose?"

"I suppose you could say that. He's a loner."

"Does he have talent—as a writer?"

I thought that one over for a moment. "He's written a couple of good stories based on his experiences in Korea. I think he has talent—yes."

"I'm glad! We need men with talent. We have the numbers, Mr. Venable, but the Negro in the South must eventually provide his own leadership. That is why I am so concerned with a man like Mr. Brown. He has intelligence—that is obvious. And you say he has talent. But still he seems to prefer to hang back from our struggle."

I was getting pretty damned restless. If I sat there smelling that jasmine smell much longer, I was going to start getting ideas, and I didn't want to get those ideas.

"I'm not sure where I fit into all this."

She turned and placed her hand on my arm, a simple and quite natural action which affected me not at all, except for wiping out God knows how many generations' aversion to miscegenation. I had this crazy spontaneous debate raging over whether or not sex was really possible in the front seat of a sports car. And all because of a goddamned hand on my arm!

"He respects you a great deal, Mr. Venable. He told me how you had persuaded him to attend our meeting last night."

Oh, Andy Brown, I thought, you lying son-of-a-bitch! I can see you now, laughing your black ass off after telling her that!

"West Brandon is critical, Mr. Venable. I think it can be the most critical town in the South. For the first time there is the definite possibility of achieving a one hundred percent integrated community in the South. We must have that, and we are going to have that, but we will need men like Mr. Brown and like you."

I squeezed the door handle convulsively. "Me!"

In case of emergency, use this exit.

"Yes. Negro and white together," she said, her hand still scorching my arm. "That is the way it must be done here, and I want you and Mr. Brown to symbolize that spirit through your words and your actions."

There have been three separate and distinct times in my life when I would have been far better off had I, at a particular moment, pushed a female out of the front seat of my car and driven off into the night with never a backward glance. I will not mention the other two due to the rather sordid aspects of the situations involved. The third was this moment with Honeypot Hungerford.

But I did not push her out of the car. I smiled my sickly, fatuous smile and mumbled something about "doing whatever I can," and we left the car together and walked right into the spider's parlor—fly and spider together.

eight

The Reverend Clifford James met us at the front door and took my hand *earnestly* in his and smiled *sincerely* at me and thanked me *warmly* for coming. Then he ushered us into his living room where the birds and the beasts were assembled.

The bald, bullet-headed, ANGRY black man was there. He was introduced as Cecil Willard, who taught history at the Carver High School. Although West Brandon's public schools were largely integrated, the persistence of a Negro residential section maintained the existence of Carver High which was entirely Negro. Mr. Willard accepted my hand with suspicion, and I instinctively recalled something my father once said about a Negro man he knew.

"I'd sure hate to meet up with that nigger in a dark alley. I'd want it to be so dark he couldn't see me!"

I had a feeling about Mr. Willard. I had a feeling that it was impossible for him to like me because I was white. And it was impossible for me to dislike him because he was black. And there was a lesson there for both of us, but neither one of us was about to learn it.

There was another teacher from Carver High School, a delicate, birdlike little brown woman with the name of

Agatha Lewis. She bobbed her head at me and flashed a quick golden smile. Miss Lewis taught Algebra.

Mac Kirkpatrick, student president of the S-Double-F, was the only white in the room other than myself, and, of course, there sat Andy Brown, ceremoniously arrayed in a conservative gray suit, complete with white tab collar shirt and black knit tie—in short, an Andy Brown it had not been my privilege to see before. As I entered the room, he bowed his head solemnly in my direction and pursed his lips thoughtfully, spoiling the effect somewhat by a secret wink meant only for me.

Andy Brown, I thought, you are pulling the assembled legs, and you are making me a part of the gag, and we are going to have words, you and I, we are going to have some serious words.

Introductions concluded, we seated ourselves in a circle while Mrs. Reverend James, a stout, nervous-looking woman, scurried in from the kitchen with coffee and plates bearing huge slices of coconut cake, all of which was served with considerable confusion before she retired to the back of the house.

To my considerable dismay, the formal business of the evening was kicked off by our host with a lengthy prayer during which I kept my plate of cake and my cup of coffee precariously balanced on my lap.

"Oh, merciful Lord in Heaven," Reverend James intoned. "We are gathered here in Thy sight to consider Thy work. Thou hast created all Thy children equal in Thy eyes, Lord, and it is to this end that we here have dedicated our efforts. We are thankful, Lord, for the grace of Thy bounty, and we pray that it shall continue to be granted unto us. But, Lord, we do know that Thou dost hate injustice. We know how Thou hast risen up in other times to help Thy children cast off the chains of oppression, and we gather here with the

77

blessed assurance that Thou art with us in our struggle for a righting of the ancient wrongs which still agonize our people. We thank Thee for the presence of our white brothers here tonight, Lord."

I was tempted to suggest that he give Andy Brown credit for one of those white brothers.

"Oh Lord, grant us the strength to pursue our struggle for the right, keeping ever and always before us the necessity for love—even for those who stand in the way of Thy will, Lord. Help us to love and to overcome through love rather than through hate, for we know that this is the only way. Grant us the power of Thy love, Lord. We ask it in the name of Thy Son who died on the cross to save us all . . ."

And the *Amens* were supplied by all of us, Venable included. That should have been sufficient warning for me, but I was too far into that room to get out of it. And when I raised my head, I was aware of the moisture in my eyes. I have this weakness. I cry easily.

"Now," Reverend James smiled at us, his communication with the Almighty completed, "you all just go on and finish your cake and coffee, but I think we had better begin our discussion. And I am going to ask our visitor from the City of Brotherly Love, Miss Hungerford, to start right in by explaining her plan to us." He made a courtly bow in her direction. "Miss Hungerford?"

She took a delicate sip from her cup and placed it next to the untouched cake on the table beside her.

"Thank you, Reverend James." She panned the room slowly, letting those great yellow green eyes touch each of us in turn. "Let me say first of all what I said at the meeting last night. My purpose in coming to West Brandon was not to tell you how to manage your affairs. My purpose was to demonstrate to you that your struggle here for a one hundred percent integrated community in the deep South is not going unnoticed by people in other parts of the country. You are not fighting alone!"

"Amen!" murmured Reverend James.

"The national organization of Students for Freedom has had a great deal of experience all over this country in assisting local groups to organize effective programs of peaceful resistance to the evils of bigotry and the suppression of the lawful rights of Negro citizens by a militant white majority. It is to pass along to you the benefits of that experience that I was sent to West Brandon.

"During the day, I have been talking with many people here, Negro and white, and I think I would sum up my impressions of the West Brandon situation in one word. You may not like that word."

Then something peculiar happened to her face, and I was fascinated at the effect which was as though she had suddenly slipped on a mask. Her face went hard and tight and cold. All the soft curves were flattened out into planes, and the sensuality of the mouth simply vanished in a thin, taut line.

"That word," she snapped, "is *complacency!*"

Cecil Willard's bullet head jerked up, and his angry eyes got angrier. Agatha Lewis made a quick, fluttering movement with her hands, and her gold teeth flashed, but not in a smile. Andy Brown squirmed in his chair, fingered the knot of his black knit tie and shot a brief, unhappy look in my direction. Reverend James put the fingers of his hands together, pursed his lips as though about to speak, and then thought better of it.

"Now," she said, "you may say to me that there is no complacency in West Brandon, and you may support this by saying that your people here have marched down Main Street carrying signs and singing songs. You may say that there is no complacency because some of your people have walked up and down across the street from the stores and restaurants

79

which remain segregated. You may say you are not complacent because you have written letters to the newspapers urging that your City Council pass a local Public Accommodations law.

"But I am saying to you here and now that you could keep on marching and picketing and writing letters until another hundred years have passed, and it would not accomplish what must be accomplished! You cannot dramatize the evils of bigotry by making meaningless and ineffectual and superficial gestures of protest. If there is a stronghold of bigotry and race hatred, then you must storm that stronghold. You must invade it physically, armed only with love and with truth, and prepared to suffer the spiritual and physical pain and humiliation which the defenders of those strongholds will surely inflict on you. But it is only through your pain and humiliation that your struggle can achieve the *dynamic* and *dramatic* significance it must have to arouse the conscience of the community and force it to take action!"

She knew when to stop and allow the fire she was building to singe us a little.

Cecil Willard was bobbing his head in agreement, and his face was a study in how to look happy though angry.

"Now you are talking, young lady!" he growled. "Folks here have been preaching *nonviolence* so hard it's come to mean *pussyfooting!* There's nobody going to pay any attention to what we're doing in this town unless we can shake them up."

Agatha Lewis clapped her tiny hands together. "That *is* the truth!"

Mac Kirkpatrick was leaning forward excitedly. "I can guarantee at least two hundred students who'll go along with anything you suggest, Miss Hungerford. Two hundred *white* students!"

And the Reverend James upped the ante. "We can produce three hundred young people who will be ready and willing to go where we tell them and to do what we instruct them to do—with love in their hearts!"

But it was not at Kirkpatrick or James that those yellow green hungry eyes were looking. It was at black Andy Brown and white Robert Venable.

"Later," she purred, "we may need those numbers, and I am proud that you can produce them. But it is a proven military fact that a great deal can be accomplished by sending a small but efficient and fearless force into an enemy position to probe his strength before any massive assault is made." She turned to me. "You would agree to that, based on your own wartime experience, wouldn't you, Mr. Venable?"

She acknowledged my cautious nod and rushed past my cowardly qualification, cutting it off at the first "However . . ."

"Now, to be more specific." She reached into her handbag and produced a piece of paper, unfolding it and placing it on the table beside her chair with the air of Eisenhower getting ready to announce his plans for the invasion of Europe. "I have a list of the places which are supposed to serve the public in West Brandon and which persist in excluding Negroes. There are twenty-five such places listed. I have talked with a number of people today, and the consensus of opinion is that the most violently and flagrantly bigoted people represented on this list are the owners of this restaurant."

One long, lovely finger jabbed at the paper.

Gentlemen, our target for today!

"It is Fuller's Restaurant, owned and operated by James and Cora Fuller, both of whom have a reputation for viciously anti-Negro activities in this community over a long period of time. James Fuller is an avowed member of the Ku Klux Klan and has been arrested several times for assaulting

81

Negroes without provocation. From all that I have been able to learn, their restaurant is of a low quality, one which few self-respecting people, white or Negro, would care to patronize."

It was time for a question. If no self-respecting person wanted to eat there, why bother? She answered the question before it was asked.

"I believe that by concentrating our initial attack on the least reputable place on this list, we might be able to shame some of the others into taking action to desegregate. We can be reasonably sure that the reaction we will get from the Fullers will be of the sort which will repel any normal, right-thinking person." She drew an imaginary circle around the name of Fuller's Restaurant on the paper. "Thus, we will let them help us create a sympathetic and aroused community."

Mac Kirkpatrick possessed the stuff of which idiotic heroes are made. He was on his feet, his pink face pinker than usual.

"I'd like to be one of the ones to go," he declared, sounding for all the world like Horatius at that goddamned bridge.

And the Reverend James made it a twosome. "We'll go together, Brother Kirkpatrick—in love and humility!"

It sounded great to me, and I was about to second all motions and get the hell out of that madhouse when up stepped brave old Andy Brown with a proposition that stood my hair on end.

"I have a better idea, folks." Andy Brown, plain man of the people, speaking. "You two cats probably couldn't get within a mile of Fuller's without somebody figuring just what's going on. Plus the fact that when folks read in the paper that you've been tossed out on your ear or fried in oil or strung up by your toes or whatever that Fuller cat decides to do, nobody'll pay much attention because you're not good copy anymore. Like they say in television, you've been over-exposed."

"Now wait a minute, Brother Brown," the Reverend said.

"We have been in the thick of the fight here in West Brandon, and we have earned the right to lead . . ."

Sly, smiling, crazy Andy Brown turned to Miss Honeypot Hungerford and asked, his voice *sincere* and *intense*. "I'm right, don't you think so?"

I was beginning to believe those two had rehearsed their act. She gave him *earnestness* and *intensity* right back along with a nod of agreement. "There is a great deal in what Mr. Brown says. We need new faces, new names . . ."

I felt compelled to make my commentary. "New *blood*."

"Exactly—new blood."

We had given the word two different readings, and somehow my facetiousness had been turned on me, because I was suddenly in the scene—which was just where I had no desire to be.

And who helped pull me in? Little Andy Brown!

"Professor, that would be perfect!"

I was being made the straight man in a bad routine, and I knew it.

Why, what would be perfect, Mr. Bones?

"You and me, Professor. We'll go out for dinner together tomorrow night."

"Perfect!" This was the Hungerford contribution.

"Wonderful idea!" Agatha Lewis put her big, golden-toothed mouth in.

"It sure sounds good to me!" We were even making Cecil Willard happy. Who says you can't please all the people?

It seemed an appropriate time to cast a dissenting vote, but Alise Hungerford never gave me a chance.

"What could be better? Ladies and gentlemen, we have the ideal team to accomplish this mission. Mr. Venable is a well-known and respected writer, a native southerner, and a war hero. Mr. Brown is a veteran of the Korean War and himself a promising young writer. They are two men who have every reason to be able to expect to be allowed to go out and eat a meal together in a public restaurant. That is all they are asking, and it will be for that simple action that they will be persecuted!"

My dissenting vote got lost in the general hand shaking and backslapping, but through it all, I kept worrying about that word *persecuted*.

As I recalled, the ordeal of the early Christians who had been fed to the lions is usually described with that same word.

nine

Shakespeare said it in *Twelfth Night*. Some men achieve greatness while some men have greatness thrust upon them. I happen to fall into the latter category. However, let it be said for Venable that once thrust upon, he is apt to react admirably. At approximately three thirty in the morning following the meeting of West Brandon's kamikaze squadron in the home of Reverend James, I awakened in a cold sweat thinking of my impending mission and determined to sneak out to catch the five o'clock bus for parts unknown. However, since it was rather cold, I stayed in bed and even managed to get back to sleep. At breakfast my hands were shaking so badly that I spilled my cornflakes all over the tablecloth. By lunch, though, I had managed to find at least one bright spot in the generally gray picture. The expedition to Fuller's Restaurant was bound to end in such a horrendous fiasco that I would be removed once and for all from the arena of conflict. And after all, I decided, how badly could I be wounded in a single engagement? It even began to look pretty good. The one-shot hero who attacks, makes a name for himself and then retires from the lists—that was my aim.

By the time Andy Brown appeared in my office at two

thirty for a strategy session, I was feeling downright cheerful about the whole business.

But not Andy Brown. He entered my office wearing the uncertain smile of a cat who, having been certain he has swallowed the canary, begins to suspect that it was really a woodpecker.

"Hi there, Professor. I wasn't sure you'd be here."

"Where the hell did you think I'd be?"

He dropped into a chair and studied me for a few moments. "Look, Professor, I've been doing a lot of thinking today—about all this jazz last night. I really pulled a snow job on that chick, and I feel kind of bad about getting you in so deep."

There is nothing which can turn a coward into a brave man as quickly as being able to recognize another coward. I smiled my cold smile and pulled the corners of my mouth back sharply in the type of grimace made famous by Humphrey Bogart.

"You want to back out, Andy?"

"Hell yes! Don't you?"

That kind of honesty can be damned disconcerting, and just for a moment I was thrown, but I made a rapid recovery.

"Back out? Of course not. There's a job to be done."

"Come on, man, don't give me that old crap. I watched you last night, and you looked like the roof had fallen in on you. Well, now I'm saying I'm sorry. It was a lousy joke, and I'm ready to call it that and throw in the goddamned towel."

"Are you scared, Andy?"

"Shit yes! Aren't you?"

The second time around was too much for me, so I reverted to type.

"Yes. I'm scared."

"So I'll call the chick and tell her we were both drunk last night, and you are really the Grand Dragon of the Klan and I

86

am a member of the Black Muslims, and we don't want to integrate."

There it was—the way out; but I could not take it.

"No!"

He gave me the rolling eyes routine and the big grin routine and the dialect routine.

"Boss, we ain't got no business messin' round with them crazy niggers. Let's git us some watermelon and stay home."

"Look, Andy, let's consider this thing seriously for a minute."

"Man, I *am* serious!"

"You conned me into this. Right?"

"Right, and I am sorry. What can I say, man, after I say I'm sorry?"

"And I will admit I was just a little peeved with you last night."

"Peeved? Man, I could feel the nasties you were thinking about me all the way across the room."

"But the more I've thought about it, the more I think you may have done us both a favor. For the last several days, I've been really concerned about this whole business and particularly about my own attitude."

By God, I was sounding *sincere,* and I am a sucker for sincerity, especially my own. As a matter of fact, I *was* sincere.

"You were right the other day when you said we needed to get our feet wet. It's our responsibility to participate, Andy. Yours because you're a Negro, and mine because I . . ."

"Man come off it! Didn't I tell you the other day I didn't have any people? Don't give me that 'because you're a neegrow' routine. I'm a guy named Andy Brown, that's what I am, and that's all I am."

"But your skin is black."

"Pigmentation, man, that's all."

"And if you try to go into Fuller's Restaurant tonight, you'll get your ass kicked out because of that pigmentation."

"All the better reason why I don't plan to go. I can get me a good meal lots of places in this town."

"Well, tonight you're going to try and get one at Fuller's Restaurant."

He shook his head mournfully. "Man, you're really serious, aren't you?"

"Never more."

"Let me ask you one thing, and just give it to me straight. Are you doing this to prove a point, or to make points with that chick, or because you're a goddamned martyr, or just for kicks?"

It was an honest question, so I searched for an honest answer. I found one, and while I didn't like it, I let him have it.

"For kicks, Andy."

He considered this and found it to his liking. "Okay, man, I'll buy it that way. For kicks I will get a boot in my ass from some redneck hash slinger, but only for kicks. I just didn't want to be riding in there on a white horse."

From that point on it was fun and games. We made like secret agents and worked out an elaborate plan whereby I was to arrive alone at Fuller's Restaurant at seven thirty that evening, go in and tell the waitress that a friend was joining me and that I would order for him. Andy would arrive at exactly seven forty-five at which time I was to go out front, meet him and come back into the restaurant with him. From that point on, we would be on our own.

"What shall I order for you?"

He grinned wickedly. "Make it expensive, man—like a big steak, medium rare. I won't get to eat it anyhow, so we might as well have them waste something good."

There were minor matters to be taken care of. I called

Alise Hungerford, outlined the plan to her, and she made approving noises in that voice of hers, which, I was pleased to note, had relatively little effect on me. I was in control of things now, going in for a one-shot, going in for kicks and local color, and getting out. She didn't know that, though, and she was pouring it on for her new convert to martyrdom.

"Mr. Venable, I know I don't need to remind you of this, but remember there must be no resistance on your part or Mr. Brown's. However they may abuse you, you must accept it without fighting back."

"Sticks and stones," I said. I am quick to come up with clever sayings like that.

There was a world of gentleness in her voice. "Mr. Venable, there may very well be more than just words of abuse."

And she was right. Jesus, she was right!

The scene of the caper, Fuller's Restaurant, was located a half-mile north of the city limits of West Brandon. A garish red-on-yellow neon sign announced its presence. The restaurant itself occupied a long one-story frame structure which had recently been painted a discouraging grayish-green. When I pulled into the parking lot at exactly seven thirty, there were three other cars there. I was dressed in my most respectable and quiet charcoal gray, three-button suit, and I was uncomfortably burdened down with a growing sense of guilt which was the result of having lied again to Cathy about where I was going. On this memorable evening I was supposed to be attending a dinner meeting with some applicants for a writing fellowship at the University.

The interior of Fuller's Restaurant was only slightly less depressing than its exterior. A large jukebox dominated the scene, and the twenty or so booths situated around the walls each contained its offspring. A cashier's stand at the front door was maintained by a woman of gigantic proportions with a hairdo apparently styled with an egg beater and a mottled, purplish face which heaved and shook under the constant and furious attack on the chewing gum which was being gnawed somewhere within that awesome head. From the descriptions given me in advance, I recognized her as Cora Fuller. She did not give me a second glance as I entered and made my way to the farthest booth from the front door.

There were ten other customers. Four men occupied a booth across the dining room from me. They were well along with their meal and with a bottle of whiskey which was thinly disguised by a brown paper bag and sitting in the middle of their table. Two booths away from mine, an elderly couple were just finishing their pie, while, in a far corner, two teen-agers were feeling each other as they waited to place their orders. The jukebox was blasting out music to become tone-deaf by.

The clock on the wall over the front door showed seven thirty-five when a harried-looking woman wearing a green dress and a soiled apron burst through the swinging doors which apparently led to the kitchen. She hurled a couple of menus at the teen-agers who managed to unhand each other and turn their attention to a choice of food.

She approached me with a menu and a tired smile which revealed a set of teeth better left unrevealed.

"You ready to order, mister? Them kids'll take half a hour to make up their minds."

I smiled my white, even-toothed, gentle smile and nodded.

"I'm expecting a friend, but I'll order for him. He should be here any minute."

"Okay." The menu was thrust at me, and she extracted a pad from her apron pocket and a pencil from her hair.

"How're the steaks?"

Her eyes cut quickly to the behemoth at the cashier's counter.

"They're real nice. Give you a real nice T-bone."

I ordered two steaks, one medium, one medium rare, and she departed, stopping on her way to give the elderly couple their check.

It was seven thirty-nine. I was beginning to sweat.

The old folks made their elderly way to the cashier's counter and paid up before making their getaway. I looked after them longingly.

Take me away with you, old folks, and I'll care for you in your declining years.

But they left me behind. Old folks can be heartless.

The waitress returned with a collection of tarnished tableware and two glasses of water.

"Steaks'll be along in a coupla minutes. You sure your friend's going to be here?"

I nodded. "He'll be here."

The front door swung open, and I grinned my best sickly grin at the nice waitress lady.

"He's here now."

And, sure enough, there he stood in the doorway—old black Andy, natty in his gray suit, a scared smile fixed on his black face—a most unlikely lamb being led to the sacrifice.

It all seemed to happen in a horrible kind of slow motion. Andy spotted me and started toward me. The waitress saw him and managed to snatch up the glasses of water and all the tableware except one fork which went clattering to the floor. Clutching this assortment of glasses, knives, spoons, forks, etc., to her stained apron, she beat a retreat to the kitchen, yelling, "Mr. Fuller! Oh, Mr. Fuller!"

The four men on the other side of the room were on their feet watching us, while the teen-agers continued to find their manual exploration of each other more interesting than anything else.

Cora Fuller, looking more and more like the bride of King Kong, sat at the cash register for several seconds with her mouth hanging open before giving out with a bellow that might have come from a wounded water buffalo.

"JIM!"

A wounded water buffalo calling to her mate.

And the music from the jukebox kept going round and round.

Andy reached me and winked one unhappy eye. "Lafayette, I am here."

"Hey, Cora, since when you been servin' apes in here?"

That contribution came from one of the men across the room.

Then the kitchen door swung open, and a little runt of a man, with a broken nose and a head of red hair which stood up like spikes, emerged. At his appearance, the woman at the cash register started her move. It was Jim and Cora Fuller—in person!

"All right, nigger. Git your ass outta here." This was Jim.

"And take your nigger-lovin' friend with you." This was Cora.

Andy was seated now. Together we looked up with what we hoped would pass for calm, polite, and detached smiles.

"My friend and I would like our dinner . . ." That was my cool, steady voice which somehow or other came out in a quavering squeak.

The men had moved in as reinforcements. "You need some help, Jim?"

"I don't need no goddamned help with these two. Call the cops, Cora. They can pick up the pieces outside."

Andy shook his head. "No need for that, sir. The police

have already been notified." He smiled at me. "Also the press. We should get front-page coverage."

After that it was pretty confusing. Fuller and one of the men grabbed for me, but I managed to get to the floor and go limp just like on television. Somebody kicked me in the shoulder, but it wasn't too bad. I could see Andy—also on the floor, and he was getting it worse than I was because three of the men were working him over. There was some choice use of language, the choicest of all coming from Cora Fuller, and I could hear the wailing of sirens coming closer. Help was on the way, but it was getting doubtful whether or not the settlers could hold out.

They could not hold out—not quite.

"Stand back. I'll fix that nigger-kissin' bastard!" That was Cora.

I shut my eyes, waiting for the kick, but there was no kick. It was worse—much worse. It was about as bad as it could be. I heard the men starting to laugh, and then I felt the warm stream of water on my chest where my shirt had been torn, and then I opened my eyes.

And you would never believe what I saw. I'll give you a clue. It belonged to Cora Fuller, and, oh God, it was ugly, and it was peeing all over me.

After that, everything was downhill.

ten

A major disadvantage of having led a relatively sheltered life in mid-twentieth century, U.S.A., is that one is ill-prepared for being peed upon in public. As a citizen of a more basic and realistic society, I might have been able to shrug and dismiss the entire unfortunate incident with a casual "So she peed on me—so what else is new?"

But I was a victim of my upbringing, a product of my environment, a creature of a sanitation-oriented society. I considered the consequences of the event beyond the pragmatic necessity of having to send my most respectable and quiet charcoal gray, three-button suit to the cleaners. I considered the social implications, and I found them staggering.

Item. What does one say to one's loving wife, Cathy? Lipstick on a collar, a trace of feminine powder on a lapel, a minor shortage in the checking account—these things can be explained. There is an established tradition one can draw on—but a urine-stained suit extrapolates wifely understanding to a dangerous degree.

Item. The children, the innocent impressionables to whom DADDY must be a god-figure, immune to the soilings of ordinary mortals . . .

"Daddy, all the kids at school point at us and laugh and holler that some fat lady did nasty on you!"

Item. One's colleagues, those giants of learning with whom one shares the sacred task of shaping young minds—and the young minds—and one's drinking companions—the man on the street, the cop on the beat—the butcher, the baker, the candlestick maker . . .

"Why there goes Venable. You know, *Venable*. He's the man who . . ."

> *The man who conquered Everest? No!*
> *The man who cured the common cold? No!*
> *The man who landed on the moon? No, no, no, no!*
> *He's the man who was* . . . PEED UPON!

Making a mountain from a molehill? Perhaps, but I have a funny self-centered streak which manifests itself at times such as this. And I felt put upon as well as peed upon. I felt put upon through all the confusion which followed Cora Fuller's by-a-waterfall-with-you act—the arrival of the police—the unintelligible questions of reporters—the blinding flash of photographers' bulbs—the somewhat soggy ride to the police headquarters—the fleeting glimpse of our comrades-in-arms at the entrance to said headquarters, including a radiant Alise Hungerford—the brief but impressive ceremony of being booked for *trespassing* (consider that word and conjure up the ironic possibilities of a charge against Cora Fuller)—agonizingly through my cryptic and uninformative "one telephone call" to Cathy, asking that she bring a lawyer and "not worry"—right up to that moment when I found myself sharing a cell with a slightly battered old black buddy of mine by the unlikely name of Andy Brown—I felt put upon.

And then the miracle.

Of laughter. Laughter bubbling up from deep within the ageless well of the black man's agony. Laughter rushing to the surface and spilling out of thick red lips, past gleaming white teeth. Laughter growing to a torrent of contagion, spreading to Venable and doubling him over in a choking, gasping, convulsive heap on the jailhouse bunk. Whooping, tear-streaming laughter. Gigantic spasms of sanity-preserving laughter.

"Man!" Andy was the first to achieve coherence. "Man, if I live to be two hundred and five, I'll never see anything like that again! She did it, man! That big fat old chick really did it!"

I nodded and managed to gasp, "On me!"

"That's right, man—on you! All they did to old Andy was kick a little, punch a little. Sticks and stones may break my bones, but urine is too much!"

I was possessed of a sudden sense of history.

"You think I have had a unique experience, Andy?"

"None like it in this world or the next!"

"You said we ought to get our feet wet, Andy, but this is ridiculous."

"You wanted material for a book, boss man. Now you got it!"

"My God, Andy, that old bitch peed on me!"

"Best seller for sure!"

"Book-of-the-Month Club?"

"Can't miss!"

"*Reader's Digest?*"

"I can see it now. The most unforgettable character who ever peed on me."

"Big movie sale, Andy?"

"Man, with that scene, movies'll really be better than ever. Wide screen. Stereophonic sound . . ."

"In warm, wet, living color!"

"Jeezus!"

96

But the miracle, as is the way of miracles in this singularly unmiraculous world, faded.

And we were in a cell in a jail. Description of cell. Dimensions about eight by fifteen feet. Decor—early depressing. Walls painted a nauseous gray. Floors likewise. Furnishings basic—a single cot with a mattress (lumpy) and a blanket (scratchy). One yellowing washbasin without either soap or towels and, in one corner, one john with a rough and scratchy brand of toilet paper. A nice place to visit, but I wouldn't like to live there.

Also situated in one wall, a window (barred) which, if one stood on the bunk, afforded a view of the outside world—specifically Cavanaugh Street which runs along the south side of the Municipal Building (which contains in addition to police headquarters and the West Brandon version of the Bastille, the City Sewage Department, Tax Collector, City Surveyor, and other vital and entertaining enterprises). First I and then Andy Brown made a brief exploration of the outside world and discovered little to cheer us there.

"You fellas hungry?"

At the cell door (also barred) stood mine host, a lean and mournful-looking turnkey. In his hands he carried two brown paper bags. And, despite his Stan Laurel tragic mask, he proved something of a wit.

"Don't reckon you all got to finish yore dinner out to Fuller's. These here ain't T-bones, but they're the best we got to offer."

I felt called upon to say something cutting.

"Are my friend and I permitted to eat together here?"

Mine host looked surprised and grieved.

"Shithouse mouse, fella, we got us a one hundred percent integrated jail here. You kin eat together, sleep together, piss together—any damned thing you want together—long as you don't raise no ruckus."

97

And so we accepted the brown paper bags and retreated to the single cot where we examined the speciality of the house —two hot dogs on cold buns sans mustard. Andy Brown considered them sadly.

"I wonder how those steaks would've been."

"Probably tough."

"No mustard, Professor. How's a man going to be able to cut the mustard when there's no mustard to cut?"

A look at my mustardless hot dogs did nothing for me. A look at my watch told me that it was almost nine o'clock, and this did something for me. It reminded me that Venable, in common with all men, was not an island. And the bell was about ready to toll. Within a matter of minutes, Cathy would arrive, and my brief telephone conversation had prepared me for the worst.

"Cathy, there's been a little trouble."

"Bob! Are you all right?"

"Yes."

"Where are you?"

"In town."

"Where in town?"

"At the police station."

"I'll be right there."

"Uh, Cathy, you'd better bring Jim Hazeltine."

"A lawyer? Bobby, what happened?"

"It's not serious. Don't worry, Cathy. Just get Jim over here as soon as you can."

"All right, Bobby. Whatever it is, darling, don't worry. It'll be all right . . ."

See what I mean? The worst. Explanation—Cathy was a WIFE.

I bit into one of the hot dogs and found it, like the bun, cold, limp and discouraging. So I composed a mental treatise on WIVES.

Wives, the treatise began, are, in the main, women. As a consequence, they are woefully unsuited for their roles as the helpmeets of men. What, after all, do they bring to this all-important task? A body which is arranged so as to arouse and accommodate the husband sexually. A convenience, admitted, but a frivolous one. The same service could be obtained at the friendly neighborhood brothel. However, as a result of this minor talent, WIVES often turn into MOTHERS—more properly the subject of another work. WIVES maintain the home—cooking, cleaning, arranging, rearranging, doing laundry—tasks which, thanks to the ingenious inventions of MEN, require little more than a superficial supervision of gadgets. WIVES are sometimes COMPANIONS to their husbands. This involves chatting with him while he tries to read the morning paper at breakfast, inquiring about his work when he comes home in the evening, and sitting in the same room with him during certain mutually endurable television programs. On special occasions, COMPANIONSHIP is manifested by a WIFE accompanying her husband to official functions and/or social gatherings where she will usually spend her time engaged in banal conversation with other WIVES.

Particularly, and very much to the specific point of this treatise, WIVES are singularly lacking in both a sense of humor and a sense of history where their husbands are concerned. They are detached from the rich tapestry of a husband's struggle with the meaningful world—incapable of grasping the deep significance of the things a husband *must* do, regardless of the costs. Tell a little lie to a WIFE—even with the noblest of motivations—and, if she catches you in it, she will fix you with a cold and reproachful eye and, without once opening her tight, angry lips, she will rub your nose in the sacred memory of the wedding vows. Tell her a backed-into-the-corner truth, and her hands will fly to her ears to shut it out, and her eyes will overflow with how-could-you-do-this-to-me (and the children) tears.

"Oh, Christ," I mumbled through the soggy hot dog. "I've got to explain this to my wife."

Andy Brown smiled his most helpful smile. "Good luck, Professor."

"I'll lie to her. I'll tell her I was picked up for speeding . . ."

"Professor, I hate to be the one to tell you, but you and I are going to be big news in the morning papers. That Hungerford chick must've worked for a Hollywood press agent. All those flashbulbs going off when they hauled us out of that second-rate hash house didn't belong to the campus camera club. They belonged to the working press, and what's more, I'll lay a little bet that there's a goodly representation of that working press waiting outside right now."

"Oh, Jesus," I moaned. "Oh, Jesus, Jesus, Jesus Christ!"

"Hey, fella!"

Mine host had returned.

"You oughta watch yoreself, fella—takin' the Lord's name in vain like that. Shitfire, what kinda bringin' up did you have?"

In the blessed conviction that somewhere in the Constitution I was protected against having to engage in discussions of moral and religious philosophy with turnkeys—even turnkeys who provided me with mustardless hot dogs—I kept silent.

Mine host was not easily discouraged.

"Pisses me off to hear a white man takin' the Lord's name in vain. Guess you college fellas think you're something special."

A dignified silence from Venable the stoic.

"Think just because you went to college yore shit don't smell, dontcha? You read the Good Book, fella. Read the Third Commandment. 'Thou shalt not take the name of the

100

Lord thy God in vain.' That's in the Good Book, fella, and don't you forget it!"

He paused, pleased with his own righteous indignation. Then, as an afterthought, he added, "By the way, Venable, yore pore wife's here to post bond for you." He produced a ring of keys and unlocked the cell door. "Now come on, less you want to spend the night with yore *friend* here."

For the first time it struck me that Andy had not made any phone call. Of course his people knew he was in jail . . .

His people!

"They'll be getting you out tonight, won't they, Andy?"

He grinned bleakly and shook his head. "Don't know, boss man. Part of the game is to suffer a little, so I may have to stay here and suffer for at least one night."

"Look, I can post bond for you. You don't want to spend the night in this rathole."

"You comin' or not, Venable? Yore pore wife's waitin' out there for you. Looks like a nice, decent woman."

Andy waved one courageous Sidney Carton-type hand. "Look, Professor, you go on now. I'll sleep fine here. Besides I never spent the night in jail before. Maybe they serve eggs with their hot dogs in the morning."

There passed through the Venable mind a fleeting but noble thought of making a stand, of insisting that he remain by the side of his black brother, of sharing a night of durance vile. It passed through, but did not linger. After all, Andy Brown had not been peed upon. In the game of upmanship, he was one step behind.

"Take it easy, Andy."

"Laws, mistuh, ain't no other way to take it."

"You're sure—about the bond?"

"Sho nuff."

"If you like, I could . . ."

"You go on, Professor." A touch of hardness in the Andy

Brown voice shriveled a bit of the Venable insides. Then it was soft and mellow and darkie again. "Don' worry bout old Andy, mistuh. Maybe ah kin make it into the school tomorrow. I do de bes ah kin."

Sweet Jesus! There would be a tomorrow—a tomorrow with breakfast and a morning paper and a wife and children and a class and the goddamned world!

I paused as the turnkey swung the cell door closed and added the steel bars to the barrier which separated me from Andy Brown. He was slouched back on that single bunk, his black face illuminated by the single naked overhead light bulb, his teeth bared in a white grin which his eyes did not choose to share. We nodded our good-byes like estranged lovers, and I followed the gaunt scarecrow turnkey down the corridor.

"What's the matter with that nigger?" he asked.

"Matter?"

"Way he talks. Half the time he talks good as you and me. Other half he sounds like a real nigger."

"He's suffering from a confused pigmentation of the brain."

"He one of them outside niggers?"

"Outside of where?"

"You know what I mean."

"Yes, that's his trouble. He's outside of everything."

"Okay, college man, jest forget it."

He pushed the door open that led to freedom.

And Cathy.

She stood beside Jim Hazeltine at the desk of the night sergeant. Jim had been in school when I was a grad student, and he had settled in West Brandon to practice law. He was the nearest thing to a lawyer I had, having once advised me on a question of copyright. He and his wife had asked us by for cocktails one afternoon. Also, I had a vague recollection of having shared an extremely drunken party with him when we had been in school together. Tall, rail-thin and balding, he was a man who appeared to be dedicated to ugliness in a Lincolnesque sort of way. For better or for worse, he was my lawyer, and he looked rather sad at the prospect.

And, of course, there was Cathy.

Cathy chose not to look directly at me—or was it that I chose not to look directly at her? It came out the same either way. We did not look directly at each other. Jim Hazeltine mumbled some legal gobbledegook about having posted a five-hundred-dollar bond. The desk sergeant made some rather pointed mention of the fact that Chief of Police Walter Scrumm was out of town that night attending a meeting and that he would probably want to talk to me when he got back the next day and that I was pretty lucky the Chief was away. He also produced a manila envelope which contained various articles I had surrendered when I had been admitted (is that the right word?) to the establishment. There was more legal phraseology which I missed largely due to the fact that I was kept so busy not looking directly at Cathy.

And we departed, pushing through a small group of reporters who waved notebooks and shouted unintelligible questions while some photographer types exploded a few flashbulbs and I felt vaguely like a character in *La Dolce Vita*—but only vaguely. Jim Hazeltine got us into his car, and we drove home in relative silence. He did the only significant talking.

"Now, Bob, you may be pestered by reporters, but my advice is to say nothing."

"Now, Bob, we'll need to talk about all this at some length tomorrow, but right now I think a good night's sleep is in order."

And, "You weren't—mistreated—in any way at the police station, were you, Bob?"

When he let us out at the house, he drew me aside and whispered, "Bob, I heard a rumor—and I'm sure it's just that—that she—well—that she urinated on you. That's not true is it, Bob?"

I had already ruined his evening sufficiently so I shook my head. He looked enormously relieved, muttered his good nights and left.

I was very tired. Jimmy and Elaine had gone to bed. Cathy fixed some hot tea and a ham and cheese sandwich for me. She did not say anything really pertinent until I had eaten. Then she stood in front of me, took my face in her hands and turned my face up to look at her. It was at this point I realized that I had been the one who had avoided looking directly at her after all.

"Bobby."

Very gentle, very patient. I knew I was in trouble.

"Bobby, are you really that concerned over this Civil Rights thing?"

Note that she did not use the obvious approach generally employed by WIVES. She might have said, "Why didn't you tell me, etc.?" or "Don't you think I have a right to know, etc.?" Cathy was a clever one. She asked a simple direct question which demanded a simple and direct answer.

"Honey, I—I'm not sure. I've always been interested, as you know, in matters relating to the constitutional rights of all citizens, and I recognize that there are certain inequities as far as Negro citizens are concerned, and I suppose . . ."

"Bobby . . ."

I was confused, as I had every right to be, at this interruption of my direct and simple answer.

"Bobby, you don't want to talk about it tonight, do you?"

104

This called for a rather involved explanation, so I gave it. "No."

And so we did not talk about it any further—except for one small item. When we were in our bedroom, she noticed the lamentable condition of my shirt and suit. Social implications be damned, this was a laundry matter, so she asked for an explanation. I was too tired to think of a good story, so I did the unforgivable. I told her the truth.

"Bobby, she didn't!"

"She did."

"She couldn't!"

"Yes she could."

"Bobby, that's barbaric!"

I went along with that point of view.

"Bobby, I think you ought to sue that horrible woman!"

"On what grounds?"

And with that she started to laugh. Having nothing better to offer, I joined her. We laughed all the way into bed—most of the way through a completely spontaneous and unrehearsed lovemaking—only at some point she was crying, and I was crying. And what with all the mutual laughing, crying, and lovemaking we passed an entertaining half hour before falling asleep in each other's arms.

All of which merely demonstrates how really sneaky WIVES can be.

eleven

For as long as I can remember, the most important single item in the morning life of the male Venable has been the morning paper. It is supposed to be there, waiting for me when I arise. Woe betide the paper boy who, for whatever reason of human frailty, fails to make his delivery to the Venable door. My cornflakes turn to ashes in my mouth without the printed word of the new day's saga propped against the milk bottle.

And so on this morning—the morning after—the eager little bastard who delivered my morning paper made it right on schedule. The paper was there, and on the front page there was the story and there was a picture. It was not a good likeness, but the limp figure being carried by three husky cops was unmistakably Venable. The story itself was terse and unimaginative, and I found some consolation in the fact that it only hinted at the *pièce de résistance* of *l'affaire* Fuller.

Venable, currently a writer-in-residence at the University, was knocked to the floor and pummeled, kicked and otherwise abused by several persons, including Mrs. Cora Fuller . . .

Otherwise abused!

Cathy insisted that Jimmy and Elaine be prepared for any

talk they might hear at school, so I gathered them to my fatherly side and put it to them in a straightforward, manly way.

"Last night—er—something happened, children. It wasn't really important—nothing really, but in case anyone should say anything to you at school today—just don't pay any attention to them, because you see . . ."

Elaine reassured me. "Are you talking about your getting arrested, Daddy?"

"Where did you hear about it?"

"On my transistor radio while I was getting dressed. It was on the news."

Jimmy chimed in, "I heard it too, Daddy. I heard them say your name on the radio."

Cathy moved in to the rescue. "Now, children, you're not to get upset over this. Daddy will explain it all to you when there's time—tonight—at dinner."

Dinner at the Venable household was the traditional occasion for airing family problems. Usually these had to do with Elaine and Jimmy and their schoolwork. Instead of grace, a typical Venable evening meal began with a "Well, how was school today?" type query. I did not particularly appreciate Cathy's booking my act in on the "I don't understand modern math" circuit. However, explaining things at dinner seemed infinitely preferable to explaining them at breakfast, so I did not complain.

The truth of the matter is that I was just a little disappointed by the calm way Jimmy and Elaine seemed to be taking this. When I said, "Your mother's right, kids. There's nothing to get upset over," Elaine replied, "Who's upset, Daddy? It sounds cool." She might have been talking about a movie she had seen. Correction—she would have sounded a lot more enthusiastic about a movie.

Jimmy, the more romantic of the two, asked, "Who arrested you? The cops?"

"Who else arrests people, dummy?" Elaine sneered.

"The Texas Rangers. The Northwest Mounties. Matt Dillon." Jimmy, the world's leading authority on law enforcement, paused and thought deeply. "And the F.B.I."

"They're all cops, aren't they, Daddy?"

"Are they, Dad? Northwest Mounties aren't cops. I saw them on the afternoon movie in this picture with Cary Cooper . . ."

"*Gary* Cooper," I corrected him.

"Yeah, one of those old-time actors. Anyway, they had Northwest Mounties in that picture, and they didn't dress like cops, but they arrested everybody."

"Oh hogfat!" This from Elaine who, in the manner of twelve-year-olds, had acquired a singularly unattractive collection of expressions.

I solved the problem. "It's time you were leaving for school. I'll explain it to you later."

"At dinner," Cathy added helpfully.

"At dinner," I agreed.

When the children were gone, Cathy eyed me with a noticeably diminishing wifely patience. "Shall I wait until dinner too, Bob?"

I nodded. "Yes, if you don't mind, honey." It is one thing to laugh and cry and make love with your wife at night. It is something else to sit across the breakfast table from that same wife in the cold clear light of morning and try to tell her the truth about something you don't begin to know the truth about yourself.

"All right, Bob. Whatever you say."

A simple acquiescence? Not on your tintype. When a WIFE says to her husband, "Whatever you say," and he feels a stabbing pain in his testicles, it is because she has him firmly by the balls—and is squeezing.

108

Confucius say, "When wife has you by balls, get the hell out of there!"

I left. Who am I to argue with the wisdom of Confucius?

Free of children, wife and home, all I had to contend with was the world. The world that morning took many shapes and forms. Old Mrs. Pearl Ponder who lived in widowed solitude across the street was standing in her front door as I left my house. I saw her see me, and immediately she vanished. Seconds later, I saw the venetian blind in her living room window tilt, and I made my way to my car with the nasty realization that those tired, prying old eyes were following my every move.

On my way to the campus I routed myself by way of Cavanaugh Street which took me by the two-story brick colonial structure where Andy Brown and I had shared a suite the night before for a brief time. In the bright morning sunlight, the Municipal Building looked very gracious, a reconstruction of the gentle past. It seemed quite incapable of concealing within its walls that depressing cell.

But the window was there. I saw the window, and as I drew abreast of it, I thought I saw a face at that window, a black face with eyes that followed me. Of course, it could have been my imagination. I have always had a vivid imagination. For all I knew, Andy Brown was long sprung from the pokey and as free as air. I could have parked the car. There was a parking space—no excuse there. I could have walked over to that window, and if Andy was there, we could have exchanged some sharp repartee for all the passing world to hear. I had made my foray into the greatest social revolution of twentieth-century U.S.A. and had, in one brief encounter with the enemy, achieved a unique martyrdom. There was nothing to fear now. Why not make an open show in support of my comrade-in-arms?

I drove on past the Municipal Building. Andy Brown, I

decided once and for all, was already out of jail. He would be in my class at ten o'clock, and I could make a public display of our comradeship there. After class we would have coffee together and talk about our adventure of the night before and have a few laughs and plan other adventures . . .

I slammed on the brakes as the light at the intersection of Cavanaugh and Main turned red. Simultaneously I slammed on other brakes.

Other adventures!

How long does a traffic light stay red? Stop and consider the total amount of time one sits at intersections waiting for a green light. What to do with all that time? Answer—think! Make decisions! Solve the problems!

Initial attack. That had been the way Miss Honeypot Hungerford had described our going to Fuller's Restaurant. That seemed to mean, as jolly old Major Bowes used to say as he spun the wheel of fortune, "This is only the beginning, ladies and gentlemen, o-o-only the beginning!" Now what happens to the shock troops who are sent in for the initial attack? *If* they get back alive, they are given a couple of days' rest, fed a little better than usual, slapped on the back by all the brass, maybe slipped a minor decoration or two—and then—hup, two, three, they're right back in the front lines again.

Item. Robert M. Venable did not—repeat *not*—consider himself a soldier in the revolution. Neither did Andy Brown. It was a worrisome thing that Andy had been willing to spend the night in jail, thus carrying the gag much too far, but he had probably had his own reasons which had nothing to do with any cause. There had been this pact between Andy Brown and Venable. *For kicks.* That was the reason and the only reason. So what's all this crap about *other adventures?*

There is an old adage about the stock market. *Get in, make a quick killing, and get out!*

Why had we gone into this thing? To get our feet wet, that's why. To get a taste of the action—not eat a full meal—just taste. Motivations—one hundred percent selfish. Interest in the cause—negligible. All right, I had got more than my feet wet, thanks to Cora Fuller. I had my taste, and it was nasty. I had seen hate on the faces of white men—hate that was directed at me. I had the experience. In the future, when I decided to argue the LIBERAL cause at comfortable cocktail parties, I could do it without reservation, because, you see *I was there*. Venable had manned the barricades.

I would undoubtedly write a book, and on the dust jacket, under the picture of that distinguished, slightly graying AU- THOR, the biographical blurb would contain these priceless lines: *Mr. Venable was actively associated with the Civil Rights movement in West Brandon and was actually jailed for his participation.* That sort of thing made points. Next year I would go back to that other university in the frozen North as a battle-scarred veteran. The Unitarian Discussion Group would invite me to lecture. The President of the University would ask me to drop by for a chat, because he is very interested in the plight of the Negro in the South and has never been south of Evansville, Indiana.

In short, I had everything I needed, and if I chose, I could tell Alise Hungerford and the rest—politely, of course—re- gretfully, of course—exactly what they could do with their *other adventures*.

And, as the light turned green, that is just what I decided to do.

Decision made, I reached the parking lot in reasonably good spirits, discovered to my amazement that it was much easier to find a parking space at eight thirty in the morning than at one minute to ten, and entered the English Building in what might pass for a jolly mood. It did not last long.

As I opened the door to my office, I saw that someone had

pushed a plain white envelope under the door. This was not unusual. Messages of various kinds were often left in this manner. It was not until I had settled myself at the desk and filled and lighted my pipe that I bothered to open the envelope. It contained a single sheet of white paper, a rather good quality of bond. And there was a message, printed in block letters—simple and to the point.

YOU FUCKING NIGGER LOVER, GO BACK WHERE YOU CAME FROM OR YOU AND YOUR WIFE AND KIDS WILL FIND OUT WHAT HAPPENS TO NIGGER LOVERS HERE.

The printing was very neat. The lines were straight, and the letters were of a uniform size. I admired that. Someone had taken a great deal of care with this message. I spread it out on my desk and studied it for a long time. There were no smudges or blurs. It was simple and easy to read and understand. It seemed to deserve an answer.

"I am back where I came from," I said finally. And, "You leave my wife and kids out of this," I said.

A rather brave response, marred only by the fact that my throat was so tight that the words came out as a quavering croak, and my hands, as I tore the paper to shreds, were shaking.

Question. Where is the dividing line between fear and anger?

But the receiving of messages for that day had only begun. The next came by phone. There were no nasty words here— only a rather woebegone invitation to come down for a chat with Dr. John Allen. Dr. John Allen being one of the last men I wanted to see at that moment, I cast about desperately for a good reason to decline the invitation, but his voice began to waver as though he might be going to burst into tears, and I hastily said I would be right down.

His office was on the first floor. On my way down, I passed

112

one of the jollier members of the English staff, a one-year-away-from-retirement old gent by the name of Curwood Farnsworth. During my graduate student days at the University, I had taken a course in Jacobean Drama from Farnsworth. He was a roly-poly little man with a thin squeaky voice and the morals of a spider monkey. If the number of coed asses which had been pinched and/or patted by Curwood Farnsworth during the thirty-five years of his service to the University could be brought together, there would be enough asses to cover every seat in the new stadium. He spotted me, waddled up to me, dug an elbow into my ribs, winked one bright baby-blue eye, and squeaked, "Atta boy!" That was all, but it warmed my heart. I turned to watch him go his merry way on down the corridor, pausing only to speak to a girl for a moment and add one more ass to his impressive collection.

Good old Farnsworth! It was entirely possible, of course, that his, "Atta boy!" had nothing to do with my immediate dilemma. Farnsworth had become a bit vague, and it was quite likely he had mistaken me for someone else—or that he had been referring to a term paper I had written for him years ago—but I chose to believe he was speaking to the Venable of that moment.

My spirits fortified, I entered Dr. John Allen's office. One look at his face brought on an acute state of depression. It was not an angry face. It was not a disgusted face. It was—God help us—a hurt face.

"Sit down, Robert."

That seemed a reasonable request. I sat down.

"The writer-in-residence program," he began, in a hurt voice, "is very near and dear to my heart."

Bullshit, I thought, for reasons previously explained.

"I fought for this program tooth and nail, hammer and claw," he continued and added his own home imitation of

113

Winston Churchill. "And I gave of my blood, sweat and tears until I achieved . . ." Carried away by his purloined rhetoric, he lifted his right hand with two fingers spread to form a V.

Dr. John Allen paused, seemingly exhausted by the memory of his gallant struggle.

Then, "Robert, you are the first writer-in-residence here at the University. As a graduate of the University, as the author of a highly successful novel, as a writer of great promise, you seemed the ideal choice. And I have been delighted with your work. The Chairman of the English Department, Dr. Cannon, has been delighted with your work. Dean Hawser has been delighted with your work."

My father thanks you. My mother thanks you. My sister thanks you, and I thank you.

He had a pretty good monologue going, so I kept silent.

"But this—" With a flourish, he opened the top drawer of his desk to reveal Exhibit A for the prosecution—the morning paper. Those little bastards had done their work well that morning, I thought. Everyone got his paper on time.

"Robert, I won't pretend to understand your reasons for getting involved in this sort of nonsense. I assume you have your reasons, but ask yourself this question. Are those reasons more important than the writer-in-residence program? Now I'm going to tell you something, Robert . . ." He was a wonderful quick-change artist—from wounded indignation to just-between-you-and-me-and-the-gatepost, in the twinkle of an eye.

"They fought me on this program, Robert. You know why? It wasn't getting the money. The money was there, Money wasn't the problem, no, sir! The problem was persuading the Dean and Dr. Cannon and others of my colleagues that it was safe to bring a writer here to work with

114

our students. A lot of people have strange ideas about writers, Robert. They put them in the same class with actors and painters and people like that. You know what Dean Hawser said to me? Now this is strictly between you and me and the gatepost, Robert, but Dean Hawser called me in last year when I was trying to fight this program through—against tremendous odds—and he said to me, 'John . . .' I've known Dean Hawser for many years, and he calls me 'John.' 'John,' he said, 'I don't think I'm very keen on this business of bringing some writer here for a whole year. I've never known any writers personally, but from everything I hear they're a pretty bad lot these days. I don't read contemporary novels. As far as I'm concerned, the last significant novelist was Hardy.' The Dean is a little narrow-minded in this area, Robert, but he is sincere. He is a sincere man—and an excellent administrator.

"Well, he went on, Robert. 'From what I hear about the novels that are being written today, the men who write them are mostly drunkards, dope fiends, perverts or Communists. Now, why should we expose our fine young people to someone like that?'

"That's just what Dean Hawser said to me, Robert. Right in his office he said that, and he was serious. And he expressed the fears of many of the responsible and respected members of the faculty and administration. And, Robert, it was with great difficulty—you might say it was with blood, sweat and tears—that I managed to convince him that there are a few contemporary writers who are not drunkards, dope fiends, perverts or Communists. I said to him, 'Dean Hawser, I am considering a man who is a graduate of this University to be the first writer-in-residence if this program is approved. His name is Robert M. Venable, and he is a teacher as well as a writer. I can vouch for him.' Robert, I vouched for you with

115

the Dean. That is the point I am trying to make. I put my own reputation on the line for you, and now this happens."

He tapped the front-page photo with his finger.

"I am sitting here now, Robert, waiting for my phone to ring. When it rings, I know who it will be. It will be Dean Hawser, and he is not going to be happy, Robert. Dean Hawser is a good man, a fair man, a good administrator. He has been Dean for almost fifteen years, and he loves the University. He is proud of the reputation of the University as a liberal and progressive institution—and he is not happy when something happens to rock the boat."

And in his contemplation of Dean Hawser's unhappiness, he fell into a brooding silence, sinking lower in his chair, his head slumped forward, his eyes those of a grief-stricken bloodhound. It was this doggy quality that finally touched my heart.

"Look, John, I'm sorry this puts you on the spot. It's not your fault, and if there's anything I can do to get you off the hook . . ."

The sad eyes lighted. Someone had shown the bloodhound a bone.

"Robert, I appreciate that, and I knew you'd feel that way. It isn't myself I'm concerned for. It's the program—the program I fought so hard for. You can help. Now, tell me just what happened last night. It must have been a mistake."

"Mistake?"

His head bobbed enthusiastically. "Exactly. I don't know what your relationship to this nig—Negro student is—what's his name?"

"Brown. Andy Brown."

He frowned. "Andy Brown. That name sounds familiar . . . Well, never mind. I don't know what your relationship to him is, but . . ."

"He's one of my students."

116

This surprised him. "Really? I didn't know any of them were taking Creative Writing."

"He also took a course from Samantha last year."

"Oh. Oh, yes. I remember her speaking of him. She was terribly upset when he appeared in her class. You know Samantha is rather afraid of them, Robert. I had great difficulty convincing her that he was not going to attack her. As I recall, she was not impressed with his potential as a writer."

"That's who I was with last night."

"You went out there with him to have dinner?"

"Well, in a way. I went there first, and then he joined me."

"You mean he came in after you were already there?"

"Yes, you see . . ."

"You mean you were already there, seated at a table?"

"Yes, but . . ."

"And then this nigger . . ."

"Listen, John!"

"This Andy Brown walked in and came to your table!"

The questions had changed to statements. He had his version firmly established.

"Yes, and I . . ."

"And then all the trouble started."

"Yes, but, John . . ."

"And you were knocked down and kicked and . . ."

"Peed on," I said helpfully.

That stopped him. "Peed?"

"On."

"Yes—well . . ." He whinnied a nervous little laugh. "This isn't the time for levity, Robert. I see my—our way out with Dean Hawser."

"John, listen to me. I went there—deliberately—to meet . . ."

117

"Stop! Please don't tell me any more. Whatever else there is to tell, don't tell me. I would prefer you didn't tell anyone, but above all, don't tell me." He was pleading now. "Let me believe it was all a mistake, Robert. Let me believe you were there minding your own business, and this Andy Brown or whatever his name is walked in and came over to your table. Let me say this is what happened, and I'll be in the clear with Dr. Cannon and the Dean. Please, Robert!"

I searched around for a principle, but I could not find one. What the hell, it would get me out of his office and away from him.

"Sure, John. That's the way it happened."

He drew a shuddering sigh of relief. "Good! I knew it must be. It could have happened to anyone, Robert. I know things may be a little tense for a few days, but they'll smooth out. Nothing to worry about—nothing at all."

"Sure, John. Now I'd better run along."

"Of course, Robert." He stood up and beamed at me. "If there is anything I can do, Robert, you know where I am."

I assured him that I did indeed know where he was. And I left.

My ten o'clock class started off in fine fashion. As I entered the room, someone started to applaud, and the rest of them joined in. It was, I think, the first time that I had felt even vaguely good about what had happened the night before—except for that moment with Curwood Farnsworth. I looked at my class and thought what a nice bunch of kids they really were. It had been that way ever since I started to teach. It was the students who made it all worthwhile. To hell with the John Allens and the Deans and the rest. And this was a particularly good group—fifteen of them, all selected because they had demonstrated a genuine talent in writing. They were my kind of people.

Only fourteen of them were in the class. Andy Brown was

missing, and this disturbed me. But the rest of them were there, faces bright—nine men and five women students with the world by the tail—and they had applauded me. They understood.

I had reached the class about three minutes past the bell. As usual, there was a small stack of manuscripts waiting for me on my desk. These kids were eager. They wrote all the time, and we had an understanding that they would turn in material as they completed it, without setting any deadlines. I picked up the day's offering, waved a hand at them, and grinned a modest let's-don't-make-a-big-thing grin at them.

"Looks like you people have been pretty busy."

Tony Miller, a bright-eyed and bushy-tailed junior with an angelic face and a half-finished novel which might just make him a small fortune someday, called out, "Looks like you've been pretty busy too, Mr. Venable."

General laughter—friendly, relaxed laughter—a jovial response from Venable who was at last among friends. Until, looking casually through the morning's manuscripts, he discovers a single, neatly folded piece of white bond. He unfolds it, and the good world goes sour.

WE ARE WATCHING YOU, YOU FUCKING NIGGER LOVER

I refolded the paper carefully, hoping to Christ my face did not betray the sickness in my stomach. The class got underway. I started to talk, and as I talked I searched those fourteen bright young faces. One of them—at least one of them—was evil. And before I had finished, all of them were evil.

twelve

"Well, Mr. Venable."

I had been wondering when she was going to get back in the act, and I thought I would be prepared for her. I had several speeches ready for spontaneous and unrehearsed delivery. The party was over—that was the gist of what I had to say to her. You can take a guy like Venable and lead him out on a shaky limb one time with a gorgeous body and a husky, honeyed voice and the whole Hollywood myth of the dusky, undulating sexpot who stands in the shadows of the bamboo hut and murmurs, "I am Tondelayo." I had gone that route already. And she was not going to catch me again.

But she cheated. She did not give any warning. It wouldn't have taken much warning—just a few minutes—just enough time to check out the defense perimeter, to make sure all systems were stop instead of go.

She sat there in my office, lovely, lonely, trustingly—waiting for Venable, because he was the one man to whom she could turn in this strange place where she could not really feel at home with her own people and where she was an enemy to the whites. Little orphant Annie had come to my house to stay and the goblins were going to get me if I didn't watch out.

120

A quick glance up and down the corridor. No one was watching. Perhaps no one had seen her come in. Shut the door. Worry about having to sneak her out later. If anyone knocks say I'm busy. Come back later.

Oh, Jesus, lady, why couldn't you leave me alone!

"I hope you don't mind my just coming in like this. I was told you were in class, so I decided to wait and try to catch you here."

Who told you? Was it someone who knows who you are?

"No—that's all right." I made my way past her, cautiously skirting those crossed and gleaming legs. I placed my manuscripts on my desk and sat down on the edge of my chair, poised for flight. "I wasn't expecting to see you so soon . . ."

"I was worried about you, Mr. Venable. I wanted to call last night, but I thought perhaps it would be best not to call you at home."

Now I should have called a stop right there. *She* had taken the first step, you understand? *She* had delivered the plot line. *Best not to call you at home.* Meaning, *I know your wife does not understand. This is between us, and we must keep your wife out of it, mustn't we?* What do you take me for, lady—a boob who doesn't know how it's done? You listen to me, lady. I have no secrets from my wife—not even about important things, and you are not an important thing, so come off it. Cathy—that's my wife, my sweet, loving, loyal and understanding wife—Cathy knows all about this, so if you must call, call me at home.

What I really said was, "Yes—I suppose you're right."

"So I decided to just come here this morning and try to catch you before you went to lunch."

There was a fleeting comic routine which Venable performed mentally as he conjured up the entrance with Alise Hungerford into the Faculty Club cafeteria for lunch. One of the principal players was good old Dr. John Allen. It was a gas.

121

"Yes, well, I have an appointment for lunch in just a few minutes . . ."

"I won't take much of your time, Mr. Venable. I wanted to see you—to find out how you are . . ."

"Oh, fine. It's been a kind of hectic day, but . . ."

Her laughter was soft and warm and intimate and scary. "I can imagine. Have you been having a very bad time?"

"Medium bad. I've had worse." It only hurts when I smile, lady. Not wounded, ma'am, but dead. And other brave sayings.

"I also wanted you to know, Mr. Venable, that what happened to you last night could not have been better. If we had written the script ourselves, it could not have come off more to our advantage."

Now I must admit that this one stopped me. I had tried to view that unfortunate sequence of events from every possible angle, but hers was one I had missed.

"You liked it?"

"Perfect! That woman—that dreadful Neanderthal woman. We should write her a letter of thanks."

Dear Cora Fuller:

In case you don't remember me, I am the fellow you peed on last night in your lovely restaurant—the nice-looking fellow in the gray suit. Remember now? I would like to take this opportunity to thank you for everything you did. It is always a pleasure to be peed on by a lady like you.

> *Gratefully,*
> *Robert M. Venable*

"A letter of thanks?"

"Yes! Nothing could have better dramatized the character of those people in West Brandon who still stand in the way of total integration than that vile act of hers. This is the sort of thing we pray for, Mr. Venable." She leaned forward, eyes flashing, her hand dangerously close to mine on the desk, and I was once again aware of that damned jasmine. "Don't you see? You are white, and any right-thinking white person, knowing what happened to you last night, must identify with you rather than with the Fullers. If it had happened to a Negro, they might be able to avoid that sense of identification. When a Negro is beaten or kicked or spat upon or even killed, a white man may feel pity or even a sense of great wrong, but he will not *identify*. It could not happen *to him*. But this has not happened to a Negro, Mr. Venable. It has happened to you, and they must identify. To do otherwise would place them in an impossible position."

I was beginning to get the big picture.

"You mean I am the good guys and she is the bad guys?"

More laughter—youthful and buoyant and delighted this time—and the hand touched and burned mine briefly. "Yes, that's it precisely. You see it from a writer's point of view, but that is the idea. That's the purpose of all this really, Mr. Venable—to reveal to a disinterested public the whole pattern of social injustice and brutality which has existed in this country for a hundred years after the Emancipation Proclamation which was supposed to set the Negro free from oppression. It takes drama to awaken most people from their apathy, and we domonstrate, we sit in, we throw our bodies in the streets and on the highways to provide the material for that drama—and what happened to you was . . ."

"A real hit?"

"Exactly!"

There seemed to be a number of comments I could make on that point—some of them fairly harsh—but I settled on, "Well, I'm glad you're glad."

"And, of course, the police acted beautifully. They charged right in and arrested you and Mr. Brown without any effort to listen to your side of things, without any regard for the fact that you had been physically abused. They threw you into jail with no chance to explain your position."

"We didn't really try to explain . . ."

"It would have been better, of course," she said, "if they had been a little rougher in their actual handling of you. That is one thing about Alabama and Mississippi, the police can be counted on to behave like absolute animals—but we can't have everything, can we?"

"Beware the Jubjub bird," I said.

"I beg your pardon," she said.

"Oh, nothing. I was just thinking of something."

At this point my phone rang. It was Cathy. I had the feeling from the instant I heard her voice. You know the feeling—guilt. I get it sometimes when I see a traffic cop—even if I know damned well I'm not breaking any law.

"Bob, something just happened."

A quick glance at Alise Hungerford showed her watching me with a slight, interested smile—the worst kind.

"Yes?"

"Bob, someone just called me." I could hear her fighting hysteria, and Cathy was not—repeat not—the hysterical type.

"Yes?"

"He wouldn't say who he was, Bob. He just said awful things—dirty, terrible things about you. Bob, he said something about a woman, a Negro woman—that she was locked up in your office with you right now. He said . . ."

"No," I said. "You just don't answer if it rings again. I'll be there as soon as I can."

"What woman, Bob?"

She just sat there, the smile still on her lips, the interest still in her eyes—but there was something more than interest. There was excitement. I had a funny, naked feeling.

"There is nothing to that," I said very stiffly in my best lying voice—because, you see, there *was* something to that.

124

There comes a time in a man's relationship with a woman when both of them suddenly recognize the fact that they are on a collision course. It happens without warning—at the least likely moment, just as it happened at that particular moment to Alise Hungerford and Venable.

And I knew it. With the lie to Cathy fresh on my lips, I knew it, and I sealed the knowledge by repeating the lie. "No, nothing to that at all."

Cathy, a qualified expert at knowing when I am lying to her, was silent just long enough to confirm that knowledge. We were being frank with each other—in our fashion. I was lying. She knew I was lying. I knew she knew I was lying. And each of us was sick—deep down gut sick. But neither of us was about to try the purgative of truth.

"All right, Bob," she said. "It's all right. Don't worry about it."

"As soon as I can," I said. "I'll get there as soon as I can."

"Don't hurry, Bob. I was being foolish."

And we said our good-byes in the manner of strangers—which, at that instant, we were. And I hung up the phone.

"That was your wife."

I nodded.

"It's none of my business, Mr. Venable, but how does she feel about your taking part in our work?"

"I—don't know." And that was the truth.

"Is she for the Rights movement?"

"I guess so. She doesn't talk much about things like that . . ."

Alise Hungerford, child of scorn, disposed of Cathy. "Then she cannot really be for the movement, Mr. Venable. There are really only two sides to fight on today. You are for the rights of the Negro, or you are against them. If you do not speak out, if you do not join in the fight for us, then you are fighting against us. You can fight against us just as viciously with silence and indifference and inaction as you can with clubs and bombs and dogs."

The pressure was building up. Venable, slow to anger, slower to take a stand on any ground, was under fire—from all sectors. Someone had called Cathy. Who? Someone who knew Alise Hungerford was in my office—someone who had seen her there, had seen me come in and shut the door. Someone who was probably outside at that moment, waiting for the door to open again. Cathy was at home, alone and frightened and sick—and I was the cause of it! And I was headed for the sack with this woman, and that scared the hell out of me, but I could not stop myself. And I was going out of my god-damned mind!

"There must," I said, "be a place for the middle-ground people. There must be a place of sanity to which we can return. I think my wife is in that place. I think I may be in that place . . ."

"No, Mr. Venable. That is a mythical place now. The people who think they can stand on a middle ground are deluding themselves. There is no middle ground. It has been cut out from under the feet of those people who claim that they are 'for the Negro's rights, of course,' but who turn their eyes away from what is happening in the struggle to obtain those rights. I tell you, Mr. Venable, they are a greater enemy than the rednecks and the Klansmen. At least the Fuller woman gives us ammunition to use . . ."

"And my wife?"

"She—what is the military term?—helps to spike our guns."

"What if I said I felt the same way she does?"

Her smile had become that of a woman who is too sure of her prey to worry—even a little bit. She shook her head. "You don't, Mr. Venable. You proved that last night."

"What if last night was just a gag?"

126

"It may have started out that way, Robert, but something happened."

Yes, something happened! I felt fear, saw hate, got hit, kicked, peed upon, and jailed and for what? Oh, you bitch of honey, don't you know? Even someone as stupid as Venable knows the answer to that. I didn't do it because I wanted equal rights for anyone. I haven't the guts to stub my goddamned toe for any cause. Pull out the stops now, Venable, and let it come because the truth doesn't have many chances with you. I did it because I want to crawl into the sticky gooey naked leg tangling belly bumping ass grabbing lip biting tongue darting comecomecomecomecome sack with you you nigger bitch! And I can't help that! God help me, I can't help it! And don't call me *Robert!* I am *Mistuh Robert* to you! Now are you satisfied?

Oh boy, did something ever happen!

"Yes," I said, "something happened all right."

"No gag, Robert?"

I shook my head. "I'm afraid not."

Again her hand touched me. "Good!" She was on her feet and at the door before I had fully absorbed the shock of that touch. "Now I know you have things to do. I'll be in touch. Oh, by the way, has a time been set for your hearing?"

"Hearing?"

"Yes. You were booked on a trespassing charge, weren't you?"

"By golly, I was." I am definitely not the type who goes around saying "By golly," so you can see what sort of state I was in.

"So you will have to appear to answer that charge. You do have a lawyer?"

"Yes."

"Good. Do you think he will cooperate with us?"

"In what way?"

She was pulling on a pair of smart leather gloves. Brisk—that was the word for her. "In various ways. We'll get together with him and discuss it. There's no need for you to be bothered about that. Who is your lawyer?"

There is something exciting about kissing brisk women. How is that for a passing thought?

"Well?"

"What?"

"Your lawyer—what is his name?"

"Jim Hazeltine."

She was the type you could see making a mental note of things—a beautiful, hungry-eyed data computer. The name of Jim Hazeltine was fed into the memory tapes.

"Is he sympathetic?"

The Venable sense of proportion suddenly got the better of his libido.

"Look," I said, "Jim Hazeltine is a lawyer. I think he is also a Methodist. I seem to remember that he used to be able to consume an impressive amount of beer, and I think he plays golf. Outside of those things, your guess about him is as good as mine."

Recognition of a ruffled Venable flickered in those eyes, but that was the only sign. "It isn't important, Robert. Just leave Mr. Hazeltine to us."

Her hand was on the door when I remembered the important question—which had not yet been asked.

"What about Andy?"

"Oh, yes, Mr. Brown. Mr. Brown will be released from jail at five o'clock this afternoon."

"The cocktail hour?"

There was a certain crisp impatient quality to the laugh this time.

"For some people perhaps, Robert. We have a very close schedule on this. There are reporters from both the press and television coming in from New York. Their plane gets in at four ten. They will need a little time to get here from the airport and get set up. There will be a press conference in front of the Municipal Building when Mr. Brown is released, and we will want a sufficient crowd on hand to make it interesting visually for the television cameras."

She might have been the hostess with the mostest, running over the last-minute arrangements for a cocktail party. And I did not want to be interested, beyond the simple fact of Andy's welfare—but this was too much for me. Why in hell should the New York press be sending reporters down to cover a small-potatoes incident like the Fuller's Restaurant caper? Alongside some of the outings in Alabama and Mississippi, this was strictly bush league stuff. So I asked her about it, and she explained it to me.

"West Brandon, Robert, is crucial to Students for Freedom. As you know, there are many organizations engaged in the Civil Rights struggle, but we have a unique opportunity here. What happened last night was only the spark. Within the next week, we are going to launch an all-out campaign here aimed at something no community in the South has yet realized—total integration in every phase of life, no matter how small or seemingly insignificant. West Brandon is going to serve as a model for the rest of the South, Robert—as a town where the Negro has cast off every vestige of second-class citizenship. No target will be too small. We are going to seek out every dirty pocket of race hatred in West Brandon and expose it for what it is, a festering sore on an otherwise healthy community. And we are going to *heal* those sores, Robert, and then we will be able to hold West Brandon up for all the South to see. And it will be Students for Freedom who have accomplished this!"

I was impressed as I always am by people who know what they want and go after it. I was also impressed by a woman

129

who could make a speech and, at the same time, be infinitely desirable. And there we were, back to the real gut issue. What I was, friends, was caught up by that wench. I was hooked, that's what I was—and the large fat Venable mouth opened and these foolish words came out.

"If I can help . . ."

Well, that was that. I went home to find Cathy reasonably cheerful, the telephone behaving itself, and all generally quiet. I said calming, peace-preserving untrue things to Cathy. The children arrived safe and sound from school. And, at quarter to five, I looked Cathy straight in the eye—well, *almost* straight in the eye—and I announced that I was going down to see Andy Brown get out of the pokey. She did not like it, but she did not try to stop me.

And so I went.

thirteen

Considering the fact that she had not had much time in which to work, Alise Hungerford of the Philadelphia Hungerfords managed to get together a fair coming-out party for Andy Brown. Gathered in the vicinity of the Municipal Building were several groups of varied origins and attitudes. Directly across the street from the main entrance, about twenty students, obviously from fraternity row, were holding an impromptu minstrel show, complete with a pair of black-face comics and a banjo-picking trio who led the entire ensemble in such old favorites as "Old Black Joe," "Darktown Strutters Ball," and other appropriate numbers. It was apparently a spontaneous group, probably sprung full-blown from an afternoon beer party and transplanted to this place where there seemed to be a golden opportunity for some good clean fraternity-type fun.

Beyond this group, actually on both sides of the street, a dozen or so white men—older and quieter—waited, lounging in and around three taxicabs. This was the West Brandon chapter of Rednecks, Inc. They lacked the numbers that more fortunate communities in other southern states boasted. More than in any other place in the South, they were patently representative of a dead and hopeless past—but they still held on, a bit dispirited, but *there*.

The official greeting party was gathered in the paved courtyard entrance to the Municipal Building. This party included the Reverend James (with Bible), Miss Agatha Lewis, a pugnacious Cecil Willard, a clean-cut Mac Kirkpatrick, and, of course, a chic and ravishing and *busy* Alise Hungerford.

And there was the press. I recognized Blanton Dillon, the editor of the West Brandon *Post-Dispatch*. Dillon was a round, erudite, and jolly little man. It had been his Jabberwocky editorial which had made such an impression on me a few days earlier. There were others, reporters and photographers and three television news cameramen. The people, by God, were going to know.

"Mr. Venable! Over here!"

The *Robert* bit, then, was for private conversation. I was relieved and ashamed to be relieved. She waved me over to her group. That morning, in my office, she had been wearing a pale blue wool suit with a white blouse that V-necked down to an impressive display of honeyed cleavage. Now she was more collegiate in a tweed skirt and an angora sweater. Students for Freedom was going to be represented appropriately. She looked very young, very fresh and scrubbed and idealistic. Central casting had sent up its best "young student social protest" type. She looked great. She looked like trouble.

Drawing me aside, lowering her voice, out of the *public* earshot, she said, "I'm so glad you're here, Robert. We need you. There has been a delay, and I think the Chief of Police may be getting ready to insist that we disperse before he will release Mr. Brown. That is a good indication that my fears were well founded."

"Fears?" I was glad the *Robert* was still with us. And I wanted no part of any fear. I wanted to ask the gal to come

132

ride away with me in my little old TR-4 and we could find ourselves a dandy place to have a picnic and be like guys and gals in college and in love are supposed to be—out of the world where there are fears and in the open meadow under a bright blue sky and young, young, young.

One of the problems Venable has is that he constantly identifies himself as a college *student* rather than a college *professor*. Those slim-waisted, crew-cut young men who can wear tapered, slim-cut white levis are the mirror in which he sees himself. He gets into trouble this way.

"What fears?"

"That Mr. Brown has been the victim of police brutality."

I was coming back from the picnic—reluctantly. "Andy? Police brutality?"

"It's a familiar enough story. They try to get rid of the press and television people because they can't stand the hot glare of publicity on their brutal treatment of Negroes. This is the first time I've come face to face with it, but I've heard stories from others who have come down here to work in the field—stories which turn your stomach." There were tears in her eyes, friends—just in case you think she was putting on an act—genuine tears. "Well, Robert, this is one time they won't get away with it. The people have a right to know the truth, and the television cameras are going to stay."

"How do you know they've done anything to Andy?"

She looked surprised. "Do you really think they'd keep him in there this long—alone—without trying to teach him the 'white man's lesson'?"

"But while I was there . . ."

"Of course! Nothing happened. Don't you see, Robert? They wouldn't dare harm you. Despite the fact that they hate you because of your sympathy for the Negro cause, you are still a white. And you are connected with the university here. Mr. Brown is just another black man to them, and they are not going to let him get away with making fools of them. He is the worst enemy they have—and intelligent, articulate, fearless Negro. He is their superior intellectually, and they cannot tolerate that. If you could read some of the reports of our workers in the South, Robert, you would know.

"Also, I have learned from a confidential source that Chief Walter Scrumm returned late last night from a meeting and came directly here to the jail. He took Mr. Brown from his cell to a room where they could not be seen or heard. I understand it is a room in the basement of the building. That was this morning, and from our inside sources, Mr. Brown has not been back in his cell since that time."

I was beginning to sweat. It sounded like the old *Darkness at Noon* routine—the trip to the cellar, the rubber ball in the mouth, the bullet in the back of the head. Comrade Brown has been executed, pass it along!

The Reverend James, a neatly packaged coffee with cream, in black suit—ready to do the Lord's work at the drop of a hat—moved over to join us, greeted me with a quick and basically disinterested smile, then asked la Hungerford, "Sister, I thought the children were going to be here to sing."

One dainty hand flew to one sensuous mouth. "Oh dear, they are *supposed* to be here. Mr. Willard—oh, Mr. Willard, where *are* the children?"

Willard's black bullet head jerked angrily. "I'll tell you where they are, Miss Hungerford. There was a high school basketball game this afternoon, and that is where they are instead of being here where they belong. I had their promise that they would be here by four forty-five, and someone is going to answer to me."

Alise Hungerford glanced nervously at the slim gold watch on her slim brown wrist. "It's almost five after now. Perhaps they can still get here before Mr. Brown is brought out. I told the network people that we should be able to set up a shot of Mr. Brown—and I think it should be shaking hands with you, Mr. Venable—against a background of singing children."

A tall, broad-shouldered, blond, handsome, and *sincere* young man in a casually *perfect* brown tweed suit—a hateful type—had come over to where we were standing. He touched Alise on the shoulder with an easy familiarity which upset me.

"Alise, sweetie, how much longer do you think we're going to have to wait? We may have to rig some lights if this drags on much more. Also, we're working against a very tight deadline if we hope to make the eleven o'clock news tonight."

She frowned him a pretty frown and shook her head. "Bill, I'm at a loss, an absolute loss, to know what's going on. They said he would be released at five. They gave me a solemn promise that he would come out of that door at five o'clock sharp. If he isn't out in another five minutes, I'll go in myself and see what's happening in there. I don't like the looks of it, though. I can tell you that the police here in West Brandon are fully capable of an incredible callousness and brutality in their dealings with any Negro who has the courage to speak out for his freedom. I think you should prepare yourself for a rather shocking experience, Bill." She stamped one handsomely shod foot impatiently. "Damn! If only the children would get here before they release him!"

Then she remembered old white Venable.

"Oh, Bill, here is the other hero of last night's story." She took my arm and his arm with equal intimacy and guided our hands together. "This is Robert Venable, the writer, who went into Fuller's Restaurant with Mr. Brown last night and was arrested with him. Mr. Venable, this is Bill Beveridge of Consolidated Broadcasting News."

His was a warm and sincere handclasp. "Nice to meet you, sir."

135

I wondered how old he was. These blond types are able to conceal those first gray hairs, and there were lines around his eyes that indicated he was no kid right out of college. *Don't give me that "sir" crap, buster!*

"Perhaps we could set up an interview with Mr . . ." He looked helpless. After all, a man in his job met so many people, heard so many names . . .

"Venable," she said quickly. "Robert Venable. The writer."

"Yes indeed. *Mr. Venable.*" He was making a point of the name, associating it somehow, and, thanks to a dandy memory course he had once taken, he would never forget it. He was also desperately trying to remember if he had heard the name before. *Writer,* he was thinking. *What did this bastard write? Should I know?*

He was going to bluff it out. "So you're the writer, eh, Mr. Venable?"

I admitted to being the writer, eh.

"By George," he said, *"Robert* Venable." His trouble was apparent. He had been confusing me with *Elmer* Venable. "Robert Venable, the writer. You wrote that—that—"

"Novel," I said helpfully—and a bit disinterestedly. I was beginning to worry about old Andy Brown.

"Sure," Bill Beveridge was beaming. "That novel. By golly, I read so many novels, but yours was really—darn it, the name is right on the tip of my tongue . . ."

I have my spiteful moments. *"Tom Jones,"* I said.

"Oh, Mr. Venable!" Alise Hungerford said quickly.

"Yeah?" He looked impressed at last. "I mean, yeah! That's it! Great book too. Great story." He nudged me playfully in the ribs. "Bet you picked up a nice piece of change on the movie sale too."

"Robert!" Her voice was low and hard and not at all happy

136

with Venable, but things were closing in on all sides, so what the hell.

"Here they come!"

Miss Agatha Lewis, gold teeth flashing in the late afternoon sun, pointed excitedly as several cars pulled up about fifty feet down from where we were standing and disgorged at least thirty Negro youngsters.

Venable was busy with a picture which had been growing in his mind of a battered and bleeding Andy Brown. Red on black was the theme. Red on black, red on black, clickety-clack, taking me back . . .

"It's about time," Cecil Willard was barking. "You kids, come on now! Where you been?"

A plump, perspiring boy seemed to be the leader. He shook his head and rolled his eyes in despair.

"Mr. Willard, I tried. I tried to get 'em all together to get here like you said, but that basketball game went into two overtimes, and they just flat wouldn't leave."

Fat little black boy, sweat pouring from his face, eyes rolling. Taking Venable back, clickety-clack, clickety-clack . . .

To round fat black Billy Joe Jackson, popeyed and sneaky. But not sneaky enough to get away with stealing a quarter from Aunt Fern's purse on the kitchen table. Uncle Jim had caught him at it, and since Billy Joe worked on Uncle Jim's farm, Uncle Jim decreed the punishment.

"No need calling the sheriff just cause a nigger stole a quarter, is there, Billy Joe?"

"Nawsuh, Mistuh Jim! Nawsuh!"

"Reckon I'd do just as well takin' bout a quarter's worth outta your black hide, don't you, Billy Joe?"

And Venable's cousin, Jimmy Junior, comes running to find the visiting city cousin. "Bobby, Bobby, come on quick. Daddy's gonna whup a nigger!"

"I tried to get 'em to leave that game, Mr. Willard. Honest I did. It was right exciting, though. We won, Mr. Willard. Double overtime, and we won!"

From the look on Cecil Willard's face, heads would roll later, but there was no time then. He herded the youngsters together just to the right of the steps leading into the Municipal Building.

A policeman appeared in the front door, peered out at the growing confusion, shook his head sadly and vanished.

Alise Hungerford galvanized into action. "Over here, Mr. Venable. I'd like you to be the first one to meet him when they let him out. Just be spontaneous. You may be shocked by what you see, but don't fight against showing how you feel. Do whatever you want. Say whatever you want. There will be cameras and microphones there to capture your reaction."

Eight-year-old Bobby Venable watched with growing interest as his Uncle Jim pushed Billy Joe up against the big oak tree. He knew Billy Joe well from many trips down to the farm. Billy Joe had let Bobby drive the mule the summer before when they were hauling tobacco from the fields to the barns on the tobacco sleds. Billy Joe had an old hound dog named Willie.

"What'd he do, Jimmy?"

Jimmy Junior, aged nine, laughed with delight and pounded his bare feet in the dust in a savage dance. "Stole a quarter from my momma. That nigger stole a whole quarter, and Daddy's gonna whup him!"

Round fat black Billy Joe Jackson caught sight of the boys and his popeyes rolled in a sad, funny plea—for what? For help, pity, understanding?

"Put your hands up on that tree, Billy Joe, and take your punishment." Uncle Jim pushed him toward the tree and yanked at Billy Joe's faded blue shirt, ripping it away from his round fat black back which glistened with sweat . . .

From transplanted fraternity row across from the Municipal Building, a sweet tenor voice rose in song.

Now some folks say that a nigger won't steal.

And a swelling chorus responded.

Way down yonder in the cornfield.

And Cecil Willard's eyes bulging angrily as he bellowed at the schoolchildren, "Sing, you young'uns, sing!" And added, "Sing real loud!"

We shall overcome! We shall overcome!
We shall overcome someday!

In the battle of songs, we were caught in the cross fire.

But I found two in my cornfield!
Way down yonder in the cornfield!

Oh, God, Venable prayed, don't let it be with Andy Brown the way it was with Billy Joe!

Billy Joe. Listening to the voice of justice belonging to Uncle Jim.

"Now listen to me, nigger. You know why I'm whupping you?"

"Yassuh, Mistuh Jim."

"I'm gonna whup you bout ten good licks with this strap. Next time I catch you stealin' anything round here, it's gonna be twice that many. Understand?"

"Yassuh, Mistuh Jim. Sweet Jesus knows Billy Joe ain't gonna steal no mo!"

And with eyes of horror and eyes of fascination and eyes of excitement, Bobby Venable watched the heavy leather strap—raised in the air, dark and mean-looking against the blue

139

sky—whistling down and cracking against that round fat black sweaty mountain of flesh. And a miracle of red appeared . . .

"Look!" Alise Hungerford cried. "I think he's coming out now!"

The redneck contingent stirred hungrily and eyed each other with sly grins. One of them, a paunchy, unshaven refugee from central casting's early Erskine Caldwell file, yelled out, "Heah comes the nigger!"

Two more policemen edged out of the front door of the Municipal Building, glanced unhappily at the crowd, and took up their places, one at each side of the door.

The television cameras were going into action. The show, as they say, was on the road, and that sick feeling was starting in my stomach. I did not want to see Andy Brown. If they had beaten him after I left the night before, then I was responsible. I wanted no part of a martyred Andy Brown. No red on black to carry me back . . .

Billy Joe started to yell after the third blow. It was not a human yell. It was like a pig—a snorting, squealing noise that never ceased. Little Bobby Venable and his cousin, little Jimmy Junior, were fascinated by the sound—and by the stripes of red raw meat etched on the fat black sweaty back.

Whooee! Whooee Whooee!

And suddenly Bobby Venable was running away, missing the rest of the fun, hating himself for his cowardice, crying in anger at his own weakness, but unable to endure any longer the red raw meat and the squealing *Whooee!* of Billy Joe who was only, after all, a nigger. . . .

> *Deep in my heart, I do believe,*
> *We shall overcome someday!*

"Let us all pray!" The Reverend James was no longer able to stay out of the act. Alise Hungerford tried to stop him.

140

"Not yet, Reverend James! The prayer should come later!"

She was too late. He was on his knees, and his voice rose in a fervent appeal to the Almighty.

"Oh Heavenly Father, whose eye doth mark the sparrow's fall, who did deliver His chosen people from the oppressor, whose mercy is everlasting . . ."

From the Benevolent and Protective Order of Rednecks came the cry, "You'd better pray, nigger!"

And the fraternity row contingent became a cheering section, led by the burnt-cork clowns, complete with somersaults.

"Gimme a N!"

The cheering section thundered, "N!"

"Gimme a I!"

"I!"

"Gimme a G!"

"G!"

"Gimme another G!"

"G!"

> *Black and white together! Black and white together!*
> *Black and white together someday!*
> *Deep in my heart I do believe*
> *We shall overcome someday!*

Someone had old white Venable by the arm and was propelling him toward the steps which led up to the entrance of the Municipal Building.

"Right over here, Mr. Venable. We'll pick it up in fifteen seconds. Just talk into the mike when I hold it toward you, and try to keep your head up as much as possible to catch the sun."

Reverend James was in prayerful orbit.

"Lord, You have been the comfort of Your children in

their time of pain. Look down now upon our martyred brother who has suffered in a cruel prison cell all through the long night of oppression. Lay Your healing hands upon his wounds, Lord!"

Two hours after fleeing from the scene of Billy Joe's whipping, Bobby Venable saw the round fat black man cheerfully chopping wood down by Uncle Jim's barns.

"You all right, Billy Joe?"

"Lawsee, Mistuh Bobby, Ah jest a mite stiff in de back. Mistuh Jim he wore me out for fair. Whooee! He wore dis nigger out for fair!"

And so it was all right. What they said was right. Niggers didn't mind getting whipped. Niggers were different after all, and Bobby Venable could sit down at the table with his Uncle Jim and eat hugely of Aunt Fern's fried chicken and mashed potatoes and corn and butter beans and tomatoes and biscuits and cold milk and sweet-potato pie.

Nigger! Nigger! Nigger!

The burnt-cork cheerleaders went into a frenzied series of acrobatics, evoking an explosion of whistles, cheers, and applause from their flock of clean-cut young men.

"Three seconds—two—one—"

The Venable head jerked up and looked into the eye of the nation. Bill Beveridge was speaking in that crisp, well-modulated, objective voice of our-man-on-the-scene.

"Violence came last night to this sleepy little college town of West Brandon. Two men—one white and one Negro—went together into a restaurant which has maintained a rigid policy of excluding Negroes . . ."

> *God is on our side! God is on our side!*
> *God is on our side today!*

Somewhere out there in television control land, a hoarse voice muttered, "Shut them kids up. I can't get a goddamned level on this."

142

"With me here on the front steps of West Brandon's Municipal Building is one of those two men, Robert Venable, well-known author of such best sellers as . . ." Those earnest blue eyes filled with horror as realization struck in the nick of time. *"Tom Jones!* You didn't write *Tom Jones,* you son of a bitch! What're you trying to do to me?"

Then recovery and, "We'll edit that out, Mac. Never mind. I'll pick it up again." He gave me a nervous how-could-you-do-that-to-me laugh. "With me here on the front steps of West Brandon's Municipal Building is one of those two men, Robert Venable, a well-known author who is currently on the faculty of the University. Along with an ever-growing crowd of white and Negro citizens of this community, Mr. Venable is awaiting the release of his companion in last night's Civil Rights episode, Andrew Brown, a Negro student at the University."

He turned those sincere eyes on me. "Mr. Venable, you were released from custody last night, were you not?"

The microphone was thrust at me, and I mumbled an affirmative reply. Speaking into microphones has never been one of my strong suits.

"A significant aspect of the situation here in West Brandon is that Mr. Venable, a white man, was released shortly after his arrest on charges of trespassing, while Brown, a Negro, has been held incommunicado until this moment. There have been widespread fears among the Civil Rights workers here that Brown has been a victim of a tough police policy aimed at striking fear into the local Negro community and keeping the West Brandon Negroes from going on with the massive new demonstrations now being planned by Civil Rights groups, particularly the Students for Freedom.

"Mr. Venable, I believe that both you and Mr. Brown were physically assaulted last night at Fuller's Restaurant. Could you tell exactly what form this assault took?"

I stared, hypnotized by the microphone. "On television?"

"For the nation to hear, Mr. Venable."

Somewhere in the distance there was banjo picking, and a sweet tenor voice rose in the air.

I hear those gentle voices calling, Old Black Joe . . .

"Well, someone hit me—and knocked me to the floor . . ."

"Yes, Mr. Venable—and then?"

It was rather nice to be able to tell that friendly-looking microphone about things.

"I think someone may have kicked me a couple of times . . ."

"Anything else?"

"A woman peed on me."

"Anything—WHAT!"

The friendly microphone was jerked away from me. It did not like me anymore.

"We'll edit that out, Mac! Jesus Christ, what did you say?"

"I said, a woman . . ."

"Here he comes!"

The camera's eye moved past Venable to capture the front door which was swinging open.

I heard Alise Hungerford's voice in my ear. "Let yourself go, Robert. Be *spontaneous!*"

And Cecil Willard's voice was thundering, "Sing now, children! Sing *loud!*"

We shall overcome! We shall overcome!
We shall overcome someday!

The fraternity boys were chanting a choral ode.

"Here comes the nigger now! Here comes the nigger now! Hit him again—harder, harder! Hit him again—harder, harder!"

144

The Reverend James' voice rose to a shrill and anguished pitch.

"Send down Your comfort, Lord, to our brother. Bathe his wounds with Your sweet love!"

Little Bobby Venable, snug and warm in his bed at Uncle Jim's that night, just before drifting off to sleep, wondering why it didn't hurt a nigger like Billy Joe to be whipped . . .

It was the greatest center door fancy since Diamond Lil. There he was—old black Andy Brown, boy martyr—fresh from the torture dungeons. With him was Walter Scrumm, the Chief of all the Police in West Brandon. And one large, beefy arm of the Chief was flung around the shoulders of his victim. And they were laughing, those two gay dogs. And in Andy Brown's mouth, clamped firmly between dazzling white teeth, was a large and expensive cigar. He stood for an impressive moment, surveying the scene. Then he saw his noble white friend and companion, Venable. Slowly, majestically, fully conscious of his place in history, he removed the cigar from his mouth and waved it in greeting.

"Professor," he said, "how nice of you to come."

Somewhere behind me Alise Hungerford was using some very unladylike language. The television cameras were taking their pictures. Bill Beveridge was strangely and uncharacteristically silent. The children's chorus was never in better voice.

And Venable? Venable was being spontaneous. Venable was doubled over and laughing, laughing, LAUGHING!

fourteen

The laughter was a good thing for Venable because, as it turned out, he was laughing *at* Alise Hungerford, and laughter is the greatest weapon going, and Venable badly needed a weapon at that time. What the laughter did was to remove Venable from the hook with Alise just about the time it was looking like lights out and beddie-bye for certain. And Venable did not want this to happen. This is for the record. Venable did not want to have hanky-panky with Hungerford. Venable was no paragon of husbandly virtue. He had an eye for the girls as they walked by in the summertime—the girls who, as Irwin Shaw put it in his short story, jiggled when they walked. Venable was not above making a few passes between martinis at large cocktail parties. His was a smooth line which hinted at the pleasures of hanky-panky, but for all this, Venable was really a rather dull and faithful husband type who found the sack time spent with his wife quite satisfactory, thank you, ma'am.

So the laughter took me home—away from a fuming and frustrated Hungerford—away from a bewildered Beveridge—away from the various assortments of choral entertainers who had assembled for Andy Brown's coming-out party. It took me home, and I took Andy Brown home for dinner because—for some strange reason—no one else seemed to want him.

Cathy had not yet had the pleasure of meeting Andy Brown.

A word or two here about Catherine Venable, formerly Catherine Dalton of the Richmond, Virginia, Daltons. When I was in graduate school, Cathy was a senior English major. We met in the stacks of the library in mutual pursuit of a book with the call number 929.239, J58. What the book was, I could not remember for the life of me, but the call number will be with me always. Having arrived on the scene simultaneously, we played Alphonse and Gaston for awhile, compromised by making a date to consider the book together, and that was the beginning. We agonized through a winter and a spring trying to discover where animal passion left off and true love began, and in the summer decided it was all hopelessly academic and got ourselves married.

Now a word or two about Cathy and Andy Brown. Cathy had as much or more of an "Old South" background as I, only she was not bugged by it as I was. The "Negro Problem," as far as she was concerned, was somebody else's problem. There were Negroes she liked and those she did not like. They were DIFFERENT, but she did not worry herself about this difference. She accepted it, just as she expected intelligent Negroes to accept it. What I am trying to say is that I had never had any reason to complain of her treatment of Negroes. If I made one of my impassioned speeches about CIVIL RIGHTS, Cathy would listen and smile and murmur something soothing, and, without my really knowing how or why, we would suddenly be talking about something else. She was *cool* about it—cool in the modern sense of the word.

So much for the background. On this particular evening, bringing this particular Negro student home, I found a Cathy who was not running true to her cool form. It had been a bad day for her, coming on the heels of a bad night. She had a certain waspish quality about her when Andy Brown and I appeared. She was particularly waspish with me, perhaps because I kept collapsing in gales of laughter, and she obviously had trouble getting with the gag.

Of course, another ticklish aspect of the occasion was the fact that I had invited Andy to stay for dinner, and I had given her no warning. She had that thing that many wives have about their husbands bringing home unexpected dinner guests—black or white or red all over. And there was the little matter that I had promised to talk to the kids at dinner about "things." All told, she had a fair number of burrs under her saddle. But Cathy was true blue and a real scout—on the surface. She said, "Glad to have you," and "I hope you won't mind taking potluck," and all manner of acceptable and gracious things. But she was not happy. I was the only one who could tell she wasn't happy, but *I could tell.*

However, things were rather bright. Good old LIBERAL Robert Venable was entertaining a genuine black Negro for the first time at his family's festive board. In restaurants, cafeterias, drive-ins, etc., Venable had broken bread with a fair number of Negroes, but in his own household, with his own complete family, at his own dinner table, never before.

And the circumstances were encouraging. It was not Venable's contribution to *Be Nice to a Negro Week.* It was spontaneous and unself-conscious and all the things it should have been. The only flaw was that Cathy had not been made a part of things.

The evening started off like a house afire. We arrived, Andy Brown still nursing the remains of that fine expensive cigar, Venable still nursing the remains of his laughing jag— two excellent fellows who had taken the plunge—gone out for a bit of a lark in no man's land—and got back with only superficial flesh wounds.

And Venable, with a fine sense of what is proper, mixed a large pitcher of martinis for consumption before potluck was served. Cathy, politely and detachedly, had absented herself to "take care of things in the kitchen."

"Well, Andy, here's to life in the jailhouse." I lifted my glass containing one perfectly mixed Beefeater's (8 parts) and Martini & Rossi (1 part) MARTINI.

"Professor," Andy grinned, "I will drink to that."

So we drank to that.

"Man, that does go down so smooth."

He had struck a sensitive and responsive chord. "Dry enough for you? That's eight to one, which I find is far and away the best ratio—stirred ever so gently so as not to bruise the gin. It's best, of course, to serve them in chilled glasses, but on the spur of the moment . . ." Venable, in company with several million other American males, was convinced that he and only he had discovered just the right formula, technique and attitude in making martinis.

Andy Brown looked impressed as he held up his glass and considered it thoughtfully. Then he revealed those pearly whites in a sad kind of grin. "I'll level with you, Professor. This is the first martini I've ever had, so I couldn't tell you if it's the best or the worst ever made."

A considerate Venable would have let it go at that. An overly exuberant, foot-in-the-mouth Venable had to make a big thing of it.

With sayings like "Never had a martini before?" and "Where've you been all your life?" and "You haven't really learned about life and drinking until you've mastered the martini!"—and other crappy comments.

And Andy Brown, sipping his martini politely and smiling patiently, said, "Didn't you know, Professor, us niggers drink our gin straight on Saturday night."

And the trouble was he was only saying what I had been

thinking without knowing I was thinking it—but Andy knew. He knew a lot about me, Andy Brown did.

So that seemed to be a good time to stop the laughing.

"Sorry, Andy."

"Sorry? Man, don't ever be sorry." He raised his glass and drained it, smacking his lips over the olive. "Don't ever, ever be sorry. This martini is smooth and good and I think I will grow to be very fond of martinis. Maybe that's the only difference between us, Professor—that little bitty dash of vermouth and that olive. Wouldn't it be nice if it turned out that was the only difference between us? Wouldn't it be a grand and glorious thing if somebody was to go around on Saturday night and add a little bitty dash of vermouth and an olive to all the gin all the black folks was drinking and lo and behold, they'd be just like the white folks? And then nobody would care who ate where or who goes to school where or who married whose daughter or sister or nothing like that there."

"What really happened last night, Andy?"

"You mean after you were sprung?" He was getting a bit thick in the tongue. "How you like that, man? *Sprung!* That sounds real hep, don't it? Like I was one of those cats in *The Untouchables.* After you got you a *mouthpiece* and got *sprung.*"

"Okay—after I was sprung—what happened then?"

He grinned a silly little grin and held up his empty glass. "Is it polite among the white folks to ask for seconds?" He had the needle out—not too far, but it was definitely out.

I poured a refill without comment, and he looked puzzled. "No more olives?"

"You want another olive?"

"Oh man, yeah. That's what makes it so good! I mean, if I am going to pass using the martini route, I want to do it right."

Getting more olives meant going back to the kitchen

150

where Cathy was fixing dinner, and I did not relish this prospect, but the man wanted an olive, so I girded up my loins and went.

"I'm looking for the olives." This to Cathy whose back was presented to me, but not in love. "For the martinis."

The back did not offer much encouragement. "They're in the refrigerator."

"Look, honey, are you sure I couldn't fix you something to drink? If you don't want a martini, I could whip up . . ."

"No thank you."

"Maybe a glass of sherry?"

"No thank you."

"Anything at all I can do to help you in here?"

"No thank you."

Talking to a back, even as attractive a back as Cathy's, which says nothing but "No thank you" can be discouraging.

"Look, honey, I guess I should have called to ask about bringing Andy home for dinner, but it just seemed . . ."

"It's all right, Bob."

"I mean, he's had a pretty rough time, and I thought . . ."

"It's all right, Bob."

"Actually, what happened down there this afternoon was funny as hell, honey. And I didn't get a chance to get it all straight from him, so I figured . . ."

"It's all right, Bob."

It was a very clever back. It could say, "It's all right, Bob," as well as, "No thank you." With a little training, I imagine it could have been taught to say, "Screw you, Robert Venable!" So, before it caught on to that one, I took the jar of olives and silently stole away.

"Okay, Andy, you have your olive. Now settle back and tell me what happened last night—after I was sprung."

He looked at his drink and smacked his lips. "Mmmm! That olive looks so good! Looks good enough to eat!"

"In the jailhouse, Andy—what happened?"

"Oh—in the jail house . . ." He took an elaborate sip of his martini and rolled his eyes. "Lawsee, boss man, that is sho sumpin!"

"Andy!"

"In the jailhouse—after you departed—there was only sweetness and light. I stretched out on that luxurious mattress for a little bit and refreshed myself with a beauty nap—and then I was gently awakened by that kindly gentleman who brought us our dinner and told me that I was requested for an interview."

"With Chief Scrumm?"

"I do believe that was the gentleman's name—yes. The Chief of Police Walter Scrumm."

"Your pal, from the looks of things when you came out."

The martinis were obviously getting to him. "Yeah, yeah—definitely my pal. Wally—he told me call him Wally—he proved to be a friend in need which, as you well know, Professor, is a friend indeed. We had us a long and interesting talk, and while we found ourselves differing on a few minor points here and there, we discovered we could reach compromises which were practical and therefore desirable. He's a very persuasive man, Wally is, and most stimulating. Most stimulating indeed . . ."

The second martini was gone, and he was chewing on the gin-soaked olive. And I detected something wrong with him, his story and the whole ball of wax.

"So you two became old buddies overnight?"

"Yeah, man." Up went the empty glass again. "Skip the olive this time, Professor." He was definitely on his way. The words were selected a bit too carefully, and the eyes were having trouble focusing. I poured his drink, and he bobbed his head. "Thankee, mistuh. Thankee kindly."

"And that's all there was to it? You had this nice talk, and you compromised your differences, and he stuck that big cigar in your face, and the two of you lived happily ever after?"

"You might say that, Professor. How'd you like that cigar? Man, it was big!"

"Those little differences you mentioned—the ones you were able to work out a compromise on, what were they?"

In addition to a drunk look, he was getting a cornered look.

"Oh, man, les let bygones be bygones, huh? You outta the pokey. I'm out of the pokey. Les everybody be happy."

"We're out on bond, friend. There'll be a trial later on, you know . . ."

"No." He shook his head slowly from side to side. "No trial later on."

"What the hell are you talking about? We were booked on a charge of trespassing. There's got to be a trial."

"Charges dropped." The third martini was gone, and Andy Brown was not far behind. His head was set at a crazy angle to his shoulders, and his eyes were almost closed. "All charges —dropped and forgotten."

"Since when?"

"Since last night and this morning, Fessor. Since nice lil talk with ol Wally Scrumm."

"And he agreed to forgive and forget?"

"Like Christian gennuman he is."

The air was heavy with the smoke from Venable's white pipe, the fumes of martinis, and the unmistakable aroma of untruth. And Venable, tireless pursuer of truth, would not relent. There was the temptation, of course—the Oedipal instinct that told Venable the truth he sought might contain the seeds of his own destruction—but in the words of Lady Macbeth, *That which hath made them drunk hath made me bold.* Venable pushed ahead.

"Bullshit, Andy!"

He opened one large eye which managed to look surprised and puzzled and hurt—no mean trick for a three-martinied eye. "What's that, Fessor?"

"In the immortal words of Harry Brock in *Born Yesterday*, Andy, 'Never crap a crapper.' Now what really happened with Scrumm?"

"You don't believe my story?"

"I do not believe your story."

His black kinky head shook sadly from side to side. "Man, thas too bad. That was such a *good* story."

"But not a true story?"

"Man, what's being true got to do with anything? What's true? Only thing that's true is what works, man. One thing works for you. You got a nice white lawyer, gets dressed up in a nice suit of clothes and comes down to the jail and pays your bond, and then after awhile he's gonna get together with the nice white judge and he's gonna say, 'Looka here, Judge, your honor sir, my client's a nice respectable white man who made just one little ol' mistake, that's all. Couldn't we maybe settle all this outside court?' And that judge say, 'Sure. I think we can work out something for your nice respectable white client.'

"Now that works for you, Fessor, so that's truth for you. On other hand, les consider truth for old Andy Brown— whilst I have me one more of those fine martinis." He held out his glass.

"Andy, these things are hitting you pretty hard. You'd better take it easy . . ."

"Easy!" His laugh was not happy—nor was it drunk. Suddenly the speech cleared and the eyes focused. "Professor, we are now embarked on a philosophical discussion concerning truth. So let me tell you a truth. The drunk act was just that—an act. I could put away about twelve of these things and never bat an eye. You are talking to the champion gin drinker of our time. No, Professor, I'm not drunk. I'm not about to get drunk. I wish to Christ I was."

So I poured his glass full again and listened.

"The truth," he said, "about Andy Brown is not as pretty as the truth about Robert Venable, but it is just as true. Sure I could get a lawyer who would pay my bond, and I could get out of the jail. But when my trial comes up—man, that is when the cheese will begin to bind. That nice white judge is going to take one look at old Andy Brown, and he is going to pick up the whole book and throw it at him. Now that is another kind of truth."

"But your story about Chief Scrumm—none of that was a true story?"

He looked wistful. "If you would only believe it, Professor, it might grow to be a true story in time."

"What really happened, Andy?"

"Professor," he said very quietly, very calmly, "the Chief of Police, Walter Scrumm by name, merely showed me the error of my ways. He is a patient and a thorough man, and he explained matters to me in terms which made the whole thing very clear to me. Like, I had a choice, you see, between saying I was sorry and promising him I would never mix in any of this damn foolishness again—in which case, all would be happy and carefree and gay, with lots of good fellowship all around; or I could persist in all this damned foolishness— in which sad case, he, the Chief of Police, would see to it that I ended up in the big pokey, the one with the high stone wall all around it, and the key would be thrown far far away.

"He had a nice way of putting things, Wally did. He pointed out the various differences between my situation as a black man and that of a white citizen like you, Professor. He painted a very vivid picture of life in the big pokey where you need the wings of an angel to fly over those high prison walls, and he kept raising the question as to how important all this really was. So, to make a long story short, in the end . . ."

"You finked out!" This was Venable, rising in righteous wrath for a cause betrayed.

Andy Brown finished the latest martini and nodded. "That is the currently popular expression for it, I do believe."

Now at this point, it is interesting to examine Venable's point of view and attitude. What was his trouble? He had apparently been delighted when Andy Brown had confounded Alise Hungerford and company by emerging from jail happy and healthy instead of bruised and bloody. Why the indignation, then?

Listen to the indignation.

"My God, Andy, you let that bastard scare you into turning your back on your own people!"

Answer—Venable was a romantic, a romantic who wanted honor and valor and courage to prevail in his heroes. Andy Brown had betrayed the hero image. He was the man who had remained in jail to suffer. And when he had come out laughing, it was to be assumed he had somehow conquered the enemy within. But Andy Brown had not conquered. Andy Brown was no hero. He had turned fink. He had betrayed the cause. He had betrayed his own . . .

"Professor, how many times do I have to tell you? I don't have any people!" He was on his feet—an agitated Andy Brown I had never seen before. "Listen, Professor, after you left that jail last night, I didn't take any nap. I sat on that lumpy mattress, and I thought for a long time. I didn't like that cell. It was interesting to see what it was like, but I wanted out. I eat three good meals a day, and if there're a few places I can't go to get one of those meals, I don't give a good goddamn. My wants are simple, Professor. I want to write and I want to have the good life and learn to make martinis and play golf and go live where I want to live. And most of all, I want to play it cool, man. I want to look out for number one, and I'll do anything, say anything I can to do just that."

Brave words. Brave Andy Brown, a black man with the guts to be yellow. But something was going wrong. He was saying those brave finky words, but the voice was quavering, and the eyes were filling up with tears.

"Goddamn it, Professor! Goddamn it to hell! Why didn't you stay with me? If you had stayed with me, we might have made it, but by myself I chickened out!"

Black and white together!

"Look, Andy, I understand . . ."

"Do you? Then I hope to God you'll explain it to me sometime, Professor, because I don't understand a goddamned thing anymore." He looked around the room like an animal looks around a cage. "Look, Professor, I've got to get out of here. I've got to think . . ."

"But dinner is almost . . ."

"Screw dinner!" He did not raise his voice. It was flat and dead and desperate. "Not *your* dinner, Professor—just dinner. I'll slip out. Tell your wife I'm sorry. I don't think she'll be sorry, but I am."

"Andy, wait a minute. Perhaps if we talked this out . . ."

"No, Professor." He was at the front door. "That's our trouble, yours and mine. We are such great talkers. We talk all the time. We—" He broke off, his face twisted now into the mask of an Andy Brown who frightened me. "Sweet Jesus, man," the mask whispered, "what am I going to do?"

But before I could give him the answer, he was out of the door, and the door was closed behind him, and he was gone, and I was standing there with egg on my face. Which was just as well, really, because I did not have any answer to give him.

fifteen

Around the campfires, they speak of that night as the "Night of the Telephone."

With Andy Brown gone out into the night, but not forgotten, Venable concocted various explanations for the fact of the departed guest, ate his dinner with his all-white family, discussed in a remarkably honest fashion with Elaine and Jimmy what had happened the night before, helped Cathy clear the table and do the dishes, struggled through Jimmy's modern math assignment, and generally conducted himself as a gentleman, husband, and DAD.

Among the items not yet taken up for discussion was the telephone call Cathy had received during the day. By children-in-bed time and what's-on-television-tonight time, the conjugal atmosphere had become so pleasant that neither party was inclined to introduce potentially dangerous topics of conversation. And so we settled ourselves before our bedroom portable television set—Ma in her kerchief and I in my cap—to watch the latest episode in our favorite "spy-for-fun" television series.

It would be inaccurate to say that all hostilities had ended, but there were the elements of a dandy truce, and Venable badly needed a truce.

The program's teaser was quite promising. What happened, you see, was we start off with this lovely, fresh, girl-next-door-type girl strolling through a park. It is spring, and she is so happy it makes you want to smile just watching her. She passes by other people—a cop, a couple of kids, an old man with a cane, a nurse type pushing a baby carriage—and they all smile at her because she's so pretty and happy. She stops when she meets the nurse type, and she is making happy noises over the baby in the carriage, and the nurse is looking very happy and friendly. So this fresh, lovely girl bends over the carriage to say "cootchy coo" things to the darling baby inside, and we go in for a tight over-the-shoulder shot, and we see there isn't any darling baby inside. There is only a cruddy-looking little doll, but in a flash, there is something else. There is an ugly snub-nosed automatic there. The girl has taken it from her purse and placed it beside the doll, and then she covers it with the blanket, and she and the nurse smile some more and say more nice things and move on. Then the titles start to roll over a shot of this fresh, lovely girl walking briskly away—and we are hooked, wondering what nasty business a sweet kid like that could be involved in and how it all relates to our hero, the cleverest international espionage agent this side of Istanbul.

And then the telephone rang.

You can get lulled into a blissfully unsuspecting state by things being pleasant, by a promising teaser to a television show, by the fact that you and your wife are comfortably settled with pipe and knitting and slippers and coffee and all those things. So when even as menacing an instrument as the telephone rings, you may not view the event with alarm. You may be so completely tranquilized by all this peace and order that you simply walk over to the damned thing, pick it up and say "Hello" without any fear at all.

I did just that.

And the voice at the other end of the connection was not

the sort to cause any concern. It was a man's voice—rather soft, distinctly southern, polite and even gentle. It said, "Is this Mr. Robert Venable?"

"Yes."

"I have a message for you." The voice remained soft and polite and gentle. "It's a message from a lot of people in this town who hate nigger lovers who—"

I slammed the phone down—hard. Across the room, Cathy gave me the curious eye.

"Bob—who was that?"

On the tube the titles were finished, and the commercial was extolling the virile virtues of a new mentholated charcoal filter cigarette. Venable's first instinct was to lie, but lying to Cathy was getting to be old hat, so he told the truth.

"I think it was your friend."

"What friend?"

"The one who—" I ventured onto the soft-boiled egg surface of the subject we had both been avoiding. "Who called you today."

She was out of her comfortable chair and her comfortable mood. "Oh no!"

"What did he sound like—the man who called you?"

"He—he had a rather nice voice really, very soft—just a trace of a southern accent—it seemed so out of character with the terrible things . . ."

"That's the same one."

"What did he say?"

"I didn't give him a chance. He got as far as *nigger lover,* and I lowered the boom on him."

"Do you think he'll call back?"

"If he does, we won't answer."

We stood there, the two of us looking at that instrument of the devil trying to fool us with its innocent pastel plastic

160

façade. But it couldn't keep up the sham. It started to ring again.

I looked at Cathy, and I could see the panic starting to build.

"Let it ring."

"Oh, Bob, you know how I am about that!"

I knew how she was. She was like the girl in *Voice of the Turtle* who went to pieces if she had to just sit and listen to a telephone ringing unanswered. I had that trapped and helpless feeling of resentment at Alexander Graham Bell and Don Ameche and all the people who were responsible for the telephone.

"Let it ring."

"It could be someone else," she said.

"Let it ring."

"Something could have happened to your folks—or mine . . ."

That was the nature of the demon. It might always be *something important*. I walked over and stood beside the son-of-a-bitch, hoping I could outlast it. It outlasted me.

All right, I thought, I will listen to you. I will pick you up and listen to your vomit. I will listen to it as long as I can, so you can spew it all out, and I can know you for what you are.

I picked it up. It had the same voice.

"Is this Mr. Robert Venable?"

I gave it its cue. "Yes."

There followed what might be called a monologue, delivered in that soft, polite and gentle voice to Venable who did not attempt to answer, but simply stood and listened—an audience of one.

"I have a message for you." Note that his opening had a certain inflexibility. "It's a message from a lot of people in this town who hate nigger lovers who go around—" I think he

161

was surprised to find me still with him, because he paused, and then he laughed—not unpleasantly. "Are you still there, Venable? Not going to hang up on me this time? You know, Venable, you'd be surprised how close an eye we have on you now. We know where you are and what you're doing most of the time. We know that nigger bitch was locked in your office this morning. We called to let your wife know. How was it to get some black ass, Venable? It probably wasn't new to you. Up north you probably got lots of black ass. Must be pretty good. Is it all that good, Venable. How does it feel for a white man to stick his . . ."

Think of something else! Anything else!

The first girl I ever fell in love with was named Peggy Hanes. We were seniors in high school. One night we'd been to a movie, and when we came home her folks were in the living room, so we went out in the garage and sat in her father's car, a Buick, and listened to the radio. Guy Lombardo's orchestra was playing the sweetest music this side of heaven, and we just sat there and listened. I had never kissed her, and I wanted to kiss her very much, but I didn't know how to ask her. It was very important that I ask her and not just grab her and make a fool of myself. Guy Lombardo was playing "When I Grow Too Old to Dream," and I finally said, "Peg, you wouldn't like me if I was crazy, would you?" And she asked, "Why?" And I said, "Because I think I might go crazy if I don't kiss you." And she sat there very quietly for awhile, and then she looked at me, and I could see her smiling in the glow from the radio light, and she said, "I wouldn't want you to go crazy, Bob." So I kissed her. It was a very corny line. The date was November 27, 1939 . . .

"What does your wife think about you fucking that nigger, Venable?"

He had an interesting vocal delivery. There was no anger in the voice. It was well modulated and regular, almost monotonous in its lack of variation of pitch, rate and force. It was difficult not to be hypnotized by it.

"We'll keep your wife posted, Venable, don't worry about that. Or maybe she doesn't mind. We noticed you took your buck nigger friend home with you this afternoon. Maybe you brought him home so he could give your wife some nigger . . ."

Once, when I was very little—about five years old—we lived in a big house at the top of a hill, and there was a little creek down at the bottom of the hill. I was playing down there with two little colored boys, Petey and Paul—I never knew their last names. Their mothers worked for women in the neighborhood. We were playing follow-the-leader, and I was the leader. I was always the leader. I started across the creek, walking from stone to stone, and about halfway across, I slipped and fell into the creek. I can remember my head being under water, and I knew I was going to die. But one of them—either Petey or Paul—jumped in and dragged me to the bank. I was trying not to cry, and when they got me to my mother, she bawled them out for leading me where there was danger, and I wanted to tell her it had been my idea, but I didn't tell her, and she sent them away with dire threats of what she would do if they ever showed their black faces around there again, and they looked scared and ran, and my mother made soothing noises, and I sobbed something to the effect that if "I'd been a bullfrog, everything would've been all right." And my mother thought this was very cute and told everyone in the family what a cute thing Bobby had said and how dangerous it was for him to play with those little nigger children. And I never saw Petey or Paul again, and I missed them very much . . .

"You know what might happen to you, you nigger-fucking bastard—what might happen to you some dark night? Some dark night, Venable, we might catch you and take a dull knife and cut off your nigger-loving balls . . ."

I made motions with my hand to Cathy to come to me. Then I wrote on the note pad beside the telephone.

Get Jimmy's whistle.

It was a real regulation police whistle he had traded some baseball cards for at school a few weeks earlier. He had blown it only once in the house, and it had been enough to send us right up the wall. Cathy appeared with it and handed it to me, looking puzzled.

The voice droned on, spilling out its filth in a steady, venomous stream. Carefully, I put the whistle to the mouthpiece, took a deep breath and BLEW.

I seem to remember hearing a kind of scream of pain before I hung up. It was a pleasant sound.

sixteen

The Night of the Telephone, lest we become confused about time, was Thursday night. When I fell asleep that night— which was about thirty seconds after my head hit the pillow because I have this dandy escape mechanism which permits me to get away from unpleasant things by falling asleep—I was in for a few dreams, none of them very happy except for one brief one in which I saw a faceless man with blood spurting out of his ear. That one I enjoyed.

And the next day turned out to be Friday.

Proving that my ability to escape was not limited to sack time, I avoided the campus on Friday, taking the kind of license we CREATIVE people are expected to take from time to time. That morning, I drove Cathy up to Addison which is a fair-sized mill town about twenty miles north of West Brandon. There are some mill outlet stores there where you can buy socks and towels and underwear and other basic goodies for a few cents less than the retail store prices. There is also a huge fabric store where Cathy went to find all manner of bargains on material which she used to make herself and Elaine skirts, dresses, coats, etc. I have never really sat down and made an estimate of what I have saved over the years by marrying a woman who could and would make her own clothes. It would probably add up to an impressive sum.

Aside from the bad moment I experienced when I saw a billboard sign which the local John Birch Society had erected across the highway from the fabric store, demanding in letters of red and blue on a white background that Earl Warren be impeached, it was a pleasant enough morning. While Cathy was prowling through the tables piled high with Dacrons, silks, woolens, linens, and the like, I strolled around the store's huge parking lot, smoking my pipe and managing to keep my mind reasonably blank while I enjoyed the sun's warmth and the smug sense of pleasure I felt from having heard on the car radio that the frozen North from which I was a fugitive had experienced another eight inches of snow the day before. In my wandering, I happened upon a gnarled and ancient Negro who was making his rounds of the parking lot with a burlap sack slung over one bent shoulder and carrying a piece of a broom handle with the sharp point of a nail protruding from one end. He moved slowly, having all the time in the world to accomplish his task of picking up litter from the parking lot.

We encountered each other and stood, for a few moments encased in a mutual pocket of the world, and talked.

Venable: "Good morning."

Negro: "Yassuh."

Venable: "Mighty nice day, isn't it?"

Negro: "Yassuh. Sho is. Yassuh."

Venable: "Looks like winter's almost over."

Negro: "Yassuh. Das a fak."

Venable: "Yes, sir. Spring'll be here before we know it."

Negro: "Yassuh. Sho is."

And we parted company, moving on, each in his own way and back to his own life, away from that little space of time we had shared in a way some people might not be able to understand.

By noon, Cathy and I were on our way back to West Brandon, laden down with half a dozen pairs of socks for Elaine, Jimmy, and me, plus a lavender towel set for a cousin of Cathy's who was getting married, plus some T-shirts for me, and assorted materials from which Cathy would make three dresses for Elaine, a skirt for herself and a couple of sports shirts for Jimmy.

By the time we reached West Brandon and considered the scenic approach to the town which is really picturesque and lovely and idyllic as you come to the top of the hill that looks across a wooded ravine to the hill on which the town is situated and see a couple of graceful church spires showing over all those pine trees against a bright blue sky and things like that, I was quite prepared to believe the world was not really such a crappy place as events of the last few days had led me to think it was.

I even managed to spend about an hour after lunch taking a nap on the living room sofa, which is my very favorite thing to do after lunch. And I maintained my insulation from the outside world, except for one telephone call which was from Bernie Spruill, my agent in New York.

Bernie, despite the usual fictional characterization of agents and despite the fact that he was as fond of making a buck as the next guy, is really a very nice person. For writers who complain about agents being con men, leeches, mother-rapists and assorted obscenities, let me say that my own homespun philosophy regarding agents is as follows. Every time Bernie Spruill makes a penny, Venable makes nine cents. Considering the fact that he has to deal with guys like Venable and maintain a plush office on Fifth Avenue and hire secretaries and con publishers and drink martinis at lunch and buy postage stamps and make long-distance telephone calls and commute from Stamford, I figure it is like the drunk said when he happened upon a graveside ceremony-in-progress one day and stumbled over to join the mourners just in time to hear the minister saying, "The Lord giveth and the Lord taketh away," which evoked the comment from the drunk, "If that ain't a square deal, I'll kiss your ass."

Bernie, it seemed, had seen a wire-service story on my adventures in Fantasyland and was bubbling over with CONCERN for me and IDEAS for MAKING MONEY.

"You're sure you're okay, Bob? No broken bones or anything?"

"Sound of wind and limb, Bernie."

"Oh, those bastards! How can you stand it down there, Bob? You know, I read about all that business in the *Times,* but when it hits someone you know—personally, I mean—it really comes home. Know what I mean?"

I assured him that I was somewhere slightly north of the Dark Ages and that this was, after all, the section of the country I laughingly called home and that all was well and he should not worry, because I would very probably never write another book that would make him any money anyhow.

The mention of writing put him into a new and happier orbit.

"Bob, you know there's always a bright side to these things, so you mustn't be discouraged—no matter how lousy things are down there. The Civil Rights movement is hot right now. I mean it is *really* hot, and you're right there on the scene—right where it is happening. You're a part of the greatest social revolution of the century, Bob. Now, from your last letter I gather the new novel is giving you a little trouble, right?"

"It is not giving me any trouble. It's just that I'm trying to stand off from it a bit to gain a new perspective, and . . ."

"Like I say, Bob, it's giving you a little trouble, so why not

168

put it aside for a little while. *That* problem isn't going to disappear and besides it'll probably have more immediacy if you bring it out during the next presidential election year." He was too polite to remind me that I had been supposed to bring the damned thing out during the *last* presidental year. Bernie had a feeling for a writer's sensitivity.

"But, Bob, you're in a perfect position now to do a quickie book on the hottest item going. Maybe a non-fiction book with a good personal slant. If you could get it out by summer, I could have at least half a dozen publishers bidding against each other for it."

I muttered something about lacking the objectivity to do a good book on the Civil Rights movement because I was too close to it at the moment.

"Bob, that's crap for the birds, and you know it. Be a reporter, that's all it takes. Reporters manage objectivity at close distances. This doesn't have to be the great American documentary. All it has to be is powerful and vital and authentic and colorful and provocative. It should strip the whole ugly business that's been going on down there to the bone once and for all. While you're at it, I think I could probably line up a couple of magazine assignments for you."

"Like *Reader's Digest?*"

"Jesus, Bob, I don't know about that. I was thinking along the lines of *Harper's* and the *Atlantic*. You know, there's not a hell of a lot of money there, but the prestige is great." He paused, and I could hear the sound of conflict that was going on in his mind between the desirability of getting ten percent of some prestige from *Harper's* and ten percent of some solid cash from *Reader's Digest*. "You think you might be able to turn out something the *Digest* would buy, Bob?"

"I could do a piece called *I Was a Urinal for the S.F.F. and Found God*. How does that grab you?"

There was one of those long, reproachful silences. "I'm

serious, Bob, so be serious, will you? What the hell kind of joke is that?"

"You wouldn't believe me if I told you."

"Okay, Bob, forget the magazine, but what about the book idea? You think you could take a crack at it?"

I was suddenly tired by the thought of the money he was spending for the call. "Maybe so, Bernie. Look, I'll give it some thought and drop you a line over the weekend."

"Or call, Bob. Anytime. Just call collect if you come up with something. As hot as this is right now, I think I might be able to get you a good contract just on the strength of a couple of chapters and a short outline."

"Okay, Bernie, I'll give it some thought."

"Good boy. How's the family?"

"They're fine, thanks. Well . . ."

"You having pretty good weather down there? I guess that's one of the compensations to go along with all the garbage down there. Boy, it's been murder in New York this winter."

"Yeah, Bernie. Well, so . . ."

"By the way, Bob, if you do come up with something, maybe you could arrange to run up here for a couple of days. Sometimes it's easier to sell something like that just by going in and sitting down and talking to an editor. I mean, you're right there on the scene, and you ought to be able to come up with some great items—significant, you know what I mean? Something that really has *immediacy*."

"Yeah, Bernie, I'll be in . . ."

"And do give the non-fiction idea some serious thought, Bob. I know you've never done that kind of book, but there's an increasing demand for non-fiction today. In fact, some people in the publishing business think the novel may be on its way out as a really big item."

"Good-bye, Bernie."

170

"Take care, Bob, and keep in touch . . ."

I hung up very quickly before he could spend any more of his money.

And I could not figure out why I was annoyed by his suggestion that I write a book about what was happening in West Brandon. After all, it was not exactly as if the thought hadn't already crossed my mind. Perhaps it was what he had said about wondering how I could stand it "down there." That took me right back to the frozen North where so many of my friends were constantly asking the same kind of question.

"I don't understand how you could even consider going back down there, Bob."

"You're from down there, Bob. What kind of Middle Ages feudalistic people are they anyhow?"

"When are those idiots down there going to wake up to the fact they're living in the twentieth century, Bob?"

All of which somehow got me around to thinking of Alise Hungerford.

As you will recall, when our hero last saw Miss Hungerford, he was laughing his head off, and she was neatly attired in a tailored fit of pique. Being blessed with a sometime talent for forced forgetting, Venable had managed not to think about her all day. But now he thought about her deliberately. And he added her to the list of people he knew suffering from the *down there* syndrome. And this helped him somewhat in tempering the thoughts which came to him when he thought of her. It helped, but it did not completely solve the problem.

But the arrival home from school of Elaine and Jimmy helped a bit more. And a rousing series of games of *Uncle Wiggily* with Jimmy who was really a nut about games in a family which, except for him, hated games, helped even more. After all, when you have to worry about whether the

171

old rabbit gentleman is going to get to jump ahead to the Five and Ten Cent Store or get caught by the alligator, you can't be bothered by other less vital things.

But even Venable could not hide behind Uncle Wiggily forever. Jimmy beat him two games out of three, and then Jimmy wanted to watch the Bullwinkle Show on television. Which proves that a man's children have no real concern for him.

And Elaine was doing her homework. And Cathy was in the kitchen. So Venable was left alone. And so he thought some more about Alise Hungerford. And Andy Brown. And what had happened that week. And what might happen the next week. And out of all that thinking came several things of note.

Venable was going to seek out Alise Hungerford. There were some things he had to say to her about her *down there* attitude. There were—some things he had to say to her . . .

Venable was also going to get in touch with Andy Brown. He and Andy had gone into something together, and they had come out of it apart, and that was not good.

Venable was going to stop being a jellyfish. He was not a *down there* guy. He was a *down here* guy, and if anything constructive was going to be done in West Brandon it would have to be done by a *down here* guy, not someone who had come south to do missionary work.

Venable was going to turn over a new leaf and become a man of resolve and purpose and ACTION.

All of which should serve as a hideous object lesson to wives and children who are heartless enough to leave their husbands and fathers alone in time of need.

seventeen

A resolution to become a man of ACTION should never be made on a Friday, because Friday is followed by Saturday and Sunday, and those two are notoriously poor days for implementing any worthwhile resolutions. To his credit, Venable did not, as a lesser man might have done under such adverse circumstances, *lose* his resolution. He simply held it in abeyance over the weekend. And he utilized Saturday and Sunday for those things which were proper to Saturdays and Sundays. He held his resolution in reserve—never really forgetting it—simply not using it. He *thought* about it a great deal. Indeed there might be unkind critics who, looking at Venable with historical perspective, might say that the native hue of his resolution became a bit sicklied over with the pale cast of thought that weekend—but then there are always those literary bastards who say things like that.

The truth is that Venable was completely taken up with the things proper to Saturdays that Saturday—such as not shaving on Saturday morning and watching the Saturday morning horror picture for children on the television with Jimmy and emptying the ashtray in the car and eating a huge pastrami sandwich for lunch and watching the last three

173

holes of the golf tournament on television and finally going over to the home of those good friends who serve martinis from the lime crush dispenser and getting DRUNK.

Drunker than usual, as a matter of fact, because those good friends were slow getting around to cooking the steaks and were determinedly gay and casual and kept avoiding any discussion of Venable's activities during the week just concluded so that the very absence of the subject caused it to hang heavily over the evening's festivities which were not terribly festive and in order to get out from under that heavy-hanging subject, Venable became the lime crush-martini dispenser's best customer and got DRUNK.

So drunk, in fact, that he experienced a total loss of memory concerning such vital items of the evening as the eating of the steak, the drinking of the brandy, the attempted seduction of the hostess, the drinking of the scotch, and the interpretive dance rendered by Venable himself to the lilting strains of an old and scratched but memorable Louis Armstrong recording of "Baby, It's Cold Outside."

These items were duly reported to Venable by his loving wife who has her own unique reportorial style for such occasions, one which is not above including a fair amount of editorial comment.

Happily, nearly the whole of Sunday was given over to the pursuit of that already discussed and all-important Sunday task—nursing the HANGOVER. And it was a dandy!

But the resolution was never abandoned—only held in abeyance and THOUGHT ABOUT.

And Monday came.

I greeted Monday with eyes reasonably clear and hands moderately steady. My soft-boiled egg and dry toast and black coffee went down remarkably well. The childrens' screaming preparations for school did *not* send me up the wall. I managed two smiles and a chuckle out of *Peanuts*. And I felt

174

pretty good about things in general because I am a sucker for new days, new weeks, new terms of school, new cars, new pajamas, new recipes for spaghetti sauce—anything which has the hope of the first time about it.

And I was in my office early to find my latest communiqué from the unknown admirer waiting just inside the door. I tossed it unopened and unread on my desk and sat down, ready to turn resolution to action, ready to call Alise Hungerford and straighten *her* out and to call Andy Brown and straighten *him* out and ready to follow all that up by straightening out the world in general and West Brandon in particular.

And I then decided I was ready to start it all off by reading my note after all. The printing was somewhat less tidy than in previous notes, and I prided myself that a shattered eardrum might have been responsible for this. The message itself demonstrated scant ability to create fresh copy.

GET OUT OF TOWN YOU FUCKING NIGGER LOVER

He *did* have a fixation on that word.

My mood was sufficiently positive to permit me to fold the piece of paper containing this deathless prose into an airplane, raise the window and, making sure no one saw me, sail it out into God's great world in the hope that some deserving person might read it and ponder the problem for me.

Then, secure in the blessed hope of a new day and armed with resolution about to be put into action, I reseated myself at my desk, addressed a scornful "Up yours, buddy!" to my anonymous correspondent, and reached for the telephone.

Which rang an instant before my hand made contact.

It was Alise Hungerford. And I could feel the initiative slipping away from me.

We were back on *Robert* terms. "Robert," she said, "I've

175

been expecting to hear from you all this weekend. You got away so quickly on Thursday that I didn't get a chance to see you—once everything started to happen so fast . . ."

It was obvious she had forgotten that she was piqued with me, so I thought I would drop a gentle reminder.

"Well, Andy and I decided we'd better check out. *Andy and I* . . ." That was the magic word, *Andy*. Now she would remember.

"Yes, I know." Where the hell was the pique? She sounded all sweetness and light. "Andy is here with me now. In fact we had breakfast together, and most of the time we were talking about you."

I had that trapped feeling. Andy Brown and Alise Hungerford, eating their cornflakes together and discussing their best pal, Venable.

How come those two were eating breakfast together?

What's been going on since Thursday night?

Why isn't *she* put out with *him* anymore?

What the hell were they talking about when they were talking about me?

What was it I was going to say to her?

"And we were wondering if we might get together somewhere for lunch—the three of us. Some things have come up . . ."

What things!

"You can make it, can't you?"

A glimmering of that old resolution returned. Get them both together and have it all out in one fell swoop. That was the way to do it! Also, it made it unnecessary for me to have to think of some reason for saying "No."

"Yes. I guess I can make it. Where?"

"Where can we all eat together, Robert?"

That seemed as good a time as any to get started. "In any eating place in town with about four exceptions." I even managed to sound fairly caustic, and that pleased me. But she apparently hadn't noticed. I made a mental note to bone up on being caustic.

"You decide, Robert."

"I'll meet you at Bernardo's." Bernardo's was a better-than-average restaurant just off the main shopping district. It affected an ersatz Italian atmosphere and served lousy pasta but good standard fare. It also had private booths and good coffee and my favorite waitress in all the world whose name was Grace and who was probably one hundred and five years old and who had been waiting the tables at Bernardo's for as long as there had been a Bernardo's and who was a real, genuine gas. I was in love with Grace from back in my student days when she had been wont to give me extra servings because I looked, in her inimitable prose, "No bigger'n a ounce o' soap after a week's washing." I had put on weight since then, but I was still in love with Grace.

"Bernardo's," Alise was saying. "Where . . ." And I heard a familiar voice in the background. "Never mind," she said. "Andy knows where it is. What time shall we meet you?"

"How about twelve thirty?"

"Fine."

The conversation seemed to be over, but the connection lingered on, and I was starting to get that uncomfortable warm feeling in the pit of my impressionable stomach. I wondered what she was wearing at that moment. I wondered why the hell Andy Brown had been having breakfast with her. And that all led to a line of thought which was nothing but BAD NEWS. I tried bailing out.

"You say Andy's there with you?"

"Yes. We just had breakfast together and . . ."

"Let me talk with him a minute." Goddamn it, I *know* you just had breakfast with him! You *told* me!

177

Then there came that old familiar voice—but changed—or was that my imagination?

"*Good* morning, Professor."

I lowered my voice. "Andy, is everything okay?"

He did not lower his. "Sure, Professor. Why shouldn't everything be okay?"

He was obviously under duress, and he couldn't talk. Maybe there was a gun being held on him. "I know you can't talk now, Andy, but listen very carefully. If there is anything wrong—anything at all, just say something like 'And how was your weekend?' " I knew all about how to handle this sort of situation. After all, I was a WRITER.

"Say what, Professor?"

Goddamn it, Andy, don't act stupid!

"Say, 'And how was your weekend?' if there's anything wrong—anything you can't tell me with her there . . ."

"Everything's great, Professor. I meant to call you, but we've been pretty busy."

He was trying to tell me something. Maybe the call was being monitored!

"Busy? Busy with what, Andy?"

"We'll tell you all about it at lunch, Professor."

"Dammit, Andy, I want to see you *before* lunch. Come by my office this morning, or maybe better, I could arrange to meet you in the stacks at the library. That way you might be able to give them the slip. You could say you had to get a book on . . ."

"Sorry, Professor. We're going to be busy all morning, but we can talk it all over at lunch."

I said several unprintable things, although I'm not sure whether they were said before or after he hung up. Then I sat and stared at the telephone for awhile, thinking black thoughts about black Andy Brown, and I finally decided what had really happened was that it hadn't really been Andy I

178

had been talking to, but someone she had planted to *sound* like Andy Brown—perhaps even to *look* like Andy Brown. Someone or *something*. There was a science fiction book I read once in which some nasties from outer space invaded Earth and started bringing in giant seedpods which grew into humanoids which were exact duplicates of Earth people— only these things had no heart, no soul, and they were here to take over. Maybe Alise Hungerford was really from outer space. In many ways, Philadelphia was a lot like outer space compared with West Brandon. And she had put one of her giant seedpods in poor old Andy Brown's basement, and during the night it had bloomed into a duplicate Andy Brown, and *that* was the thing she'd had breakfast with. And *that* was the thing I had talked with on the telephone. And Christ knows what had happened to the real Andy Brown!

But the thing that really scared hell out of me was that she was probably going to try to put a Robert M. Venable-type giant seedpod down in my basement.

So I stewed a lot during the rest of the morning which brought forth nothing more startling than a call from a member of the local Junior Chamber of Commerce remind- ing me in a "If you're too busy, what with *things,* we could get someone else" way that I had promised to serve as one of the judges in the upcoming Miss West Brandon beauty contest which was a preliminary to the state contest which was a preliminary to the MISS AMERICA CONTEST. He obvi- ously was opening the door for me to chicken out, possibly because when I had been asked to take on this challenging responsibility, the name of Venable had been that of a visiting WRITER and had not been smeared across the front pages of newspapers as a TROUBLEMAKER.

The point should be made that, under ordinary circum- stances, I would have been glad to seize the slightest oppor- tunity to get out of the job. I am a sucker for agreeing to do things like that when they are a couple of months in the future. It seems civic-minded and public-spirited and the way one is "expected to behave"—and besides, it is a long way off, and, what with the way science is progressing, the world may have been blown up before then, so what the hell.

However, I did not take the offered opportunity to get out, thus flying in the face of established precedents. I stayed in. Because the Venable back was up, I was not going to be read out of society just because my name and my picture had been in the papers. I told the nice Junior Chamber of Commerce man that I was *looking forward* to being a judge, that I was *proud* to have such an *important* responsibility, and that he could *count on me*.

The poor guy thanked me, calling me a real friend and undoubtedly thinking to himself that with friends like Venable he sure as hell didn't need any enemies. For a few minutes after he hung up I basked in the pleasant glow of the knowledge that I had just done a *positive* thing.

But the glow had vanished when I reached Bernardo's a few minutes before twelve thirty. When I came in, Grace spotted me and came bustling over to greet me.

"Hey there, Mr. Venable. Where you been keeping yourself so long?"

"Here and there, Grace. You miss me?"

"Day and night, honey. You look like you could use some decent food. Ain't that wife of yours feeding you?" Her ancient face was contorted in a sly wink. "Maybe she don't like you going round getting your picture in the papers."

"You saw that?"

"Sure did, honey. It wasn't what you'd call a good likeness, but I could tell it was you. You oughta be ashamed of yourself anyway, going to a trashy place like Fuller's to eat."

I promised her it would not happen again and told her I

180

was expecting two more people to join me and that we would like a booth in the back.

"Those folks you're expecting, honey—they black or white?"

"As a matter of fact, Grace, they are both colored."

She shook her head disapprovingly. "Now that ain't the reason you want a booth in the back is it? I mean this here ain't Fuller's, you know. No reason why you shouldn't eat right out at a table with those folks if'n they're decent."

"That's not why I want a booth, Grace. We have some— business to discuss, and I just wanted a little privacy."

She did not look convinced, and I did not feel very convincing.

"Okay, Mr. Venable. I'll fix you up. You wanta wait back in the booth or out here?"

I glanced around. The place was about half filled with students who made up most of Bernardo's clientele. After all, I thought, my picture had been in the paper, and the word about what had happened to me was out on the campus, and there were probably plenty of students there who either knew who I was or would recognize me, and I was never a great one for being stared at.

"I'll wait in the booth, Grace. There're a man and a woman."

"Don't worry, I'll show 'em back when they come in."

As I went toward the back, not one of the eating students paid any attention to me—not openly anyhow—which goes to show how sneaky students can be.

The booth was small. The table was covered with a red and white checkered tablecloth because Bernardo's was ostensibly an Italian restaurant, and to further verify this fact there was a Chianti bottle on the table with a candle on it and lots of wax drippings coating the straw basket. I ordered a beer and lighted my pipe and wondered whether Alise would sit next

181

to me or Andy and how she would look and how he would look and what the hell I was doing there.

And without finding any answers, I passed about ten minutes before they arrived. We said a variety of polite things. Andy and Alise sat together across the table from me. She looked, in answer to my question, very lovely and very young and very fresh in a skirt and sweater and a cloak of innocence. Andy Brown—or rather the humanoid she had hatched from a giant seedpod to replace the real Andy Brown—looked relaxed and proper and QUIET. The two of them seemed to belong together, and this did nothing at all for the Venable sense of security.

We sparred a bit while Grace bustled with our orders.

"Oh, it has been such a really beautiful morning, hasn't it? I don't feel like eating much—perhaps a salad." Alise Hungerford, lover of nature and calorie watcher.

"Got a real tasty Chef's salad." This was Grace, hovering alongside and being helpful regardless of race, color or national origin.

"That sounds wonderful—with just some vinegar and no oil. Robert, I'm sorry we kept you waiting, but we were held up."

"How's the lasagna?" Andy Brown, with an Italian bent.

"Terrible. That cook just don't know how to cook Eye-talian food even if his name is Tony." Grace was winning Brownie points for candor.

"I have the most marvelous recipe for lasagna, Andy," said Alise, the girl homebody. "You use cottage cheese."

"I think I'll try the vegetable soup." Venable wanted Grace gone.

"Lord, honey, you don't want that stuff today. It's weak as Yankee dishwater."

Andy and I finally settled on hamburger steak which Grace assured us was "real good."

"What'll you all have to drink?"

"Hot tea, please," said Alise. "With lemon."

"Glass of milk." That did it. I knew then for sure this was not the real Andy Brown.

I ran a final check. "Bring me another beer, Grace. Come on, Andy, you want a beer, don't you?"

"I don't think that's a very good idea," Alise answered for him. "Are you sure you wouldn't rather have tea or coffee or milk, Robert?"

In minor skirmishes of will, Venable does occasionally emerge victorious. "Beer," I said, "is what I will have."

"I'll stick with the milk." Was I mistaken, or was there a note of unhappiness in Andy's voice?

"One hot tea with lemon, one milk and one beer," Grace chanted, with what I took to be approval of my stand. "Want that beer now, honey?"

"Yes." And with what might qualify as defiance, "I'll probably want another one later."

Then we three were left alone.

"I didn't mean to sound prudish about your having beer, Robert," she said, sounding prudish. "It's just that people in our situation are very vulnerable to criticism. There are many people who can twist the most innocent things into something dirty. A man and woman being together can lead to the vilest claims of sexual behavior—if one of them is white and the other Negro. Our sitting here with beer on the table could end up being reported as a drunken debauchery."

Was I mistaken, or did I detect one Andy Brown eye closing in what seemed to be a wink? Hope flickered . . .

"Well," I said finally. "Here we all are."

"Yes," Andy nodded. "Here we are . . ."

There is a rather nice little one-act play entitled *Here We Are* which is about a young couple on their honeymoon, and we seemed in danger of stealing most of the best dialogue from it, but Alise saved the day. She had a new line.

"Robert," she said, "we might as well get right down to cases. Andy and I have been talking . . ."

She stopped while Grace placed a glass and a fresh bottle of Miller's by my place, poured the ice water from its glass into the empty one and deftly filled the chilled glass with beer. Grace knew her onions, and I briefly considered leaving the party and taking her on a picnic in the woods.

I didn't do that, but the interruption caused by her arrival did give me a chance to seize the initiative.

"Before we go any further," I said, timing my delivery to beat my honeypot seedpod fancier to the draw, "I want to make one point very clear." There were no objections from the floor. I had them nailed. Smiling a tight, hard, Bogart-type smile, I let them wait while I took a slug of the Miller's, spilling only a very little on my tie. They still waited.

"There are a few things about what has been going on I don't like," I said, continuing the famous Venable imitation of Bogart. "The thing that'll kill any Civil Rights movement in this town dead in its tracks is the impression that people from the outside are coming in and organizing and stirring things up. The people who live here are proud, and I think they have some cause for that pride. If there are things wrong here, and there are, then I say the leadership for correcting those things should come from southerners who . . ."

"Exactly!" This interesting word came from the tempting lips of Miss Hungerford who was, oddly enough, leaning forward with her eyes shining.

"Of course!" This unexpected echo came from old black enthusiastic Andy Brown.

"And furthermore . . ." The Venable express was slowed. "Furthermore, I—I . . ." It ground to a lumbering STOP. "What was that?"

"That is precisely what Andy and I were discussing this morning, Robert."

"What?"

"That's right, Professor. Alise here and I agree that it was a mistake for her to look like the leader. It should be a white man and a Negro who come from this part of the country."

"You agreed on that, huh?"

Alise smiled—open and honest and appealing.

Andy smiled—man to man and shoulder to shoulder, marching along together.

Venable fed them the cue. "What white man and what Negro?"

"Why you, Professor," responded Andy Brown, "and me."

That wink had not been a wink. It had been a speck of dust in the unhuman eye of that fully developed product of the Andy Brown giant seedpod.

Stormy weather!

eighteen

As previously noted, when five-year-old Bobby Venable used to play with Petey and Paul, his leadership in all games was an accepted fact. There had been no general election held to establish this particular order of things. The three boys had first met one summer afternoon when Bobby Venable had sneaked away from his house for a forbidden exploration of the neighborhood and ended up in an alley which ran behind the houses in the next block from where he lived. Suddenly and frighteningly, from behind a row of garbage pails, he had been ambushed.

"Ho theah!" Petey was the larger of the two Negro boys— probably eight years old, tall, skinny, sooty black, with slightly crossed eyes and an expression of fierce and unwavering menace.

"Ho!" Paul was short and squat and was someday going to become a mountain of flesh. He was six—or so he thought. Lighter in shade than Petey, he was invariably and magnificently soiled from the crown of his kinky head to the bare and dusty tips of his toes. But he was probably the happiest child ever born of woman. It is doubtful that Paul ever went two minutes without laughing—even when he was asleep.

"Ho!" he said again and collapsed in mirth.

"Whut's yo name, white boy?" Petey edged around the garbage pails and advanced on an uneasy Bobby Venable.

"Name's Bobby. What's yours?"

Paul giggled. "Mah name Paul. His Petey."

"You wanta play something?" Bobby Venable had a feeling that it might end up being a choice between playing and fighting.

Petey considered this for a moment. "Mebbe. Whut you wanta play?"

"Soldiers."

"Whut kinder soljurs?"

"Americans and Germans."

"Dat sound awright to you, Paul?"

It was the funniest thing Paul had ever heard.

Petey nodded then. "Dat sound awright to us."

There was still one more question to be decided. Bobby Venable raised it. "Who's gonna be general?"

"Whut's de gineral?" Petey asked suspiciously.

"The leader of all the soldiers."

There was a quick conference between the two little Negro boys, and then Petey announced their decision. "You be de gineral. You de white boy."

So, from his earliest days, Venable had been groomed for a position of leadership in biracial affairs.

One of the things Venable had learned from a careful study of some of our most dynamic national leaders down through history—men like Warren Harding and Calvin Coolidge and Dwight Eisenhower—was that the first rule of effective leadership is to GO SLOW. Sit back and listen for awhile. Let things take shape and form. The chances are, in any emergency, that things are not really as bad as they seem to be, and given a bit of time and patience and disregard, they will *probably* work themselves out. But first and foremost, a

187

leader must seek the support and advice and approval of the ESTABLISHMENT.

"What we must have," I had said to Alise and Andy, "is the backing of key people in the town. There are plenty of them who are in complete sympathy with the Civil Rights movement. It is just that they have not been given an opportunity to participate in it in their way. We need a law—a town ordinance which will outlaw any and all discrimination in places of public accommodation."

Alise had little faith. "You won't get a law like that without really shaking the very foundations of this town, Robert."

"Wait and see. Give these people a chance. I know them, you see, and you don't."

There is nothing smugger than a smug Venable.

Bright and early on the morning following luncheon at Bernardo's, I galvanized into action—well, perhaps *galvanized* is not the exact word. I had prepared a list of people I would see—people who represented the element in West Brandon which must be brought into the struggle for a one hundred percent discrimination-free town—people who were and always had been LIBERALS—people with standing in the community—people who had somehow been bypassed by the sudden and unexpected eruption of Civil Rights demonstrations in the streets of their town—people who had every right to be disturbed because they felt the pressure which had been brought to bear was unjust and unwarranted.

People like Blanton Dillon, editor of the West Brandon *Post-Dispatch*. At eleven o'clock on Tuesday morning, I was seated across the desk from him in his office which fronted on Main Street and afforded a view of the passing scene through a large plate-glass window. Dillon had a regular column which he called *Window on Main Street*. It contained an assortment of folksy bits and pieces of the day-to-day happen-

188

ings to West Brandonites of all walks of life. Sitting there with him, exposed to the passing parade, I enjoyed one of his cigars—a rather powerful blunt—and a steaming mug of coffee which had been served by his secretary.

My acquaintance with Dillon was slight, but most of what I knew about him I liked, despite the fact that when I had first arrived at the University in the role of Writer-in-Residence, he had done an interview with me and published it, referring to me throughout as *Robert H. Venerable.* Aside from minor sins of that sort, he put out a rather good small-town newspaper—one which, more often than not, took the LIBERAL road. As already noted, he was given to using literary allusions in his editorials. He had a sense of humor, and an abiding passion for West Brandon was reflected in his paper whether he praised or damned things. He also passed out good cigars and a pretty fair cup of coffee.

"Blanton Dillon," I had told Alise and Andy, "is a man we must get to stand with us."

"Blanton Dillon," Andy Brown had commented, "will stand exactly where Mr. Fenway Thurston tells him to stand." Fenway Thurston was the owner and publisher of the *Post-Dispatch,* a man of shadowy business antecedents but very firm immediate assets.

"Blanton Dillon," I had retorted, "is too good a newspaperman to allow himself to be dictated to by his publisher."

And this, being the word of the LEADER, was the attitude which had prevailed and brought me to Blanton Dillon's office with a view of the passing parade.

We had indulged ourselves in the customary opening pleasantries which are essential to any kind of serious dialogue in the South and were ready to get down to brass tacks—whatever *they* are.

"What I wanted to discuss with you, Blanton," I said—

having been admonished by him that I must call him *Blanton,* "is the future of the Civil Rights movement here in West Brandon."

Seated there in his swivel chair behind his oversized and incredibly cluttered desk, cigar clenched between his dentures, he was the picture of a right jolly old elf—round and pink and shining of countenance.

"Hi there, Miss Annie!"

For a moment I thought he was talking to me, but he was merely waving and shouting at an ancient little woman who was being escorted past the window by an oversized Saint Bernard.

"Bless her heart," Dillon chuckled. "Main Street wouldn't be Main Street without Miss Annie." Then he turned his attention back to me. "The Civil Rights movement, huh? I figured that, Bob. From the looks of things, you've got yourself right in the middle of that."

"Well," I said modestly, "I do try to have a sense of responsibility."

He grinned and clicked his teeth and jabbed his cigar in my direction. "You writer fellows always trying to get material for another book. You know something, Bob, it's like I was telling you when I interviewed you last fall, I've always had a hankering to write a book myself, but I never seem to have either the patience or the time to turn out anything longer than a three-column feature. Maybe what I ought to do is get a lot of my *Window on Main Street* columns together and publish them—sort of a collection of impressions from over the years here. This is the place to see things all right, Bob." He waved a hand at the window. "Right by there, they all come by sooner or later."

He sat for a moment considering the street with a faraway smile. Then he swung back around to look at me. "Is that

190

what you're after, Bob—a book? If it is, then I can see some sense in what you're doing."

"And suppose I'm not after a book?"

He leaned back and grinned at me over his cigar. "Then, I guess I'll have to figure you for a damned fool. No offense, of course."

"Of course," I said in an offended tone. "Why a damned fool?"

"I wrote an editorial about a week ago. Maybe you read it. Lots of my own editorials I don't like, but this one I did. I headed it *Beware the Jabberwocky*. You happen to read it?"

"Yes, I read it."

"Did it make sense to you?"

"At the time . . ."

"That's what I liked about it. Old Lewis Carroll knew how to make sense out of nonsense. In my own way that's what I was trying to do."

"But since then . . ."

"What's happened since then? It's still the same town. The people are the same." He studied me for a moment. "Look, Bob, I figure you for an intelligent guy. Maybe that's because I'm a sucker for writers. I figure any writer is intelligent—in some basic way. Now you know this town pretty well. You know what its traditions are, its history, its way of life. I've lived here most of my life, and I'm damned proud of this town. It's not perfect, but no town is perfect. We've got our share of bigots and rednecks who live here and do business here, but the thing that makes West Brandon different from so many little towns in the South is that those people are in the minority.

"Now they aren't going to change. We aren't going to be able to wave some magic wand and make them different somehow. We're going to have to live with them until their breed dies out.

"Bob, the main point is that the colored people here have always had it pretty damned good. We integrated our public schools, on a token basis, two years before the Supreme Court decision. We've always had a mutual respect between the whites and the colored here, but now it's starting to break down."

I wished to hell I didn't always get involved in debates with people who were more persuasive than I. "Well," I said, "a mutual respect can be based on something that is wrong."

"Come on, Bob. Look out there at Main Street. Watch the colored people who walk by here. Walk down the street and watch the colored people you meet. Do they look oppressed to you? Do they back off the sidewalk when a white man comes along? Hell, they walk just as tall as you do."

At that moment, outside on Main Street, an aging Negro man backed to one side as a well-dressed white man passed him. The Negro ducked his head and raised his hat and waited respectfully until the white man had passed before resuming his own shuffling way. Dillon chuckled.

"Okay. Sure there're still a few who'll give you that 'Yas-suh, Boss' routine, but they're the old ones. They wouldn't know any other way. Nobody is going to sell those people equality. They don't want equality. Look across the street there at those colored women who sit out in front of the bank and sell flowers. They've been in business there ever since I can remember, and that's a long time. Does the fact that they sit there as sidewalk peddlers make them oppressed? They want to be there. That's their way of life, and they're just as honored and respected a part of Main Street as Fred Williams, the president of the bank, is. West Brandon would be the poorer for their loss.

"There's a new generation coming up, Bob, and when that generation is our age, there won't be any race problem—not here. There'll be some sad things that go along with that—

like the fact that those flower women will probably be gone. A lot of good things will be gone, but it has to happen. It'll happen gradually—naturally and easily—unless we let people from the outside, people who have no real understanding of or stake in West Brandon, continue to rock the boat and drive a wedge between the white and colored communities here."

He was quite a talker, once he got started. Venable was beginning to weaken, but he continued to hang in there.

"All I'm asking, Blanton, is that the *Post-Dispatch* take a more positive attitude toward this thing. It's easy for you to say, 'Wait. It'll all work out in time,' but it's not so easy for a black man to wait. He's been waiting. What I'm suggesting is legal action to remove those few remaining pockets of discrimination in places that are supposed to serve the public. If the town of West Brandon could pass an ordinance which prohibits such discrimination, then it could stand without shame. There's a federal law coming. We all know that. Why not lead the way? It's all well and good to point to the whites whose hearts are in the right place, but that doesn't help the pride of a black man who still finds himself refused service in his own town for no other reason than the color of his skin."

Now, that wasn't a bad bit of talking either, but it didn't get very far with Blanton Dillon.

"Let's let the federal government do it, Bob. That's not a proper function for a town. The *Post-Dispatch* will always be on the side of proper liberal causes, but a revolutionary sheet it is not. I work for a publisher, and that publisher is a businessman in this community, and his bread is buttered on the side of peace and quiet and order. So that's the way I run his newspaper.

"When a bunch of long-haired, wild-eyed people march up and down the middle of Main Street out there and invade private property and try to cram something down this town's

193

throat, then I'll speak out against it. And I'll do that because I love West Brandon." He grinned pleasantly. "And, of course, my job."

So he sat there, round and fat and jolly and intelligent and unmoving. And Venable sat there, painfully afflicted by the disease which had plagued him all his life—the crippling ability to see merit on both sides of an argument.

And we finished our cigars and said some unimportant things and watched the people passing by on Main Street, white people and black people, and then I left. Just before I left, though, Dillon gave me some advice.

"Think it over, Bob. It's easy to get yourself trapped in something like this. It's not really your fight, you know. I have a notion you love this town. It's a very lovable town. It's taken quite a few storms and come out pretty well. Remember the Communist scare ten or twelve years ago. A lot of people got stirred up over that, but it blew over. West Brandon and the University weren't hotbeds of Communism. Neither are they hotbeds of prejudice. Stand off a little from this mess. Look at it, if you like, and write yourself a book about it and make some money, but don't get trapped in it.

"It's easy to get trapped, you know. Hell, almost got caught myself not long ago. Somebody went to Fenway Thurston and told him I had been seen out singing freedom songs with a lot of crackpots, and he hauled me in on the carpet. I had to admit I had been singing, but, hell, I just happen to be a sucker for group singing, and they were a pretty good group, so I stood around and contributed my golden tenor for a few numbers.

"There are a lot of people like me in West Brandon, Bob. We don't hate anybody. We just love this town, and we don't want to see it torn to pieces when it doesn't really deserve it. It's a good boat, Bob, so don't rock it."

194

And I walked back out onto Main Street, carrying Blanton Dillon's advice, the image of Venable the Leader slightly askew. That was the first of a planned series of interviews with RESPONSIBLE white citizens. The specifics of each interview varied, but the general results were the same. A sampling should suffice.

Sample one. Raymond Mullins, owner of Mullins Furniture and Appliance Store and Mayor of West Brandon, serving his fifth consecutive term in that office.

We talked in the display room of his store, surrounded by automatic washing machines.

Venable: "Why not put the town on record as being officially and legally opposed to discrimination?"

Mullins: "Look, Mr. Venable, I was elected mayor of *all* the people in West Brandon, and I do my best to serve *all* the people. If there's one thing I've learned from serving *all* the people for five terms as their mayor, it is that they don't want things crammed down their throats. Now we have a nice little town here. We work out our problems gradually.

"I am all for the colored people getting a fair shake. I employ a colored man here in my store as a salesman, and he's a dandy. Good old James Boyd . . ."

Venable note. There is a story about the white people who invariably point with pride to the "Negro I employ." This has led to the suggestion that Hertz start a "Rent-a-Negro" plan for people who want to show how unprejudiced they are. End of note.

Mullins, continuing: "Above all, Mr. Venable, we don't want to rock the boat."

Sample two. Horace Blasingame, prominent builder, realtor and insurance executive, former member of Congress, member of the West Brandon School Board.

Venable: "We need to have men like you speak out in support of the Civil Rights movement, Mr. Blasingame.

195

When you were in Congress, you supported Civil Rights legislation down the line."

Blasingame: "Young fellow, *that* is why I am no longer in the Congress."

End of conversation with former Congressman Horace Blasingame.

Sample three. Mrs. Priscilla Uggams, driving force in the League of Women Voters, mother of five, member of the City Planning Board. A handsome, graying, courageous-looking woman. Venable attacked with hope.

Venable: "You could bring a great deal of pressure to bear, Mrs. Uggams. From everything I've heard you have always been a consistent fighter for worthy causes here."

Mrs. Uggams: "Mr. Venable, you are a most attractive man, and so I am going to be honest with you. If you quote me on this, I will probably swear you are lying. I think that what you suggest is very probably a good idea. I have always tried to support the advancement of our good colored citizens. Now some of them are just plain worthless, but there are some very deserving ones. But I am not going to go along with you, and I'll tell you why. I am in line for a position I have wanted for many years—the presidency of the local chapter of the United Daughters of the Confederacy. My mother once held that post, and it was always her wish that someday I might gain the same honor. And I'll tell you something else, Mr. Venable, because you *are* a terribly attractive young man. I think the United Daughters of the Confederacy is really a very foolish organization, but I am going to be elected its president if I possibly can."

Venable: "For your mother's sake."

Mrs. Uggams: "Yes, for my dear dead mother's sake. I am sorry, Mr. Venable. If you had come to me any other year but this, I think I would have been behind you one hundred percent."

196

But the rejection which really broke my back came from George Jones. George Jones represented what was probably the most respected store of wisdom and integrity in all of West Brandon. Teachers, merchants, students, clergymen, and common laborers alike sought his company and opinion. During most of the daylight hours, George Jones could be found in the vicinity of the post office, a location he had selected because it made him available to a representative cross section of the community. Few people allowed a visit to the post office to pass without pausing to have a few words with George Jones, and he patiently gave of his time to all who stopped.

It was after my meeting with Mrs. Uggams that I finally sought out George Jones. He turned away from a little boy—George Jones was extremely fond of children—and regarded me with the wisest pair of eyes I had ever seen.

"George Jones," I said, "I want to ask your advice about something that is very important."

He considered me for a moment, then turned and led me over to one of the columns at the far end of the post office entrance where we could have a bit of privacy.

And he listened while I poured out my message. When I had told him what I had in mind, I asked, "Now I want to know, George Jones, don't you think I'm right?"

George Jones gave me his reply in two ways. First he lifted his left hind leg and peed on the column. Second, he bared his aging fangs at me and snarled—not viciously, but conclusively. Then he turned his back on me and began to scratch at a flea which had dared locate itself behind his right ear.

nineteen

I was becoming discouraged—and in doubt—thus bringing into play an old Venable axiom: *When in doubt, chicken out!* Which was exactly what I had in mind doing.

"I've had it," I said to Cathy. One advantage offered by wives is that they are handy and generally inclined to be sympathetic. And on the evening of that dark day when George Jones had offered the final and crushing rebuke to the Venable crusade among West Brandon's RESPONSIBLE citizens, I was in sore need of sympathy.

Cathy put down the book she was reading and looked at me across the uncrowded room, her expression somehow conveying the fact that this was not her idea of some enchanted evening.

"I," I repeated with emphasis, "have had it. They can count me out. I know when I'm licked."

Now Cathy might have made a speech, but she can be remarkably terse when the mood is on her to be terse. She did not make a speech. She simply sat there and looked at me for what seemed to be a very long time. Then she spoke tersely.

"Yes, you certainly do, don't you?"

Then she resumed reading her book.

One of the things I have learned from being married to Cathy a number of years is that there is seldom any point in trying to understand why she disapproves of something I have done. On various occasions I have tried to pursue such questions, and invariably I have ended up more confused than when I started. Now it was painfully obvious from that one terse comment that she disapproved, but WHY? I knew it would be a mistake to ask her. Because she might just tell me.

So I asked her, "Cathy, why do you disapprove of my getting out of this damned fool business? I wasn't aware that you were very gung ho about it."

And she told me. "Bob, you're my husband, and I love you very much . . ." That should have been sufficient warning, but I let her continue. "But . . ." There it was. The next word is always *but*. "But you are a quitter." She said that very quietly, almost sadly—the way parents sound when they give kids that crappy routine about "This is going to hurt me more than it does you."

"I've watched you quit things ever since we were married. Some of them were very small things like that end table you were making when Elaine was a baby. Some of them were big things like your first novel . . ."

"Wait a damned minute! I finished that novel!"

"No," she said. "You didn't finish that novel. You brought it to a stop, and you were lucky enough to have what you had written make sense. It made money, and it was published, but it was not finished. I remember the way you talked about it when you were first getting started, and if you had written the novel that way it could have done more than just make money. It could have been a very fine novel, but you quit on it. Now you're quitting again. I can't possibly feel the way I think you feel about the Civil Rights thing, Bob, but I admire the stand you took on it. I was very proud of you that night you were in jail—because I knew you had done something that was difficult and humiliating and painful in a cause you believed in.

"I haven't said anything about this because I wanted you to do it on your own—without any pushing from me. I thought you might make it, Bob, because you did seem to believe in it, and I haven't seen too many things I felt you *did* believe in since we've been married. I wanted you to see this through—no matter how much I might disagree with you."

A cornered rat is faced with two alternatives. He can squeal, or he can fight. I fought—a fact which did not affect my status as a rat.

"So you decided to put me to the test, huh? You wanted to confirm your opinion of me, is that it?"

"Oh, Bob . . ."

"Don't give me that! You just sat back and let me get so damned far out on the limb I couldn't possibly get back without crawling—so you could verify the fact that you're married to a gutless wonder!"

"Don't make it worse, Bob . . ."

I was on my feet and hurling things around—and I was putting on a pretty damned good act—only it wasn't all an act. I could tell because of the way my throat tightened up on me and the silly goddamned way I couldn't keep the tears from my eyes.

"Forget it! You've said it all. I'm a quitter, a fink, a spineless son-of-a-bitch who runs when the shooting starts. How the hell have you been able to stand being married to me all this time?"

"Because I love you."

That is precisely the sort of unfair answer a wife gives in moments of stress, and I wasn't about to let her get by with it. She was out of her chair and moving across the room toward

200

me, and I knew that if I let her reach me, I would also let her take me in her arms and make it well, and I didn't want her to make it well, because that would only prove that what she had said was true, and even if it was true, I didn't want any goddamned part of it, so I got away from her.

"Bob!"

I was out of the room, out of the front door and in the car, gunning the engine and hauling ass away from the truth and away from Cathy and away from the chicken-shit bastard I could see reflected in her eyes.

And where did I go? And what did I do? Well, it's like this.

There was this phone booth, see, and in my wallet there was this piece of paper with this number written on it. So I went into this phone booth and extracted this piece of paper from my wallet, and I dialed this number. And I waited with my heart pounding from a number of causes until the ringing stopped and the voice answered.

"Hello . . ."

"This is Robert—Robert Venable."

"Robert!" There was music—not background, but in the way she pronounced the name. "I've been wondering when you would call. How did things go?"

I wasn't about to say how things had gone. I wasn't interested in *things*. "I want to see you—now."

There is no silence like the silence in a silent phone booth. It is a silence of confinement, of separateness from the outside world. It is a stuffy, trapped, other-world silence that can be broken only by that voice at the other end of the line. It hung around me and suffocated me. Then . . .

"All right, Robert. Shall I meet you somewhere?"

"I'd rather come there—to your place."

A beat—then, "All right. How long will it take you?"

"Five minutes."

"Five minutes, then."

I hung up the phone and pushed open the door of the booth. In the world outside the night air was chilly, and I started to shiver as I stood there.

Question. What had happened to Venable's lust for Alise Hungerford? It may be recalled that at one point he was merely waiting for the bedcovers to be turned back before leaping into the sack with her.

Answer. Not a damned thing had happened to that lust. It was still there. It hovered around him whenever he was with her. It slipped into his bed with him at night and wove dreams of honeyed flesh for him. But Venable was an easy victim of circumstances, of the lack of opportunity, of a paucity of initiative, of a chronic fidelity to his wife, of the problem of just how to broach the subject, and of a number of things like that. Also, and this is pertinent, the lady, beyond being gorgeous and sexy and desirable, had never *really* offered him any encouragement. Whatever passionate exchanges had passed between them had passed thus far solely in one exotic area of the rich Venable imagination—a world in which a suave and fantastically virile Venable frolics his way through entire populatons of ravishing females, establishing himself as one of the greatest swordsmen of all time.

As I started the car my teeth were chattering. In moments of great stress, my teeth are given to chattering. I was suddenly cast in a drama of danger and intrigue, because I was in a night world of people who were watching me, hiding behind trees, around corners, trailing me in black limousines. Every car that passed mine contained someone who recognized me and would later testify that they had seen me on that particular night, going in that particular direction—and the people who pass judgment on the guilt of guilty husbands would be able to put all the pieces together and trace my path to where Alise Hungerford was waiting for me.

202

Already the image of her was forming in my mind. She had been awaiting this moment as surely as I had. That first night I had seen her, I had felt her eyes on me. She had seen me then, and she had *known* then that this was going to happen. I pictured the room she was in. I knew she was living in one of the new apartment developments in the more affluent section of the Negro district. Her apartment number was 18-D. I would manage to reach the door without being detected, and I would push the bell, and soft chimes would whisper inside, and the door would swing open. She would have been too wise to have a light on—on, possibly a soft lamp somewhere in the background, and she would murmur, "Come in—quickly!" and I would be inside and the door closed behind us before I really saw her in the half-light—wearing something long and clinging and silken, with nothing underneath. And there would be so many words which should be spoken, but there would be no time for words.

"Don't talk!" she would whisper fiercely. "Don't talk now!"

And there in the semidarkness, we would come together with an insatiable urgency and the silken, clinging something would fall way from her tawny body, and somehow, miraculously, my clothing would be gone, and we would sink to the thick carpet—one frenzied flesh, and all around us would hang the scent of jasmine . . .

Oh, Christ, make my teeth stop chattering!

A quitter!

By God, we would see who was a quitter! I just want you to know, Cathy, that you drove me to this, so when your damned spies come to you with the word—and I know they're out there—put the blame where blame is due. The truth is that you are being damned unfair anyway. That end table would have been finished, except that something went wrong with the belt on the power saw, and you know damned well

203

how long it takes to get something like that replaced, and then I got terribly busy on something, and we moved, so it wasn't really a question of my quitting on it.

The apartment building was lighted up outside like Grauman's Chinese Theatre for a world premiere. It looked remarkably new and neat and well kept—just as nice as you would expect to find in a white neighborhood. There was a well-lighted parking area, but I drove around the corner and parked the car where it was reasonably dark.

There was really no reason for me to feel so self-conscious about walking into that apartment building. After all, there were probably plenty of white people who came and went on business—or perhaps socially. We weren't still living in the Middle Ages, for Christ's sake. I couldn't find a side door, and the two well-dressed Negro women who were coming out of the front door as I entered had no damned reason to stare at me the way they did. For all they knew I might be selling something. Door-to-door salesman did come around at night as well as in the day.

If I could have stopped my damned teeth from chattering, I would have asked them about buying something—maybe some magazines or some Fuller brushes—and that would have thrown them off the track.

Where the hell was apartment 18-D? The trouble with these damned places was that there was absolutely no discernible plan to the numbering system. Why should 21-F be on the first floor, for Christ's sake?

I found apartment 19-E, oddly enough, one floor up from 21-F. There is a strangeness about being in the hallway of an apartment building. You know that behind each closed and numbered door, life goes on in a world you cannot possibly imagine. And you wonder about that world, and when you approach the door to ring the bell, you have a terrible feeling that the person who opens it may want to destroy you.

18-D turned out to be on the third floor. Someone else will have to figure that out. It was a menacing-looking door, with a menacing-looking light coming out from under the door and a menacing silence all around—except for my teeth which had started to chatter again.

Actually, it wasn't the teeth that really bothered me. It was the fact that my legs were trembling and making me slightly unsteady. *Stop for a moment! Take several deep breaths! Think calmly!*

RELAX!

Inside of that door there is a woman. The sparring is over, and the main event is about to take place. Conjure up that picture of the long, clinging, silken garment again—and the soft, indistinct lighting—so that nothing will have to be real. It will be dark and shadowy and mysterious and dreamlike and a far, far better piece than you have ever had, and it will serve Cathy right for calling you a quitter, and all you have to do is press that little old bell and the door to honey heaven will open and what the hell are you waiting for!

I PRESSED THE BELL!

It did not produce the whisper of chimes, but instead, a strident buzzing which should have tipped me off right away that things were not going exactly as I had planned.

THE DOOR SWUNG SLOWLY OPEN!

twenty

"Come in, Robert."

Someone had fouled up in the lighting and scenery and costume departments. There was a bright overhead light on in a room furnished with functional modern-efficiency-apartment-type furnishings. There was no thick carpet on the floor. There was not even any thin carpet on the floor. In short, it was very much like the reception room of your neighborhood dentist. And there was the receptionist—Miss Alise (Herself) Hungerford. Only she was not wearing a starched white uniform. Nor was she wearing something long and clinging and silken. She was an "At-home" Hungerford in the best Vassar tradition—faded and sloppy jeans, rolled up at the bottom, scuffed sneakers, a man's shirt, hair done up neatly in a towel, and a scrubbed, shiny and unmysterious face.

Jesus Christ, I thought, I have come to seduce the girl next door!

"Come in, Robert."

I came in, and the door closed behind me. I was able to examine the room in more detail. It was a dandy—a modern sofa with wooden legs and foam-rubber cushions, a severe coffee table, two uncomfortable-looking chairs, one end table with a ceramic-base lamp on it, and two genuine simulated copies of bad modern art hanging on the walls.

It was a room, in brief, created for romance.

"Nice place you have here," I remarked with that flair for originality which marks many Venable conversation openers.

"Oh, I think it's terribly sterile, Robert, but I am grateful for it. The local committee went to a great deal of trouble finding this place for me to stay while I am in West Brandon. Usually we have to live in someone's home, and this does give me a little privacy."

"Oh, it looks very nice," I mumbled. "How many rooms?"

"Well, this serves as the living room, and I usually eat in here too. Then there's a little kitchen alcove over there." She pointed to a little kitchen alcove. "And, in there," pointing to a closed door, "is the bedroom and bath."

"Not bad," I mumbled, "not bad at all."

"No, and I am grateful for it. Sit down, Robert." I sat down in one of the uncomfortable-looking chairs which lived up to its promise. "But I do so miss having my own things. I think that's the hardest part of this job, really." Now she was seated in the other uncomfortable-looking chair and being *chatty*. In about one minute I knew damned well she was going to ask me if I'd like a cup of tea. She had that look about her.

"I have the most marvelous little apartment in Philadelphia—just crammed with books and records and, well, junk. It's mad and messy and impossible, but I love it! And when I'm there, I always have just scads of people in, and it's a perfect madhouse. But this—" With a sweep of her hand she indicated the interior of Cell 18-D. "This is so cold. I don't spend any more time here than I have to—usually just to sleep and fix breakfast. I probably wouldn't have been in now, except that I simply had to wash my hair tonight, and I hope you'll excuse the way I look."

"Oh, you look fine. I . . ."

"You're sweet to say so. Look, could I make you a cup of tea?"

I made a desperate grab for my fading dream world. "You wouldn't happen to have anything stronger, would you?"

The girl-next-door face was touched with a frown—not a big frown, just a little frown. "Well, I do have some sherry in the kitchen. I always keep some sherry around for when I have cramps. I could get you a glass of that if you like . . ."

Now here is a sign of our times. When I was in my roaring twenties, the girls did not talk about their *personal* problems —not to me anyway. And in my quaint old-fashioned way, I was still hideously embarrassed by this sort of thing.

"A glass of sherry would be better than a cup of tea."

"Do you drink a good deal, Robert?" It was not exactly a disapproving question, but it did reveal a trace of concern.

And I was getting edgy.

"What do you mean by a great deal?"

"I don't know. I just think it's too bad when a person comes to depend too much on stimulants . . ."

"Don't you drink?"

"Just a little sherry when I . . ."

"Yes," I said hastily, "I know."

"Just a jiffy, I'll get it for you."

And she was back in the little kitchen alcove, switching on another bright light to go with the bright light we already had, and bustling with cups and glasses and boiling water and a *little* glass of sherry—all of which she finally brought into the living room where the picnic continued.

There is a line in the Thurber play, *The Male Animal*, where the Dean's wife says, "A little sherry is such fun." That is a lot of crap. A little sherry is a little nothing. What I

208

desperately wanted at that moment was a good belt. I wanted something that would dim the lights and blur the edges a little and stir the blood a little, because, damn it to hell, I had come there in good faith to have my blood stirred and to show Cathy I was a man who knew how to go after what he wanted and get it, and to show myself I was not a quitter and to SEDUCE A WOMAN!

And I needed something a lot stronger than a little sherry, because the truth of the matter was that it had been a hell of a long time since I had seduced anyone. In fact, it had been about eight years, and that last time had not actually been much of a seduction, because both parties were pretty smashed, and she was the wife of a very good friend who was even more smashed than we were and had passed out, and Cathy was away visiting her parents, and these good friends had invited me over for dinner and we had all gotten smashed and I had just gone to the john when this gal had appeared in the doorway looking smashed and sexy and we had sort of slipped and fallen to the floor and fumbled our way through what must have been the clumsiest screwing of all time, after which we were both horribly sober and re- pentant and guilt-ridden and unable to look one another in the eye for at least a month. It was not a very satisfactory seduction, but it was all I had.

"Is your sherry all right?"

"Yes, fine."

"I'm afraid it isn't a very good sherry—just a cooking sherry actually. I'm not much of a connoisseur of wines. I never drank anything until I was in college, and then I had a roommate who told me it would help when I had cramps, so I tried several things and sherry seemed to be the only thing I could stomach. I tried drinking some whiskey once, but I just upchucked everything."

Romance!

209

Venable badly needed a little encouragement, but he wasn't getting any. So, being no quitter, he decided to take matters into his own hands.

"Would you mind if we switched off that overhead light and turned on the lamp?"

"Of course not," Alise said, just the way she was supposed to, and she switched off the overhead light and turned on the lamp, which greatly improved the general atmosphere, and Venable felt encouraged to continue.

I raised my little glass of sherry to my lips and smiled a suave, mysterious smile—a much easier task in subdued lighting. "That's much better. Here's to you, Alise Hungerford."

She apparently knew the rules of the game, raising her teacup and responding, "Thank you kindly." And she took a little sip, letting her eyes remain on mine over the rim of the cup—which is good form for situations like that, diminished a bit by the fact that she was drinking tea and I was drinking a very inferior brand of cooking sherry, but what the hell!

And then there was the proper moment of silence, that period of hesitation during which both parties wait tensely to decide who shall make the first move. There are a number of acceptable techniques for coming off this interval. For example, the lady can shiver and murmur, "My, it's getting chilly."

Or, the man can look terribly sad and grim, thus causing the lady to ask, "What is it? What's the matter?" Ladies are suckers for men who suddenly look sad and grim. And then the man says, "It's nothing. Suddenly you—you reminded me of someone . . ." And she leans forward, interested. "What someone?" And he averts his face and murmurs, just loud enough for her to hear, "Someone from very long ago." "A woman you knew?" she asks. "A girl really. We were both very young," he replies. "Were you—in love with her?" "Oh yes—for the first time—and the last." "What happened?" And then the man sets his jaw, and, if he is really skillful, summons up a trace of moisture in his eyes and says, "She died."

By this time, of course, the lady should be close to him, and she will certainly want to touch him, because he has suffered and she owes him comfort, so she will reach out her hand and touch his hand, and she will say, "I am sorry—so truly sorry. I didn't know." And he will smile a little and return the pressure of her touch ever so little and say, "How could you? I've never told anyone else." And then he will look at her, and wonder will grow in his eyes, and he will whisper excitedly, "Yes! You do! You look so much like *her!*"

By this time, simple physical maneuvers will be in order, and only a few basic and largely incoherent words necessary.

There are more direct approaches, of course. The man can simply walk over to the lady and say, "I'm going to kiss you, baby, so slap my face now, if you want to, because once I get started I don't like to be interrupted."

Or the lady can say, "Do you want me to get undressed all the way?"

Problem—what technique would Alise Hungerford and/or Robert M. Venable use?

I placed my little glass of sherry on the coffee table and asked, "Is it chilly in here to you?"

She said, "No, I'm very comfortable, but I can turn up the thermostat if you're cold."

She was obviously above a corny routine like that, and I admired her for it. So I took another sip of my sherry, extracted my pipe from my pocket and filled and lighted it, managing at the same time to work myself into a condition of grim sadness. Then, with complete spontaneity, I raised my eyes and looked at her. My eyes widened for just a moment, and then I really looked sad and grim.

And she noticed this right away. "What is it, Robert? Don't you feel well?"

I got as far in my lines as, "It's nothing . . ." and she cut me off.

"Is it your stomach?"

"No, it's just that I . . ."

"You didn't have much luck, did you—with the people you were going to see?"

"Suddenly," I said with dogged determination, "you reminded me of someone . . ."

"Poor Robert." She smiled. "I could have told you what was going to happen. If those people were going to do anything to help us, they would have come forward—the way you did. The only thing that will reach them is action, Robert."

"I said, suddenly you reminded me . . ."

"I reminded you of someone? Who, Robert? And don't look so serious. It's not the end of the world just because you were turned down by the people you were so sure would help us. Now we have to pull together and make this march so successful that they will be forced to pay attention."

Venable was no quitter.

"Someone from very long ago."

"You look warm, Robert. Shall I open a window?"

"It was a girl, really. We were both very young . . ."

"We're going to have to work night and day, though, Robert, if the march is going to have the impact it should have."

"We were in love, I guess. I—*what* march?"

She laughed. "Oh, Robert, I am sorry. We've been so busy making our plans that I had forgotten that you haven't been in touch the last couple of days."

Since she had made no move to come to me, I had been considerate enough to get up and go over to stand behind her. Also, the cue lines had been confused, so I helped her out a little.

"I suppose you want to know what happened to this girl . . ."

"It will be a really massive effort," she said. "We're going to assemble some distance outside of town, because we'll need a lot of space to get things organized. Oh, it should be very exciting, Robert—like a military campaign. You should enjoy that, because you were a soldier, weren't you?"

I had situated myself directly behind her, still holding my little glass of sherry, and I leaned over her chair so that my free hand just barely touched her shoulder, and my voice was husky with sadness. "I was a fighter pilot," I said huskily. "You want me to tell you what happened to this girl?"

"Then we are going to march into West Brandon until we fill the business section with our people—pack it solidly with human beings, black and white—so that no traffic can move, so that no place of business can operate—and when the police come and drag those people away, there will be another wave of marchers ready to come in and take their place."

She was transfixed—a honey-colored Joan of Arc, caught up in the rapture of voices and visions.

And Venable? Whatever else he was, and contrary to popular opinion, Venable was no quitter.

"Okay, I'll tell you what happened to her."

"You see, Robert, we must speak with a single voice, demanding that every last vestige of discrimination be removed from West Brandon so that it can stand as a shining example for the entire South!"

I could smell the jasmine, and it was only a matter of time. Words, words, words—that was all that stood between us, and I was ready to put them aside.

"Alise . . ."

"Robert! Be careful with that glass. You almost spilled some sherry down my front."

"Okay, I'll tell you what happened to her. She died!"

"Why don't you drink your sherry, Robert? Who died?"

"That girl—from so long ago."

"Oh, I'm sorry. Was it someone you knew?"

"L-l-listen, Alise . . ."

My goddamned teeth were starting to chatter again!

"Are you all right, Robert? You sound like you have a chill. Now listen carefully, because this is very important. When we have shown those people—the very ones you tried to persuade with words—*shown* them, not with words, but with deeds—then they will have to realize that this town cannot afford the luxury of waiting— Robert, what is the matter with you? You're starting to wheeze! Perhaps then they will realize that the time for waiting is— Robert!"

"She died! Dammit, don't you understand? She died—this girl from a long time ago—the one you remind me of—and I want—"

"Robert!"

The time for words was past, and I knew that only ACTION would serve, so I lunged forward, but she chose that moment to demonstrate her goddamned footwork. A slow-motion replay of the video tape shows exactly what happened.

I am a little off balance as I go forward over the back of her chair, and you can see how she just barely manages to slip out of my reach, get to her feet—pivoting at the same time to face me. Now she circles to her left—a trick she probably learned from Cassius Clay—and I miss her completely, but my forward momentum carries me completely over the chair— notice that I am still holding that glass of sherry—and there I am, sprawled ass over tincup on top of the coffee table.

"Robert! Really!"

Even as romantic and dashing a guy as Venable finds himself at a distinct disadvantage when he is tangled up in a combination of chair and coffee table and is trying to keep from spilling his cooking sherry from its little glass. And

214

Alise was sympathetic and a real sport—give her that. She even started to help me get up, taking the glass from me and pulling the leg of the chair clear of my left foot and trying to get me off the table . . .

"Ouch!"

"Robert, what is it?"

It was my goddamned back, but I wasn't about to admit it to her. The Venable back had a sordid history of going bad at crucial moments, and this time it had really picked a dandy. And when the Venable back goes bad, there is only one thing to do for it—lie flat—and I mean it *must* be done. The only alternative is to scream with agony, so down to the floor I went and lay flat.

"Robert! What on earth are you doing?"

I managed a sickly smile. "I am practicing to lie-in. Isn't that what we're supposed to do?"

"Robert, get up from the floor. You look ridiculous."

"You look very tall from down here," I said, feeling the need to make trivial conversation.

"Robert, I don't understand what's come over you tonight. I think you were making a pass at me."

That was good. She was a bright girl—observant, sensitive.

"Were you making a pass at me, Robert?"

My old Aunt Emma used to say, "Tell the truth and shame the devil."

"Yes."

She sank into a chair and started to laugh. She had a nice contagious kind of laugh, and it made me sick. "Oh, Robert, how very sweet of you!"

From my prone position, I replied, "Thank you very much."

"No, it was! I really mean that, Robert. I had thought at one time you probably would make a pass sooner or later, but I was beginning to wonder. Now get up, please. What if someone were to come in and find you like that. Come on, Robert . . ."

"I prefer to stay here awhile. Besides, who would come in?"

There was no need for her to answer that one. The someone who might come in, came in.

"Anybody home?" It was a familiar voice. All at once I picked up the referee's count at eight, so I started to struggle to my feet. "Who the hell is that?" Then I saw him, and he saw me.

I was on my knees. "Ouch!" It was no good trying. I dropped back to my favorite position, flat on the Venable back, and I looked up into the honey face of Hungerford and the black face of Andy Brown.

"Professor! What're you doing down there?"

It was a question which seemed to deserve some sort of answer.

"Everyone," I said, "has to be somewhere."

And the referee counted me out.

twenty-one

Once upon a time there were two men. One was a white man named Robert M. Venable. The other was a black man named Andy Brown. These two men were very good friends, and they enjoyed doing lots of things together. One of their favorite things to do together was to walk down the middle of the street which was wide and pleasant and SAFE. Then one day they happened to notice that on either side of the street there had been installed conveyor-belt-type sidewalks, moving very rapidly and very dangerously, each going in opposite directions. Venable and Brown were frightened by these moving sidewalks. They preferred to walk in the middle of the street in the same direction and at their own leisurely, pleasant, SAFE rate of speed. But they were dismayed to note that the street was not as wide as it had been. Indeed, it appeared to be getting smaller and smaller. And on either side, those sidewalks were moving faster and faster and faster . . .

"I say, screw the waiting," Andy Brown said. "We've been waiting long enough. The fat-ass ofay bastards in this town aren't about to do anything for us. The only way we can make any impression on them is to turn this goddamned town upside down and shake it."

"Andy, I wish you would try to be a little less crude," Alise Hungerford said. "Are you feeling better now, Robert?"

"I am feeling fine," I said. "Even if you happen to hurt a lot of innocent bystanders in the process, Andy?"

"Robert," Alise said, "in this struggle, if a person is a bystander, then he cannot be considered innocent."

"You mean a person is either for you or against you? What kind of black and white attitude is that? It isn't that simple."

"It's a black and white situation, Professor," Andy said.

"And what ever happened to the varying shades of gray?"

"Gray isn't a good color this season. This is a black and white season."

"Oh, Jesus!" I said. "Oh, Sweet Jesus!"

"Is your back bothering you again?" Alise asked solicitously. "Can I get you some more aspirin?"

"It's not his back," Andy growled.

"My back is fine," I snarled.

"Would anyone like another cup of tea?" Alise asked.

And so we three had met again, without the benefit of thunder, lightning or rain, and the hurly-burly was sure as hell not done. We were having a mad tea party—and the side dishes were heavy portions of hostility.

"You've seen for yourself what their reaction is, Robert," Alise said. "You did your best, but the only thing these people will really understand is action—not words."

Andy Brown stirred restlessly, angrily. "Too many words—that's the goddamned trouble."

"You're a writer, Andy. You can't give up on words."

"I *was* a writer, Professor."

Quick intimations of danger—a speeded-up montage of red flashing lights, warning buzzers, caution signs—whirled through my mind. And the middle of the street grew smaller . . .

"Look," I heard myself saying, "I can't help but feel that

218

those people I talked to have a little something going for them. We aren't going to accomplish a damned thing by getting the entire white community against us."

"You're a member of the *white* community, Professor," Andy murmured. "Are you against us?"

It was a loaded and DANGEROUS and HOSTILE question. This was not the casual Andy Brown. It was an Andy Brown who had been unhappy at finding me in Alise Hungerford's apartment when he had walked in, *without bothering to knock.* And he was watching me and waiting to see which way I was going to jump when the time came for jumping.

"That's not a fair question, Andy. Robert has already proved he is with us." It was Alise who poured her own brand of oil on the troubled waters as she poured more tea into our cups. And Andy Brown subsided, looking at her in a way that hinted to Venable of things that go bump in the night. Because the suspicion was growing in the rich Venable imagination that old black Andy Brown had, to employ the language of the streets, been getting in there. He looked too much at home in her apartment, and remember that he had just walked in. No knocking at the door, no ringing of the bell—just open the door and waltz in. And when he looked at her it was the look of a belly-to-belly relationship. And when he looked at Venable—it was not, repeat *not,* a friendly look.

Venable, who was not about to succumb to the weaknesses of the flesh, had placed the entire affair on an intellectual basis. The only reasonable explanation I could accept for the change in Andy Brown was that balls had triumphed over brains. It was inconceivable that Andy Brown had developed ideals, I kept telling myself. He would not fink out on his cool world by developing ideals.

And, if he was getting in there, how did that fact affect the shrinking middle of the street?

219

Hold on to my hand, Andy Brown! If you turn me loose, I may hate you, and I don't want to hate you!

"So what do we do now?"

I asked the question with something of the same enthusiasm Napoleon must have been able to muster on the morning after Waterloo. It was a famous tag line for losers—*So what do we do now?* Freely translated it means, "How the hell did I ever get myself into this mess in the first place, and which way is the nearest exit?"

"We face facts," Alise said, thereby redoubling my determination to escape, since I had faced my share of facts on that particular evening.

"I say we blow the lid off this goddamned town," Andy Brown growled, and I had the uncomfortable feeling that he was really talking about Venable. "I'm sick of all this pussyfooting around."

"Extreme measures are certainly called for." Alise nodded. "Of course, there must be no violence—not on our part."

The new Andy Brown she had hatched from that giant seedpod was a real terror. "I'm not so sure about that nonviolent crap either. The army taught me how to kill a man twenty-seven different ways, and they told me it was all right to kill him if he was my enemy. When I walk down the streets of this town, I'm starting to see a lot of enemies."

And he was looking at me. I tried to wish back the old Andy—relaxed and loose and smoking his cigar and sipping his beer and talking his fine, cool talk. I missed that black man.

"Come on, Andy, look on the bright side of things."

The look he shot at me was hard and mean. "I'm a *dark* man, Professor. It's hard for a dark man to see the bright side of things."

"You're a *man*, Andy. That's all that really counts."

220

Stay with me, Andy! If you stay with me, we can hold out here—if we only stick together!

But it wasn't Andy who was calling the shots any more than it was Venable. Alise Hungerford, with her own brand of cool, brushed aside our differences.

"That's enough, Andy."

She did not have to raise her voice. However she had trained him, she had done the job well. There was only one way to train a man like that, and you did it flat on your back. And Venable pictured *that*—black Andy Brown making the beast with two backs with the honey woman Venable wanted for himself. And she had turned Venable down—well, the truth was, she had turned him down for a—BLACK NIGGER!

We were a happy little group—Hungerford in the middle, pouring tea and keeping the peace and making plans—with Venable to the right of her and Brown to the left of her, volleying and thundering.

Was there a man dismayed—not though the soldiers knew someone had blundered!

"The march is the answer," she was saying. "It will be massive. It will focus the attention of the entire state, of the entire nation, on West Brandon. That is what we need. The time for decision in this country is almost here, and we desperately need one shining example of *total* success—one southern town in which *all* racial barriers have been swept aside by the force of an aroused and organized minority. West Brandon is the proper target, Robert, because West Brandon is *possible*."

Faster and faster, the middle of the street was slipping away under my feet!

"And the fact that West Brandon may not deserve being singled out . . ."

"West Brandon is being singled out as a mark of honor, Robert. We are going to have every Negro man, woman and

221

child in this town marching with us. We are asking for one hundred percent, and we must give no less."

"You can't get all the Negroes here to join anything like this. Alise, you don't seem to understand. The majority of them don't really give a damn about Civil Rights or anything except eating three square meals a day and having a roof over their heads."

The white man's creed, and Venable was clinging to it by his fingernails!

Andy Brown snarled, "Don't forget the watermelon!"

"They will," Alise said. "They are already beginning to care. For the past two days, Robert, while you were out discovering how much the white establishment here really cares about the condition of the Negro, we have been busy. We can and will bring pressure to bear on every Negro in West Brandon to join us. If they are able to walk, they will walk with us. If they are able to be carried, others will carry them."

The room was starting to close in. The pressure was building up. And the street under my feet was almost gone along with the days when my heart was young and gay. And I looked at Andy Brown, and he was almost gone too, but he was not so far gone that he could not return my look with a look of his own which said, "You were trying to get in there too, weren't you, Professor? That's black man's territory. You keep out!"

"Because," she said, "they will be afraid not to be with us."

"Afraid?" I asked. "I thought this was going to be non-violent."

"There are things to fear other than violence, Robert. They will join us. And there will be whites along with them. Mac Kirkpatrick has assured me that he can deliver at least five hundred students provided we hold the march on a

222

Saturday. And Saturday is the best day—the day when Main Street will be the busiest."

"Five hundred students? Alise, you know what that bunch will be like—the scruffiest, dirtiest bunch of wild-eyed nuts on campus. They'll come out of the woodwork . . ."

"Perhaps. But there will be sincere ones among them, and we need the numbers, Robert. We need volume. There will be people coming in from other parts of the state, too, and some from as far away as New Jersey and New York. We will have at least three thousand marchers, and we will come in waves of a thousand each, so that if the police arrest one thousand, another thousand will take their place, and then another. It can be done, Robert! We are going to do it!"

I believed her.

And then she got around to the jackpot question. "Will you march with us, Robert—with me and Andy at the head of the first wave?"

She had that look in her eyes—the look that had brought me to her apartment that night—that look which offered something, promised something—something I had mistaken for all the honey in the comb. And I knew in that moment just how wrong I had been. She was offering and promising, but it wasn't a roll in the hay. It wasn't all that honeyed flesh. It wasn't words you whispered in the dark—not to me it wasn't. I got in a quick glance at Andy Brown, and I couldn't be sure about him. He still had that look about him that told of sex, but was it sex he had known or sex he had been promised—or sex he *thought* he had been promised?

"Will you, Robert?"

Venable looked down, and the middle of the street was just about to disappear. He looked at his old friend Andy Brown who had already made the jump to one of those rapidly moving sidewalks and was fading out of sight in the distance. *Oh, Jesus!*

223

And the time had come, Venable knew, and what he did must no longer be *thought* about but *done*. And a question roared in his head.

What would have happened if she had opened that door tonight and opened her arms to me? Would I have taken her? And if she had held my face in her hands afterwards and asked me to march with her, what would I have said then?

But those were questions which had no answers.

So, sure enough, Venable jumped too—not on the sidewalk that was carrying Andy Brown off into the unknown, but on the other one—and the distance between Venable and his old friend became greater and greater and then . . .

"No," I said. "I will not march with you."

And the last Venable saw of Andy Brown was a black face full of black hate, and then Andy Brown was out of sight, and Venable wondered if he would ever see his old friend again.

And then Venable saw the honey face of Alise Hungerford, full of questions—most of which she seemed to be asking herself.

And then Venable had to turn his face in the direction he had chosen—toward an unknown he had never *wanted*, but which, when the chips were down, he had *chosen*.

twenty-two

Oh, what is so rare as the joy and satisfaction which marks the return to the fold of a prodigal! A sinner redeemed, the strayed sheep returned to the flock, a Venable who has seen the error of his ways. And a note to those who wish to realize the full spiritual and temporal benefits of redemption—publicize the fact.

The morning of the day following my flight from Alise and Andy, I had a call from my fearless journalistic friend, Blanton Dillon.

"Bob, I've just learned that you damned fools are going to try to stage some sort of big demonstration a week from Saturday. Now, Bob, remember what—"

"Correction," I said. "The word *you* should be changed to *those*."

"What?"

"*Those* damned fools."

"You mean you're not involved in this?"

"I am not involved."

"But you know about it?"

"Yes."

"And you don't want any part of it, right?"

His voice sounded so friendly and approving that I was eager to confirm his supposition.

"That's right. I'm out of it." There followed one of those awkward moments in which I found myself faced with the necessity of putting into words something I had not yet completely accepted myself. So, as of that moment, I accepted it and put it into words. "I'm completely out of it, Blanton."

"Good boy!" I warmed to this wise, round little man who obviously *understood* and *appreciated* me.

And I suddenly wanted to please him even more. "I tried to tell them how foolish they were, but they wouldn't listen to me."

"I'm glad to hear it, Bob. The *Post-Dispatch* has never tried to stand in the way of the Negro struggle, but this sort of thing is going too far. What those damned fools—*those*, Bob—what they're doing is to set back their own cause in this town, and the *Post-Dispatch* will make that clear."

"Well, I'm glad to hear you've washed your hands of that bunch, Bob. Next time you're on Main Street, stop by and let's have a nice talk."

"I'll do that, Blanton. Thanks."

And I hung up—warm and secure and *on the right side*.

The next morning I reaped the benefits of having told it to a newspaperman. On the front page of the *Post-Dispatch* was a story dealing with the plans for the march, and in a bordered box alongside that story was this item.

VENABLE DENOUNCES MARCH

University Writer-in-Residence, Robert M. Venable, recently associated with Civil Rights activities in West Brandon, has refused to support the proposed "massive demonstration" of Students for Freedom. In a statement to the *Post-Dispatch*, Venable termed the plan "foolish" and stated that he is withdrawing from any participation in the activities of the local Civil Rights movement.

I experienced a few moments of discomfort akin to the feelings of the man who was attending an outdoor performance of Shakespeare in the park and had to pee. He slipped away from his wife, found a convenient spot behind a clump of bushes and relieved himself. When he returned, he asked his wife how the last scene had been, to which she replied, "You ought to know. You were in it." The public exposure of a private act always brings that kind of feeling. At least, I *thought* that was the reason I felt the way I did.

Cathy read the paper without comment. In fact, Cathy had been remarkably silent to me since our little conversation of a couple of days back, and Cathy's silences were never golden. So it was nice to know that Blanton Dillon loved me.

I was to discover, later on in the day, that a number of unlikely people loved me. On my way into the English Building, I ran into Dr. John Allen who practically galloped over to me and pumped my hand and nudged me in the ribs and said a number of jolly things.

"Proud of you, Robert—very, very proud! I knew you'd see the light. Talked with the Dean just a few minutes ago, and he is very pleased. Wanted me to tell you he is very pleased, Robert. I told him that I never had the slightest doubt that you would conduct yourself in the best interests of the University. You know something, Robert, it takes a real man to admit his mistakes, and both the Dean and I recognize that. Now, just put all this behind you and settle down with those fine students of yours. Got to uncover those future Hemingways, you know. That's what the writer-in-residence program is all about, and I know you're the right man in the right place at the right time. That's what I told the Dean. 'Robert Venable is all right,' I told him. Well, take it easy, Robert, and let's get together for lunch real soon."

Dr. John Allen loved me, and the Dean loved me.

And someone else loved me too.

When I opened my office door, there it was on the floor—the neatly folded piece of white paper.

"Oh boy!" I said to myself. It had been several days since I had heard from him, and I was beginning to think he had forgotten me. It is comforting to know you have not been forgotten.

The printing was as neat as it had been the first time.

SAW THE PAPER. CONGRATULATIONS ON BECOMING A WHITE MAN AGAIN.

I wouldn't go so far as to say this made me feel warm all over. After all, a fan letter from Dracula can be only so reassuring, but in a strange way, even this served to reaffirm the Venable conviction that he had *done the right thing*. Because, you see, it extricated Venable from an unpleasant involvement. And Venable would do damned near anything to get out of a situation he found intolerable. During the war he had once shot down a Japanese plane for no better reason than that he wanted out of an unpleasant involvement.

After that little note, I was reasonably sure that the next thing on the agenda would be a call offering me a free meal at Fuller's Restaurant. Instead, the call that came was from my Junior Chamber of Commerce friend, Mr. Taylor Huntsworth.

"Hi there, Mr. Venable," his friendly voice said. "Just wanted to let you know that you and the other judges for the Miss West Brandon contest are supposed to meet at the Brandon Inn at eleven thirty on the morning of the twenty-seventh. That's one week from this coming Saturday. We'll spend about half an hour briefing you, and then at noon you'll be having a little luncheon with the contestants—sort of give you a chance to talk to each of them and get acquainted—give you an opportunity to form some sort of preliminary opinion of their poise and things like that. Then that evening we'll have the formal contest which consists of the judging of the talent and the bathing suits—now that'll be a real chore won't it, Mr. Venable—and the evening gowns. That'll take place in the high school auditorium.

"It ought to be a really exciting afternoon and evening, Mr. Venable, and I want you to know how much we appreciate your help. All of us in the Jaycees have been working right around the clock to make this the best and most exciting Miss West Brandon contest ever, and we have every confidence that this year, for the very first time, West Brandon is going to be sending its winning girl right on to represent the state at Atlantic City!"

He was fairly panting with excitement at the prospect.

"And, Mr. Venable, if you'll permit me a personal comment—and I'm sure I speak for all the Jaycees and the contestants and their parents and friends—I was very proud—very, very proud of what I read in the paper about you this morning."

I had done it, and without any help from Dale Carnegie, I had *won friends, and I had influenced people.*

Of course, there was some criticism. Great men must always expect sniping from undesirable elements. When I went out to my car at noon, someone had written in the thin layer of dust that coated the sides of the car.

FINK

Well, I thought, I need to get the car washed anyway. Like Lady Macbeth said . . .

A little water clears us of this deed.

twenty-three

In the pamphlet of instructions to judges of a Miss America Preliminary Pageant, the following admonition is issued.

We know you are going to find the responsibility of deciding the winners of this tremendous scholarship program both challenging and gratifying. We ask, therefore, your careful study of the system of judging which will be used to select our winners.

The morning of Saturday the twenty-seventh found Venable ready to face this challenging and gratifying responsibility. He was fully convinced that nothing could be more important than selecting a Miss West Brandon who could go on to win the state contest and eventually take that magic walk down the runway in Atlantic City while Bert Parks sang "There She Is, Miss America," and Venable would be watching the tube and get that choked-up feeling that comes with the knowledge of a really significant job well done.

And even the black and ominous headlines in the morning paper could not cloud the clear picture Venable had of his duty that day.

TOWN BRACES FOR GIGANTIC CIVIL RIGHTS MARCH

230

Because Venable had become a man, and he had put aside childish things, and he was going to DO HIS DUTY to God and country and the Junior Chamber of Commerce.

During the week just past, Venable had achieved a rare and other-world kind of euphoria in which he was able to arise in the morning, eat his cornflakes, make conversation with his wife and children, meet his classes, sit at his typewriter and contemplate the keyboard, watch television—all the things which real live people do—and still remain untouched by a nasty reality on which he had turned his back.

Andy Brown? He is a black man I used to know.

Alise Hungerford? Oh, yes—well, the name is familiar, but I can't quite place her.

Civil Rights? Yes, I understand there is something of that sort going on, but I've been so busy with a number of really important projects that I haven't had time to keep up. You know, I'm to be one of the judges in the Miss West Brandon contest, sponsored by the Junior Chamber of Commerce, and that involves a responsibility which is both challenging and gratifying.

There were pinpricks of annoyance, of course. I was moving in one plane, and Cathy was in another. We lived in the same house, ate at the same table, claimed the same children, even shared the same bed at night—but we handled each other with the care of strangers. And there was this one dream I managed to forget most of—something about standing on a street corner and watching an endless line of people going past, all looking at me with the face of this black man I used to know—not saying anything, just looking at me. But these were only minor disturbances.

"You know I won't be home for lunch today." Cathy had come into the bedroom while I was in the process of deciding whether my gray suit or my blue suit would be most suitable for the challenging and gratifying task which lay ahead of me that day.

"Yes, I know." She moved past me, gathering up some of the children's clothing she had been ironing.

"And I'm not sure about plans for dinner. We'll probably be tied up until at least three this afternoon, making our evaluations of the girls' poise and general deportment, and then we judges are supposed to sit down together and discuss our various reactions and try to reach some sort of consensus. It could conceivably go on until the dinner hour, in which case we might decide to grab a bite somewhere together and just go directly to the high school for the final competition."

"Whatever you say, Bob," she said, stacking Elaine's blouses neatly in one pile. "If you're not here by six, we'll just go ahead with our dinner."

"What d'you think, Cathy—the blue suit or the gray suit? I'm getting a little tired of the gray, but it does have a better cut . . ."

"They both look very nice, Bob."

"Actually, the toughest part of the whole job will be tonight. I understand there're twelve contestants, and we have to judge them in three categories—bathing suit, evening gown and then talent."

I decided on the blue suit.

"Although," I went on as I started trying to decide which tie would look best with the blue suit, "I must admit that this afternoon has me a little scared. I mean, we have to talk with these girls and try to form some sort of opinion of their poise and personality and general deportment while we're eating lunch with them. And we have to carry those impressions with us tonight as a kind of *overall* factor which we can apply in case we have any really *tough* decisions to make in the bathing suit, evening gown and talent competitions. I mean

232

this is a pretty challenging responsibility, when you stop to think about it."

"Yes," said Cathy, starting in on a pile of Jimmy's shirts.

"Of course it will mean a great deal to the girl who wins," I said, "and it is a matter of considerable importance because West Brandon has never had a girl in the state finals, so the decision we make tonight really carries a lot of weight."

"Yes indeed," Cathy said as she placed Jimmy's shirts in a basket along with Elaine's blouses.

"So, even though it is a tough and challenging responsibility, it should prove to be gratifying," I said, deciding on a regimental red and gray striped tie.

And then Cathy said something that I did not quite understand, and I am sure it wasn't what it sounded like, because that is a word I have never heard Cathy use, and it *was* sort of muffled, so I was undoubtedly mistaken. Then she was gone, carrying the children's blouses and shirts to their rooms.

I did not see Cathy again until after my bath—which was a long, hot, soaking affair during which I managed to keep my mind almost completely blank and indulge myself in a sensuous contemplation of my soapy navel. I did have a bit of fun thinking how impressed those twelve young contestants for the coveted title of Miss West Brandon were likely to be when they actually met Robert M. Venable, who was a real AUTHOR and not the least bit unattractive—what with that distinguished touch of gray hair and that devil-may-care, boyish smile. There would be four other judges, but Venable would undoubtedly be the one those girls would want to please, because they could easily see that Venable could be more than just a judge to them.

Lying submerged in that hot, soapy water, I could hear them whispering to each other.

Gosh, will you just look at him!

Do you think he'll like me?

If he looks at me while I'm up on the stage, I'll die!

And then that moment—when the contest is over, and the new Miss West Brandon has been crowned and has cried and walked around the stage wearing her crown, and Venable is trying to slip out of the auditorium unnoticed, because he hates having people make over him—then the winner will spot him, and she will tear herself away from her parents and friends and the photographers, and she will run over to Venable and take his hand in hers and look up at him with her big blue or brown or gray or green, tear-filled eyes and murmur, "As long as you liked me, Mr. Venable—as long as I was *your* choice—then that's all that matters."

And Venable will smile his crooked, devil-may-care, but kindly smile and nod his head and squeeze her hand ever so gently and say, "Good luck, my dear. I'll be pulling for you in Atlantic City."

And she will want to kiss him, but he will simply smile again and turn and walk rapidly away, shoulders squared, chin set—content with the knowledge that he has done his job.

By eleven o'clock, Venable was patting the Yardley's After Shave Lotion on his cheeks and carefully knotting the regimental-stripe red and gray tie and making a final check of the boyish, yet dangerously exciting smile—and ready to go forth and DO HIS DUTY.

At this point, Elaine appeared on the scene, the bearer of dangerous notions.

"Daddy, couldn't you take us to watch the demonstration today? It was in the paper. There's going to be a real big demonstration. You promised you'd take us to one, and this is going to be a real big one!"

"Daddy has to do something else today, Elaine."

"But you promised!"

"Sweetheart, I'm sorry."

"Then maybe Mom can take us."

"Your mother doesn't want to get mixed up in anything like that."

Children aren't what they used to be.

"I'm going to ask her anyway!"

Exit Elaine with alarums and flourishes.

By eleven fifteen, Venable was at the front door, ready to tell his family good-bye, only no member of the family was in evidence. He waited for a moment at the door, reflecting on the nature of families in general and of his family in particular. And that moment's hesitation proved to be a mistake.

First Elaine appeared, Jimmy having joined forces with her.

"Mom said she'd think about it," Elaine announced.

"I'd rather go to the movies, but a demonstration would be fun too," Jimmy said.

And before I could exploit his preference for the movies with a good concrete suggestion, the telephone was ringing, and then Cathy made the scene.

"It's for you."

Long years of experience with telephones had taught me caution. "Who is it?"

Cathy has this terrific deadpan delivery which neatly eliminated any chance I might have had for telling just what she was thinking. "It's that student of yours—that Andy Brown."

The distant sound of bugles echoed faintly from the hills, but the white settlers had a good deal going with those Indians who were circling the wagons, and they weren't about to let themselves be saved—not if they could help it.

"Did you tell him I was here?"

"I told him I would see."

Stop for one full beat, just long enough to make sure the mind is clear of any dangerous convictions.

"I don't want to talk with him. Tell him I've already gone."

"That would be a lie, Daddy." Jimmy had this nasty fixation on telling the truth. Somewhere, somehow, I had failed him.

"By the time you get back to the phone, that'll be the truth."

"All right, Bob."

"Well, I'm off."

"Yes, Bob."

"Cathy, you don't want to take the kids to that mess down town today."

"I don't?"

"No. There's no telling what might happen."

"We'll see, Bob."

"Cathy . . ."

"I have to get back to the phone."

"We want to go, don't we, Jimmy?"

"Yeah!"

"Now listen, Cathy . . ."

But I was looking at her back, and then she was gone, and, left to the hostile stares of Jimmy and Elaine, I waved my magic wand and disappeared. I could have wondered why Andy Brown was calling me at this particular time on this particular day. I could have, but I was damned if I was going to.

The Brandon Inn is really a motor hotel, and its eight-story height makes it the tallest structure in West Brandon which has always been more or less committed architecturally to a kind of pseudo-Colonial style. It is situated on Main Street and takes up nearly half a block adjoining the shopping district. I did not approach it from Main Street, because —for reasons I was not going to think about—I did not wish to get any closer to Main Steet on that particular Saturday than

236

could be helped. Instead I drove directly to the Inn's parking garage which was at the rear of the building, left the car with an attendant and took the elevator to the fifth floor where I had been told by my jolly Jaycee contact man, Taylor Huntsworth, we judges would hold our preliminary meeting in Suite 517.

In Suite 517, there was already a real swinging group. Taylor Huntsworth, his face shining with perspiration and excitement, met me at the door and ushered me into a large room which was noisily occupied by about fifteen people, all of whom I had to be introduced to. The other four judges were already there. One of them I knew slightly—Roger Saddler, a member of the University Music Department. He had been in school there when I was doing my graduate work and had had a small dance band. There had been a fair amount of campus speculation then as to whether or not Roger Saddler and his group smoked marijuana, and that was about all I could remember about him. He was balding and had a slight tic and looked as though he might still be smoking marijuana. There was the women's editor of a newspaper from a neighboring city—a gaunt, red-faced, hoarse female with the name of Hallie Hawkins. She pumped my hand enthusiastically and called me "Sweetie," which instantly endeared her to me.

The other two judges were Mrs. Egbert Teasdale, a wispy, sixtyish old gal whose husband owned a considerable amount of real estate in and around West Brandon as a result of a lifetime of shady dealing, and Latham Billsworth, a fragile and limp young man who operated the Billsworth School of the Dance for children under twelve.

The remainder of the occupants of Suite 517 were local Jaycees, a couple of Jaycee wives, and one representative of the State Contest Committee, Mr. Caswell Upchurch who, by the very expression on his fattish face, admitted to be rather important.

Taylor Huntsworth appeared to be in charge. "Well, folks, we might just as well get started." He indicated a long table which had been set up with several plates of hors d'oeuvres which were being devoured earnestly by all concerned and an ample supply of Pepsi-Cola which was getting less than enthusiastic attention.

"Sorry we couldn't offer you folks something a little stronger, but the rules are very strict about not serving hard liquor *before* a judging session. Now later on, after the contest tonight, we're going to be right back in this same room, and I can promise you we'll have plenty of food and booze."

Hallie Hawkins had worked her way over to my side, and she whispered hoarsely in my ear, "My God, sweetie, I couldn't face this without a little nip. I have a flask in my bag, so if you get some of that Pepsi, I'll fix it up for you."

That seemed like a good idea, so I bellied up to the bar and poured myself half a cup of the stuff that makes you come alive.

"Okay, folks," Taylor Huntsworth was saying. "If you'll just make yourself comfortable, we'll run over a few things."

By this time my Pepsi-Cola was liberally mixed with a healthy slug of bourbon from Hallie Hawkins' flask, and I found myself a place on the arm of a sofa and looked attentive.

"First off, I want to take this opportunity again to say how much we all appreciate you judges giving so generously of your time to make this year's Miss West Brandon contest a success. You are five pretty important people, and I know this is a real sacrifice to you, and we appreciate it.

"I don't know of anything we Jaycees do during the year that is more important than this contest, and I want all of you judges to know that we've been working night and day to make this year's contest the biggest and the best ever held in West Brandon. In a little while now, it's all going to be up to you, and I want you to know how much we appreciate it."

I was getting that nice warm feeling that comes from drinking bourbon and being appreciated.

"In just a few minutes now, we're going down to the Colonial Room where you'll have lunch with the twelve lovely girls who're competing for the title of Miss West Brandon. We want to give you this opportunity to meet the girls and talk with them and eat with them, so you can form some idea of each of them as far as things like poise and manners and personality are concerned.

"Of course, I don't have to tell you that they are twelve pretty nervous young ladies right now. This is probably the biggest day of their lives, and they just wouldn't be human if they didn't have a few butterflies. But I know you judges will be as impressed with them as all of us have been. They represent the very best in our community—twelve beautiful, modest, wholesome, and very talented girls."

I was enthralled. And then—somewhere in the world outside Suite 517—I heard the distant wailing of a siren. I wondered if anyone else in the room had heard it. No one seemed to pay any attention to it. I wondered what it meant— not *thinkingly;* I could not bring myself to *think* about it—but there was an instinctive wonder and fear and dread.

"Now," Taylor Huntsworth said, "before we all go to lunch, I want to introduce Mary Ellen Thigpen who has been working with the girls all week getting them ready for the big day. Mary Ellen is Josh Thigpen's wife, and not too many years ago—back in 1958—she was our own Miss West Brandon. That was when she was Mary Ellen Haggle, and I might say that there were a lot of people at the state contest who felt it was pretty doggoned strange that Mary Ellen did not reach the finals at least. She was one of the best darned baton twirlers I've ever seen, and she had a specialty number with a flaming baton that was just spectacular. If it hadn't been for the fire chief coming in and setting up a lot of silly rules just before the state contest started, the story might have been a lot different—but that's water under the bridge, and I'm sure Mary Ellen would be the last one to want me sounding like sour grapes over something that happened back in 1958.

"Well, anyhow, Mary Ellen knows all these girls. She knows how hard they've worked, and she knows just how important being in this contest is to these girls. So I thought a few words from Mary Ellen might be helpful to you before we all go down to lunch . . ."

"Slip me your cup, sweetie." Hallie Hawkins was a born St. Bernard. I palmed my cup and handed it to her, and in a moment it came back to me, this time without any Pepsi to louse up the bourbon.

Mary Ellen Thigpen, *née* Haggle, Miss West Brandon of 1958, had undoubtedly been a pretty and vacuous girl in 1958. At the present reading she had managed to retain her vacuity, but various unpleasant things had happened to the prettiness, such as hardening of the old features and spreading of the old hips. One thing that she had, though, and that was ENTHUSIASM.

"The most wonderful moment in my life," she exploded, "was the moment I stood on the stage of the high school auditorium and knew that I was Miss West Brandon! At that moment, I knew that nothing more wonderful could ever happen to me. But, in many ways, working with these twelve wonderful girls in this year's Miss West Brandon contest has been even more wonderful. I don't want to take up too much of your time, because I know how anxious you all are to go down and meet these girls and get underway on the wonderful schedule of activities which the Jaycees have planned for you."

The sirens were getting louder and closer.

"How you doing on that, sweetie?" Hallie whispered. I handed her my empty cup, and she winked broadly like the good old broad she was. "Jesus," she muttered, "I'd hate to do anything like this sober, wouldn't you, sweetie?"

I took my cup, once again filled with bourbon, and nodded. Maybe, I thought, the bourbon will make the sirens go away. It was sure as hell worth a try.

"And so," Mary Ellen concluded, "let me just say this. Judge these twelve wonderful girls carefully and strictly. You won't have to apologize to anyone for the one you select as Miss West Brandon, because each and every one of these girls is a winner. That is the theme we stress in working with the girls. None of them can possibly be a loser, because the very fact that they are participating in this wonderful contest makes each of them a real winner—and therefore not one of them can possibly be a loser—not when they have all won so much . . ."

I was getting pretty confused by this, so I finished off that cup of straight bourbon which enabled me to see the sense in what good old Mary Ellen had to say.

And so—with those meaningful words of Miss West Brandon of 1958 ringing in our ears and the sporadic wailing of assorted sirens in the background of the world outside and a substantial quantity of Hallie Hawkins' bourbon in the Venable system—we departed Suite 517 for the Colonial Room which was located on the mezzanine of the Brandon Inn. The Colonial Room was large and very colonial. A number of tables were set up—several of which were on the far side of the room just adjacent to a row of windows which looked out over Main Street. I noticed this the moment I entered the room and made a very strong resolution not to make the mistake of looking out of any of those windows. Because there were noises that managed to penetrate from the outside, and I did not like those noises. So I concentrated on what was *inside* the Colonial Room.

This led to a feeling which was akin to what the early Christians must have felt when they were led into the arena where all those hungry lions were waiting. Twelve—count 'em—twelve young women, ranging in age from eighteen to twenty-one, awaited us. And they all looked exactly alike. Oh they had on different colored dresses, and some of them were blondes and some brunettes, and two were redheads, and a few were short while most were tall, but these were only superficial differences. They were lined up at the door of the Colonial Room, waiting to be *personally* introduced to each of the five judges before we were all turned loose at the trough, and so help me God, I could not tell one of them from the other.

Introductions filled the air. "Mr. Robert Venable, this is Sue Anne Cogdill. Sue Anne, this is Mr. Robert Venable. Mr. Robert Venable, this is Francie Alice Fullem. Francie Alice, this is Mr. Robert Venable . . ."

And like that.

Amid all this introducing and counter-introducing, Venable was *noticing* things and *hearing* things. Like the fact that the corps of waiters who were lined up waiting to serve us was made up entirely of white boys. And like the fact that Venable overheard a harried-looking man who appeared to be in some sort of managerial capacity saying to one of the Jaycees, "It's that damned Civil Rights march. Every last one of my niggers just up and walked out this morning—without any warning. I had to round up a bunch of college boys to serve." And like the fact that there was a growing tension in the room which seemed to concentrate itself right in Venable's throat which, for all of Hallie Hawkins' medicinal bourbon, was getting tighter and dryer—because of the *something* unseen and outside and away from this Early American feeding place, this little bit of Colonial times in picturesque West Brandon, but still making itself increasingly FELT by Venable.

Eventually, Venable found himself seated at a table, face to face and smile to smile with three of the WONDERFUL GIRLS. The other four judges were at four other tables with groups of two or three of the contestants, and all of the judges' lunches were on trays, because, you see, at five-minute intervals the judges were rotated to a new table, thus making sure that each judge would be exposed to an intimate and penetrating conversation with each of the girls. If this sounds confusing, that's because it was. Anyhow, these particular three Wonderful Girls sat there with their plates heaped in front of them and toyed with their tomato juice and demonstrated their poise and personality and general deportment, all for Venable's benefit, while we all had CONVERSATION.

Like this.

Venable: "Well, I guess you girls are pretty excited, huh?"

1st W.G.: "Oh, Mr. Venable, I just can't tell you!"

2nd W.G.: "My heart is just pounding so hard, I can't breathe!"

3rd W.G.: "That's the way my heart is pounding too—so hard I can't breathe!"

Venable: "Well, I guess I'm supposed to sort of ask you girls some questions, so I can . . ."

At this point, Mary Ellen Thigpen bustled up. "Time to move to the next table, Mr. Venable. Did you girls have a chance to get to know Mr. Venable?"

And I had my tray and was herded over to the table from which Hallie Hawkins was being removed. I wondered if she had been considerate enough to leave any of her bourbon at her abandoned place. No such luck.

243

Waiting for me at the new table were three new girls—who, of course, looked exactly like the three I had just left, which did give things some sense of continuity.

Venable: "Well, this is all pretty exciting, I guess."

4th W.G.: "Oh, Mr. Hawkins, it's the most exciting thing that ever happened to me!"

Venable: "No, I'm Venable. That nice lady who was just here is Mrs. Hawkins. She carries nice things in her purse." I felt obliged to put in a plug for good old Hallie.

4th W.G.: "Oh, Mr. Venable, that's just *awful* of me. It's so *important* to be able to remember names, and I feel like a fool, having made such a terrible mistake!"

Venable: "Well, I know you girls are pretty excited about all this, and I guess it's a pretty traumatic experience . . ."

5th W.G.: "It's fabulous, really fabulous! We've been spending all this week just working together and getting to know each other, and I've never known a sweeter bunch of girls!"

Venable: "But tonight one of you has to win, doesn't she?"

6th W.G.: "Oh yes, but you know, Mr. Venerable, it really doesn't matter who wins. It's just the thrill of being in this contest with all these wonderful girls. And there really isn't any one winner, because we all win, you see. None of us can really lose, not with this wonderful experience . . ."

Venable: "*Venable—not Venerable.*"

5th W.G.: "What *is* all that awful noise?"

All that awful noise was coming from the outside world where there were no wonderful girls or creamed turkey on toast, and that awful noise was getting to be very loud noise—so loud that it was no longer possible, even in the Colonial Room, to ignore it. Because the awful noise was singing, and there were a lot of singers.

From another table, Taylor Huntsworth was calling, "Try not to let that bother you folks. It'll pass soon."

But it was bothering us folks, and the three wonderful girls at my table were up and looking out of the window, and so were the wonderful girls from other tables and, much against his better judgment, so was Venable.

And there it was, just below us on Main Street. A solid mass of people that seemed to stretch as far as the eye could see—and they were all singing, and along the sidewalks were other people, some yelling and others simply watching.

Oh, sweet Jesus!

4th W.G.: "Look at them, will you? Isn't that the most disgusting thing you've ever seen? Of all the days to pick to do *that!*"

Somewhere down there, Andy Brown. I know you're somewhere down there, but I can't find you. All marchers look alike to me.

5th W.G.: "Sally—that's my momma's colored girl—didn't even show up this morning, and you can imagine how busy Momma was, trying to get me ready. I hope she fires her!"

And the walls of the Brandon Inn could not keep out the words of the song.

> *Oh freedom, oh freedom,*
> *Oh freedom over me!*
> *And before I'll be a slave*
> *I'll be buried in my grave*
> *And go home to my Lord and be free!*

Then Mary Ellen Thigpen was beside me, trying to get the train back on the track. "Time to move along to another table, Mr. Venable. Time to get back to your table, girls." She looked down on Main Street and swore softly under her breath. "Those sons-of-bitches! They're going to ruin this whole wonderful program!"

Then I saw them!

It was three-fourths of the Venable family on an outing, moving along the sidewalk watching the parade—Jimmy and Elaine all dressed and scrubbed for the occasion and Cathy looking lovely and motherly and interested. I cursed her and blessed her and wanted her—not an easy combination, but I managed.

"Really, girls, come along now. Mr. Venable . . ."

And then I saw him!

All marchers may look alike—all, that is, but one. He wasn't at the head of anything or anybody. He was right there in the goddamned middle of things. He wasn't with Alise Hungerford. He was there, all by himself, with a thousand others—ANDY BROWN!

> *Where did you come from, baby dear?*
> *Out of the nowhere, into the here!*

"Come along, Mr. Venable!"

Those marchers aren't moving very fast. He couldn't get too far!

"My mother didn't sleep a wink last night, and when I left home this morning, she was just bawling, she was so happy!"

"This is Mr. Venable, girls. Your turn with him now."

But why would you be doing it, Venable? Why!

"Mr. Venable, I thought you ought to know, I have this terrible case of laryngitis. I don't know how I'm going to get through my talent tonight. I sing this medley of songs . . ."

When I was a kid, I used to love parades . . .

"Mr. Venable, did you really write a book? I think that's just wonderful! Don't you, girls? Isn't that wonderful?"

I remember watching a parade once with the Negro Elks and my father saying, "Nobody knows how to strut like those niggers." So it could be just the fulfillment of a childhood wish . . .

246

"Listen, girls, there're some more sirens. I'll bet the police are going to arrest that whole bunch of troublemakers out there, and I hope they do!"

If I did, would it be because of Cathy? Or Andy?

"It just makes me furious that they'd pick this day, of all days to do something awful like this!"

Maybe, it would just be because of me!

"Mr. Venable, is anything wrong? You look sort of— Mr. Venable!"

Mr. Venable was out of his seat and heading for the nearest exit with a whole host of wonderful eyes watching him.

"Mr. Venable!"

Mary Ellen Thigpen was on her feet and looking dangerous.

Always leave 'em laughing!

"Mrs. Thigpen," I said, turning to face the entire assemblage—fellow judges, Jaycees, distinguished guests, wonderful girls and all. "Ladies and gentlemen, in the course of this luncheon I have learned to my dismay that one of the wonderful girls who is competing for the coveted title of Miss West Brandon is an impostor. She is, as a matter of fact, working weekends at a local house of ill repute. In the light of this intelligence, I feel I must withdraw myself as a judge rather than be forced to reveal the identity of this unfortunate girl."

Mary Ellen's Thigpen was moving toward me, his voice rising in a truly remarkable demonstration of strong language. Among the wonderful girls and the other luncheon guests there seemed to be developing a distinctly anti-Venable attitude. So I left, and my exit, though lacking in dignity, was not without its impressive aspects.

I reached the ground floor in an understandable hurry and left the Brandon Inn, probably for all time, to find outside mass confusion and sanity-restoring chaos. I couldn't locate Cathy and the children, but I pushed my way through the hecklers and spectators who lined the sidewalk and into the crowd of marchers who moved in a slow, irresistible mass toward the heart of West Brandon. Arms linked together, eyes set straight ahead, they shuffled forward, and they sang.

> *We are not afraid. We are not afraid.*
> *We are not afraid today.*

Andy Brown was in there somewhere, and I had to find him!

> *Deep in my heart, I do believe*
> *We shall overcome someday.*

"Excuse me, but have you seen a fellow named Andy Brown? He's a big black . . ."

> *God is on our side. God is on our side.*
> *God is on our side today.*

"Hey, Professor!"

> *Deep in my heart, I do believe,*
> *We shall overcome someday!*

"Andy!"

"What're you doing out here, man?"

"Same thing you are."

"I thought you were somewhere looking at chicks."

"How come you're not up front, leading the parade with Alise?"

"Man, that chick gave me the brush same as she gave you."

"You mean you weren't . . ."

"Naw. Wish I was, but I wasn't. She's engaged to some lawyer up in Philadelphia."

Black and white together! Black and white together!
Black and white together someday!

"What were you calling me for this morning?"
"Man, I thought I'd see if you'd like to come along, like old times."

Deep in my heart, I do believe,
We shall overcome someday!

"Hey, Professor, I never knew you had such a mean tenor!"
"Look, Andy, there she is!"
And the leader of us all, Miss Honeypot Hungerford, gleaming in the midday sun, was coming along the ranks, checking the morale of the troops. And she saw Venable and Andy Brown, their arms linked together, and a dazzling smile told us we were good men and true and if it weren't for that lawyer up in Philadelphia, she'd be honored, but that's the way it was, and WELCOME ABOARD and WELL DONE!
"Man, she is a chick, ain't she, Professor?"
Then, beyond Alise, I saw another chick, a Cathy chick with two little Jimmy and Elaine chicklets, and they saw me at about the same time and Jimmy and Elaine were jumping up and down and yelling and Cathy was looking right at me and although she wasn't laughing out loud I could tell she was laughing inside—a good laugh, partly *at* me and partly *with* me. And that made me fell GOOD.
"I decided to come along," I said to Andy, "maybe just because I've always liked parades."
"Me too, Professor."

We shall overcome! We shall overcome!
We shall overcome someday!

249

Andy Brown's baritone was not a thing to sneer at.

Deep in my heart, I do believe,
We shall overcome someday!

So we had our place in the big parade—not at the head of the parade, but right in the big fat middle of the parade—which might not have been the most important place to be—but for Venable and for Andy Brown, it would do.